Ephraim Clark was raised in the United States. After he obtained his undergraduate degree at the University of Notre Dame, his wanderlust itinerary took him from Latin America to the UK and Europe, where he earned his way as a karate instructor, nightclub bouncer, pop singer, and recording artist. He has post graduate degrees from the University of Madrid and the University of Paris, where he obtained his PhD in Financial Economics Summa cum Laude. As a full professor in finance, he has authored or coauthored nine books and over one hundred papers in top academic and professional journals. *Agents Scorned* is his third spy thriller. His first two, *Requiem for Betrayal* and *Cult Stalker*, were Amazon Best Sellers. *Requiem for Betrayal* was a finalist in the Thriller category for the National Indie Excellence Awards. Visit www.ephraimauthor.com for more information and to join Ephraim Clark's reading club.

Also by Ephraim Clark

Requiem for Betrayal (2025)
Cult Stalker (2025)

A BRAD JAMES THRILLER

AGENTS SCORNED

EPHRAIM CLARK

To my little sweetheart Maria.

Acknowledgments

Sincere thanks to my wife, Maria, for all her patience and support; my little sister, Chrissie, and my friends Konstantino Kassimatis, David Bernthal, and Oussama Bader for their many helpful suggestions on the text and plots; and Vince Font for his great editing and insightful suggestions throughout the entire publication process.

Prologue

Mario Yrigoyen fingers the smooth vanilla folders containing photos and certified copies of documents filed with the legal authorities on the island of Jersey. This folder is his last chance. It is all that is standing between him and a painful death.

His mouth is dry. His stomach is churning. His shirt is soaking wet from the sweat dripping from his armpits. He wonders if anyone notices. Looks around.

The Rincon Argentino Café is half empty. It's the only place in Paris that serves genuine Argentine mate. Two gangbangers slouched over a vino tinto in the corner are giving him the evil eye. His bodyguards know these guys. They've been hanging around Mario's apartment building for the last week. They're biding their time, waiting for the order to make their move.

The waiter arrives with a pot of hot water and a silver encrusted, wooden gourd. Mario lifts the calabash to his nostrils and breathes in the heady aroma of mate mixed with honey and ginger.

The gangbangers push back their chairs and get to their feet. Mario tenses. The four bodyguards stand. The gangbangers smirk out some kind of a taunt and swagger out onto the street. The bodyguards sit down and start to argue.

It's not a false alert. It's a message. Makes his decision so much easier. Mario has always known that once he makes his move, he might actually find himself closer to a premature death than he was before. The message the gangbangers are delivering has made it crystal clear. He cannot get any closer to death than he is now.

Mario reaches into his briefcase and extracts a small metal cylinder—a bombilla. It serves as a straw and a filter. Tipping the calabash forward, he creates a well in the mate and inserts the bombilla. Normally, the mate would be shared around in a kind of social ceremony. That won't happen today. Today, Mario is all alone.

He reexamines the photos and documents in the folders as he sips. They contain the details of secret, private bank accounts held on the island of Jersey by influential bureaucrats and politicians in South America and the United States.

His attention focuses on Bellweather, SA, a company domiciled in Jersey with a capital of one thousand bearer shares with a face value of one U.S. dollar each. It has an account containing over one hundred million U.S. dollars. This investment fund is the default account for José Lopez Rega's "golden parachute."

Mario knows Jersey well. It is a bailiwick of the British crown, a free-wheeling offshore financial center offering a rare combination of political stability, legal security, and personal anonymity on a conveniently located island right off the coast of Normandy.

Mario had anticipated his own impending downfall. Perón was old and ill. His days were numbered. As Perón's right-hand man, Mario was top dog in the ruling hierarchy. He represented Perón's authority and wielded his power accordingly, often to the detriment of Rega's personal agenda. There was no doubt in his mind. Perón's death would extinguish Mario's power base. Rega, Isabel's right-hand man, would become the new, uncontested top dog. In the context of the Argentine dog-eat-dog political arena, Mario's position of power would be a thing of the past and he would become the main course of Rega's next meal. It's not personal. Rega doesn't do personal. It's all about power.

Mario doesn't do "personal" either. It's all about saving his skin. He neglected to deliver the Bellweather shares to Rega. Without those shares, Rega can't access the money. Mario smiles as he sips. So far, Rega doesn't seem to have realized this.

He savors the last few drops of his mate. He catches his reflection in the mirror and smooths back his dark hair. His mind is made up. It's time to act. Rega has almost finished consolidating his power in Buenos Aires. His next move will be to purge the embassies. Mario knows he's dude number one on that list. He's also dude number one on the list of the foreign bureaucrats and politicians he's dealt with through their accounts in Jersey. Out of power and on the run, he knows too much and threatens their anonymity.

He's already contacted the Americans with the information that should take him off their target list. Now his immediate concern is the neutralization of the very real, mortal threat of Rega's vengeance. His program to prolong his biological life beyond his impending political death is simple, but therein lies its ultimate strength. He will inform Rega he is holding the bearer shares in escrow. He shivers with satisfaction knowing that Rega's fury will be boundless when he realizes that access to his one hundred million U.S. dollars is contingent on Mario Yrigoyen's continued good health.

In a burst of perverse pleasure, Mario imagines José Lopez Rega, impotent and livid, stomping around, cursing and swearing, pounding his frustration on the table. The image dies quickly. He knows his life will be hanging by a fragile thread, a wager on Rega's greed, the wager that one hundred million dollars in the Bellweather investment account will be enough for Rega to keep him alive. Then only the one thousand bearer shares will remain standing between him and oblivion.

He signals the waiter. His bodyguards are still arguing. The old bodyguard jefe—chief—bangs his fist on the table, and two of them slink outside with the gangbangers.

That's it. Half of his protection team just defected to the enemy. The other half is conflicted, watching him, searching for signs of weakness. Jefe's been around the block a few times in his forty-year career. He's wondering if it's time to change sides.

Mario feels the panic. His heart is pounding. His hands are trembling. His breath is coming in short gasps. He calls up his willpower. Takes a deep breath. Doesn't let himself hyperventilate. All his instincts are telling him to run for his life. His brain tells him this is not the time to surrender to his instincts. He is going to run for his life, but first, he has to make sure he has a good head start.

He signals his two remaining bodyguards to sit tight. He goes to the bar and asks for the telephone and a long-distance line. He makes one call—to Rega. Leaves a message. Hangs up the phone. Closes his eyes. He's relieved. The game is on. Rega has been notified.

Mario heads for the men's room. It has a window that opens onto a courtyard with access to a building on another street. He takes a leak, washes his hands, and slicks back his hair.

Someone starts pounding on the door. He jumps from the window into the courtyard and starts to run.

Chapter 1

Greta Papachristou was the bereaved widow of the late Georges Papachristou, vice president of the Crédit Lyonnais and undercover CIA agent. She was a handsome woman, mid-fifties, a perfectly coiffed brunette graying at the temples. Her eyes were swollen and her nose was red. She had been crying.

Brad felt slightly embarrassed to be there under the circumstances. Her husband had just been buried after committing suicide. The suicide was as unpredictable as the way he did it. He threw himself from the penthouse terrace at a cocktail party organized by the Argentine embassy. Landed on his face eight stories down.

Brad was there representing Latorre Legal on behalf of the embassy. Charles "Chuck" Hall, the managing director of Latorre Legal, had just arrived and was doing the talking. Brad took advantage to explore the premises.

Security was heavy. Too heavy as far as he was concerned. There were two men stationed at the entrance to the apartment, two more in the living room, and two on the terrace. Brad wondered who had hired them. They were aggressive and arrogant. Rubbed him the wrong way. They behaved more like they owned the place. Greta Papachristou kept casting furtive glances in the direction of the head honcho every time she spoke.

Brad sidled over for a closer look. The crack of a slap and a hail of piercing screams from the main hallway stopped him in his tracks. The biggest guard, the one with the scarred face and flat nose, was dragging a little kid six or seven years old by the arm.

"How you get in here, *cabronito* (little bastard)?" The accent was Spanish. The vocabulary was South American.

"*Mon grand-père, mon grand-père* (My grandfather, my grandfather)!" The little kid was terrified, and he was hurting.

The big guard drew back for another slap. Brad grabbed his arm and threw him against the wall. "Leave the kid alone."

The kid scampered away. The guard went for his baton. Brad went for the guard.

The head honcho grabbed the guard. Pointed to the kid. "Who is this?" The accent was Spanish.

Greta Papachristou cuddled the boy. "He is our concierge's grandson. He's looking for his grandfather."

"Shouldn't be here. How did he get in?"

"Through the service stairway, probably."

Head Honcho glared at Brad. Stabbed the air with his fat forefinger. "Never, ever interfere with my men, *gringo*."

Brad was pumping adrenaline. He bit it back and smiled. Soft-spoken. Looked him in the eye—cocked and ready. "Your men should watch the stairway, not bully little kids." It was a challenge. Dead silence—Mississippi one, Mississippi two, Mississippi three.

Head Honcho blinked. He turned to his men in the hallway. "*La pinche escalera de servicio, cabrones. Que pasa* (The goddamn service stairway, shitheads. What's going on)?"

Greta Papachristou smiled at Brad. She took the boy's hand and led him out to the landing. "Your grandfather is downstairs." Back in the room, she seemed relieved and took up her conversation with Chuck as if nothing had happened.

Brad ignored the menacing looks from the bodyguards and continued his search of the living room. Photos galore. Georges with athletes. Georges with starlets. Georges with celebrities. Mostly Georges with politicians.

Georges had a picture with every politician Brad had ever seen or heard of. He seemed to have been especially friendly with Juan Perón and a tall, balding gentleman with thick, shaggy eyebrows and a crooked, slapstick smile. In fact, they looked like a trio. There they were, in picture after picture, the three of them together, dining, drinking, laughing, singing. Brad wondered where Greta was when all the photos were taken. She was not in any of them.

Chuck was closing down the visit. "Mrs. Papachristou, it was a pleasure to meet you. If I can do anything, anything at all, please do contact me."

Greta Papachristou was expressionless. She was running on autopilot. "Thank you so much for coming by, and thank my friends at the embassy for sending you."

Brad said his goodbyes and they were out of there. Out on the street, Brad was uncharacteristically melancholy. "It's really sad. She's all alone. Her only family is her son and his family. They live a busy life on the corporate fast track in New York. They won't have much time for her. Her friends are all spouses of her husband's colleagues and clients. With him gone, it won't be long before they drift away. She's a looker, and three will be a crowd as far as the wives of any of their acquaintances are concerned. She's gonna be a lonely little lady."

"Yep. She was devoted to her husband. She told me she can't

understand why he would take his own life. Doesn't believe he did. She's in shock. She even seemed afraid. That's about it. How about you? What's your take?"

"Same conclusion as you. One thing did grab me. There was no physical evidence of her existence in the apartment. The apartment was decorated like a man cave. You know, the whole room was crammed with photos of her husband at work and at play. She's not even in one single photo."

Chuck nodded. "Yeah, she said she spent a lot of time in London."

"Those gangbangers she hired as bodyguards are another big question mark. They behaved like they own the place."

"Yeah. I don't think she approves of them. It looked like she was hoping you'd clean that guy's clock."

"Chickenshit bully, beating up on a little kid."

Chuck's pink Thunderbird parked on the street was drawing a group of admirers. One of them yelled, *"Super caisse* (Super wheels)."

Chuck grinned like a goose. *"Merci beaucoup."*

Chuck was romantically attached to his set of wheels. Only twenty thousand 1957 T-Birds were ever made, and only ten were pink. He got it for a song from an embassy hotshot who fell in love, got married, and needed a bigger, cheaper car. It was a definite attention-getter.

Brad's warning broke the spell. "Somebody's in the car."

"Shit. I forgot to lock it."

Chuck slipped to the left onto the street. Brad stayed to the right on the sidewalk. Cautious approach. The admirers felt the tension and began melting away.

Brad could make out the head and shoulders of a man through the tinted window. It was a casually dressed, elderly man with a full head of silver hair. He was sitting in the passenger seat staring off into space.

Brad came level with the door. Jerked it open. Chuck jerked open the driver's door. The man paid no attention as he climbed out of the car. He shook Brad's hand, said, *"Au revoir,"* and wandered off down the street. Brad watched him till he turned the corner. Chuck hadn't moved. He was still holding the door handle.

They were both puzzled. Checked out the car. Nothing damaged. Nothing out of place. Just a brown A4 envelope on the floorboard, and it was filled with pictures.

*   *   *

There were four black-and-white photos. The setting for the four photos was a swanky reception room decked out in chandeliers, mirrored walls, marble pillars, and fancy antique furniture. It opened onto a vast terrace overlooking the shimmering wonders of the Eiffel Tower and Paris by night.

One photo captured the reception room full of the elegant guests sipping, seducing, laughing, and talking. Another captured a similar scene out on the terrace. The third photo featured two men and two women—one a striking, big-haired blonde, the other a beautiful brunette. They were in a corner at the edge of the terrace laughing together. In the fourth photo, the blonde and one of the two men were alone together in the corner edge of the terrace. The man was Georges Papachristou. He was laughing. The blonde was serious.

Brad was trying to make sense of the photos and their visit to the widow of former undercover CIA agent Georges Papachristou. If the photos hadn't been dropped on them that way, Brad would have written off the visit as a waste of time. The widow's behavior was slightly strange, but well within the bounds of normality for the spouse of a surprise suicide victim. The photos, and the way they were delivered, changed all that. The widow's strange behavior now looked more like fear than shell shock. At least that's what Brad was thinking. After all, the reason they made the visit in the first place was because the embassy found the suicide suspicious.

"Whaddya think, Chuck?"

"I think she's behind the photos."

"Yeah, but why the unconventional delivery system? Why not just hand them over to us herself?"

"She might be afraid of something. If it wasn't suicide, maybe she thinks she's being watched. Maybe it's the bodyguards who have her spooked."

Brad took a few seconds to think that over. "Agreed. We have to figure out what those photos mean. I think it's more than just pictures of Papachristou's last moments. There's some kind of message in the photos."

"A message? Like what?" Chuck's lackadaisical expression and high-pitched tone were signaling skepticism; he wasn't noted for his imagination. His resistance to Brad's imagination was nothing new. Nothing bad, either. Kept things on the straight and narrow.

"You know," Brad said, "like a movie. Photos one and two set the background scene—swanky cocktail party, elegant guests, warm starry night, amazing view of the Eiffel Tower and Paris by night from an enormous terrace. Photo three shows the crime scene, the conspirators, and the victim. Photo four shows the perpetrator and the victim at the crime scene."

"Sounds good, but we need proof, movie daddy."

"I know it's a stretch, but still. We know he fell from that corner of the terrace. He and the blonde were alone." Brad was troubled by the blonde. She was a handsome woman, but there was something about her that turned him off.

Chuck shook his head and tried to close that road right down. "We've identified the man. He's an Argentine embassy official and the brunette is his wife. No info on who the big-haired blonde is, but Papachristou was big and strong and an accomplished athlete. He was in shape, man. No way a little, big-haired blonde is gonna throw him off the terrace."

"Yeah, well, first of all, the blonde is not little. Take a look at the picture. She's as tall as Papachristou. Taller if you count the hair. Got a pair of shoulders on her, too. You're probably right, though. But I still think the answer is in those four photos."

Chuck stared out the window, thinking it over. The view from Latorre Legal's offices on the sixth floor at number 78 avenue des Champs-Elysées relaxed him. The far side of the street below was bathed in soft shadows cast by the afternoon sun shining through the branches of the trees lining the sidewalk. Pedestrian traffic was relatively thin on that side of the Champs-Elysées. Shops were relatively scarce and it was too early for the cinemas this time of the afternoon. His side of the avenue was a different story. More shops, galleries, and commercial passages. A river of strolling humanity flowed back and forth through a festival of buskers, street performers, souvenir hawkers, restaurants, and sidewalk cafés. Chuck closed his eyes and shook his head. When he opened them, he clapped his hands and called out to Betty, his office manager. "Hey, you ready for a coffee?"

"Don't think you're fooling me, Charles Hall. You know I don't drink coffee. Just ask politely. I'll be glad to get you some coffee."

Chastened and chagrined, Chuck turned to Brad. "Gotta be careful about what you ask your female hired help to do these days." His sheepish grin said it all, and Brad loved it. Chuck was a former Marine, five feet nine inches tall and two-hundred-twenty pounds of pure muscle. Over three tours in Vietnam he shot, stabbed, strangled, and stomped his way to three hundred confirmed kills. He won three Purple Hearts, three Silver Stars, and was rewarded with embassy duty in Paris. In 1969, he cashed out of the Marines and partnered up with Brad. He went back to school and got his MBA from the prestigious HEC Business School in Paris. Now he was running Latorre Legal, a consulting firm catering to an American expatriate clientele. With all this background, he was still no match for little bantam Betty, the hundred-and-one pounds of fun who ran his office like the Berlin branch of the German Gestapo.

Betty rolled the coffee tray into the office and left without a word. Brad snatched his espresso off the tray and knocked it back. He went over to the desk and picked up the framed picture of Chuck in his full-dress Marine uniform. The strong, dimpled chin, high cheekbones, and crooked nose made him look arguably like Napoleon Solo's *Man from U.N.C.L.E.*

Chuck whipped around. "Hey, man, don't touch that. It's sacred."

Brad was smirking, but he had to admit, Chuck had come a long way since he cashed out of the marines in 1969 and hooked up with Brad, who was in Paris to meet up with his soulmate, Alice, after a master's degree in Madrid. Brad stifled a smartass reply and limited himself to "You've changed." He replaced the photo. "Okay, let's leave it at that and see what Gary has to say. I've got an appointment with my PhD supervisor now."

"How is it coming along? You've been working on it since I met you."

"Slight exaggeration. I only started three years ago. Almost finished. Writing it up."

Chuck had become interested in further education since he earned his master's. "What are you gonna do when you finish?"

"Don't know. Probably carry on as usual. It just gives me more ammunition if I have to change."

"Well, you're definitely gonna have to change. First time I heard you sing, I knew you were gonna need a day job to stay alive. My opinion hasn't changed."

"Stuff it, dork. See you tomorrow."

Chapter 2

EARLY MAY 1975, LEVALLOIS-PERRET

Viewed from the sixth-floor safe house, the rue Voltaire was humming with mid-morning activity. The sun was out. Streams of people exiting the Metro Anatole France were flowing down the sidewalks. Cars were zooming around, honking and jostling for position. Drivers were cursing and shaking their heads in disgust. The meter maids were out in force, slapping tickets on any vehicle that wasn't moving. The exception to all the hustle, bustle, commotion, and chaos was a line of twenty or more clients waiting patiently to get into the corner *boulangerie* (bakery). Fresh bread was a French *sine qua non,* or an indispensable requirement for life on earth.

Brad was scanning the street for Gary, the Paris CIA station chief. He was uncharacteristically late—not late like five or ten minutes, late like thirty minutes. Brad checked out the café across from the *boulangerie*. It was doing a bang-up business. The terrace was full and the two waiters were strutting around with their shiny tin trays distributing coffees, calvas, croissants, and *chaussons aux pommes,* those delicious apple tarts found only in France.

As Brad scanned the clientele, the corner of the café just behind the terrace caught his eye. He looked again and rubbed his eyes. He had to confirm this. "Hey, Chuck. Check this out—back corner of the terrace on the right."

Chuck came over to the window, squinted, and leaned forward for a closer look. "That's Gary in there with a broad."

"Yeah, and he should have been *here* thirty minutes ago."

"He better get a move on. I've got places to go and things to do."

"Wait. He's gettin' up. Here he comes."

Two minutes later, the doorbell rang. It was Gary. You couldn't miss him in a crowded stadium. It wasn't only his size. Gary Richards stood six feet five inches tall and weighed 225 pounds, with broad shoulders, massive hands, and enormous feet. It was the mop of bright-red hair that set him apart. He had been a super jock back in the day—all-state basketball in high school and first-string forward for the University of Dayton in college. He still worked out and stayed in good shape.

Gary had recruited Brad back in 1969 when he came to Paris from Madrid on his vintage, vertical, single 220cc Indian Arrow motorcycle. They continued working together when Gary returned to Paris as station chief. He was a no-nonsense professional spook with an impressive record of victories over what he called the black hats. Had nothing to do with race, religion, nationality, or sex. The black hats included anybody and everybody working against the interests of the United States of America. Brad liked and respected Gary. He was a cool dude with a contagious sense of humor. He was also loyal, and Brad trusted him as much as you could trust anybody whose job it was to lie, obfuscate, manipulate, and deceive.

Gary stomped into the apartment. Not his usual self. His lips were tight and his jaw was set. Dark circles around his eyes made him look like a cartoon character. "Hi, guys. Sorry I'm late. Last-minute complication." The word "complication" received a special emphasis. "Got any coffee?"

"It's all ready for you. Four sugar cubes." It was common knowledge that when Gary was nervous or upset, he scarfed up coffee-soaked sugar cubes. Meetings like these were automatic four-cube events.

Gary took his steaming cup of coffee and sat down on the leather sofa to perform his ritual. He dumped two sugar cubes into the cup and stirred. The third cube he dunked into the brew and ate like candy. Then he took a big slug from the cup and gulped it down. Brad watched him closely, but Gary didn't flinch. That coffee was hot enough to scald a Tetley tea bag. Brad never ceased to be impressed.

The coffee loosened Gary up. He clapped his hands. "Alright! Ready to go." He was trying to gear himself up for the meeting. "Hey, we beat Alabama."

He was referring to the Notre Dame football team, something he and Brad had in common. Brad was a graduate of Notre Dame, and Gary loved their football team. Notre Dame had beaten Alabama in the Orange Bowl in January.

Chuck was a wet blanket. "Yeah, but USC kicked Notre Dame's ass in the last regular season game." Chuck came from the West Coast and had no particular affection for the Fighting Irish. He also loved to needle these guys.

"Whoa, Chuck, whadda *you* know? You're the guy who thinks Notre Dame is a big church in Paris." Snickers all around. Then Gary turned serious. "We've got a traitor. One of our top agents. But he gave us the slip just before we were going to take him down. Managed to get into the Soviet embassy in Washington."

Chuck shook his head. "What's the story?"

"Seems he was selling sensitive information: financial information, names, dates, and addresses. He was a big shot on the Latin American desk. We managed to track down most of the info he sold and plug the holes. It compromised a couple of undercover operations and we lost a few human assets, but we thought we had everything under control."

Gary stopped and looked down at the floor, gathering his thoughts. When he looked back up, his jaw was set.

"We thought the Papachristou suicide was suspicious. That's why I sent you guys over. I just got confirmation there's strong reason to believe it was linked to the traitor who gave us the slip. What did you find out from the wife?"

Brad turned over the photos and briefed Gary on the bodyguards, the wife's behavior, and the strange way the pics were delivered.

Gary thought it over, got up, and looked out the window. "Looks like the wife has suspicions of her own. Thankfully, if the pics are from her, she gave us something solid to chew on. The big blonde might just be the lead we're looking for."

Brad was circumspect. The shadows of the pigeons strutting around on the metal windowsill flashed across the wall and drew his attention to the sunlight streaming through the windows, lighting up the room. Helped him concentrate. He had one crucial question. "What's the link between Papachristou and the traitor?"

"Papachristou worked closely with the traitor in the past, and his area of competence was Latin America."

"Yeah, but why would that make him an assassination target?"

Gary nodded sadly. "You're right. This doesn't look like a Soviet job. We have a *de facto* understanding with the Soviets. Contrary to what you see in the movies, we don't run around killing each other except in exceptional circumstances. However, this is not true for the Latin American revolutionaries and drug dealers allied with the Soviets. Their modus operandi is 'kill or be killed.' We're afraid the Soviets shared some intel with their Latin American allies and this is just the beginning of a long, bloody chapter of tit for tat. Worst of all, it would extend the theater of operations to include Western Europe. Everything's on pause and it's all-hands-on-deck on every channel until we find out what's going on. The big blonde is the only lead we have for the moment."

"I had the feeling Papachristou's wife was hiding something," Brad said. "Like she was afraid. The more I think about it, the more I think it was the little boy's grandfather, Madame Papachristou's personal concierge, who delivered the pics. I think she sent him because she knew she was being watched—probably by those bodyguards. Those dudes were totally aggravating, swaggerin' around like they owned the place."

Brad turned to Chuck. He could see Chuck still had something on his mind. "One last question, Gary. Who was that woman in the café with you?"

It happened so fast that Brad almost missed it. Gary twitched, then shrugged and squeezed out a sheepish smile. "So you spotted her, eh? She was head of security for that compromised information. It was compromised on her watch and the traitor escaped on her watch. She weathered the storm, did her due diligence, and certified that all the holes had been plugged. Then, just when it looked like everything was under control, this 'suicide' came up. Her career's on the line."

Gary stopped as if that were the end of the story. He looked away, reached for his sugar cube, and mumbled, "She'll be coordinating things over here." He knew this was a real stink bomb.

It was like a slow-motion scene from a Fellini flick. Nobody moved. Finally, Chuck cocked his eye. He was incredulous. His laconic smile said it all. Brad was more verbal. "You mean she didn't get fired?"

Gary went to his default defensive maneuver. He plucked another sugar cube from the package, dipped it in his coffee, and scarfed it up. "Things are changing. Not enough women in upper management. She was on the fast track. Made some plausible arguments. Some plausible threats. The people mentoring her didn't want their reputations spoiled by her failure. So here she is in Paris with a big portfolio and another chance. You'll be meeting her soon."

Brad raised his eyebrows and pursed his lips into the most sarcastic expression he had in his playbook. "So the woman who screwed up in the first place is going to come over here to investigate whether or not the screwup was so bad it caused a larger leak that, in turn, caused the Papachristou death? This will definitely be a thorough, in-depth investigation. It will especially be a huge relief for everyone when her thorough, in-depth investigation ends with the rock-solid conclusion that the leak and the traitor have absolutely nothing to do with Papachristou's death."

Gary had to smile. "You might be onto something there." He was sensitive to Brad's suspicion of authority in general—and politicians, bureaucrats, and lawyers in particular. "It is what it is, but I've got to go with the flow. You've got to go with the flow, too, Brad. You can't fight City Hall."

That was when the doorbell rang. Brad and Chuck snapped to attention. The only person who came by the safe house unannounced was Brad's nosy neighbor who used her delicious pastries as an excuse. It couldn't be her because she was in Clermont-Ferrand visiting her daughter.

Gary checked his watch. "That must be Madison." When there was no reaction, he added, "Madison Samson III is the agent we've been discussing."

The doorbell rang again. She was impatient. Brad went to the door and looked through the peephole. It was a woman in a pantsuit, early thirties, brown hair. She had teased it up to get the big, bouffant look. Her hand was on her hip and she was tapping her foot. Madison Samson III had arrived. On the warpath, painted for war. Bright-red lipstick. Dark makeup base. Blue eyeliner. Black mascara. Heavy, black-rimmed glasses accentuated the slight hump in the nose. It was perfect warpaint for the frown she was focusing on the closed door.

He opened it. "Hi, please come in."

She blew by him before the words were out of his mouth. "Where's Gary?"

"Straight down the hall to your right. Nice to meet you, too." She didn't even flinch.

Gary was uncharacteristically charming. He stood, took her hand, and said, "Madison, I want you to meet Brad and Chuck. You can call on them if you need help."

There was tension. Madison cocked her head. She felt it. She was a ferocious warrior with intuition and third-generation security antennas.

"Thank you," she said. "I'll be as polite as I can."

That was her first jab. Brad knew the dangers of sparring with women. They were born with the talent they honed to perfection through years of honey-coated putdowns in the home, in the classroom, in the office, and with their friends. Madison was a black belt in the art. Brad imagined the intricate inbreeding it would take to produce three straight generations of Madison Samsons. He smiled but didn't laugh. Her tailored gray pantsuit jacket had a dark stain at the shoulder. *That* made him laugh.

She shot a glance at the two of them and nodded. "I won't be needing any help." Then, more diplomatically, "It's a pleasure. I will use the Barbary Coast Saloon to get in touch if I ever do need anything from either one of you. In the meantime, don't do anything unless you hear from me—understood?"

With those words, all the tension was sucked out of the room. Madison Samson III had unceremoniously sent Brad and Chuck off the field. Their synchronized sigh of feigned disappointment was not enough to fool Madison. They were relieved their contact with her would now be negligible and nonexistent.

Brad sat immobile and silent, scrutinizing the face of the female facing him. Outside of the wrong foot she got off on, there was something charismatic about her. He could see where Madison Samson III would appeal to a gallery of aging bureaucrats in Washington. She had a nice figure and feminine hand moves, but she was a bulldozer, not a souped-up sports car.

With her authority established, she warmed up ever so slightly and conjured up a smile. It was a nice smile. "Do you have anything for me?"

"Gary's got everything. Nothing more to add." Brad's written reports were usually submitted after all was said and done. Gary insisted it was never a good idea to write down anything that couldn't be proven or at least shown to be highly likely. He called it CYA for "cover your ass."

She reared back. Looked down her nose. "Some things Gary told me are unclear and probably misleading. I have to see where you're going wrong."

Brad stifled a guffaw. This was coming from the person responsible for the original security breach. Unvarnished chutzpah. He could feel the irritation gathering steam down in the pit of his stomach. His knee-jerk reaction was to blow her off, but his good manners and her well-hidden charisma told him to bite it back, see how things unfolded. He had a feeling there was more to Madison Samson III than met the eye. One thing was for sure. Madison Samson III was an ominous presence, like a stick of dynamite in a box of fireworks just waiting for someone to light her fuse.

No sooner had that thought crossed his mind than she threw him a change-up. "Do you mind if I make us another pot of coffee?" She jumped up and headed for the kitchen.

How many high-flying alpha females had enough confidence to pull a stunt like that? The answer was "probably not many," and it changed the chemistry.

"She might not be that bad after all," said the voice in his left ear. The voice in his right ear jerked him back to reality. "Don't be a sucker. This woman is toxic."

Chapter 3

EARLY MAY 1975, PARIS, THE BARBARY COAST SALOON

It was almost time for the dinner show at the Barbary Coast Saloon. Brad turned down the rue Jules Chaplain, a quiet L-shaped lane nestled between the rue Bréa to the south and the rue Notre-Dame-des-Champs to the north. At number 11 stood the Barbary Coast Saloon. Nothing but the moniker had changed since 1969, Brad's first day in Paris. Then, it was called Jacky's Far West Saloon.

The street door opened onto a small vestibule. The long, rectangular barroom was one step up to the left. Brad took a quick look inside. The polished oak bar sported shiny brass fittings, and the stools were solid metal frames upholstered with soft, round, black leather seats. A dim red light glowed behind a wooden wall rack stocked with bottles of spirits, liqueurs, wines, and beers. The shades of the lamps placed strategically in the four corners of the room were designed to resemble the sails on the buccaneer boats of old. The room was empty. It was too early for customers.

Brad took the flight of stairs that led straight down to the main room that served as a restaurant until eleven and a discothèque thereafter. The lights were on above the massive hickory wood bar that occupied the left wall. The back wall featured a colorful mural of pirate ships on a stormy sea and a black grand piano that stood majestically to the side.

Devi Bastien's office door to the right of the stairway was open. Devi was the proprietor, an aging ingénue with a story to tell. Her voice was loud and clear. The other voice was a soft feminine purr. Sounded like an interview. Brad heard the words "reincarnation" and "Cleopatra." He had to smile. Her spiel hadn't changed over the years. Brought him back to their first encounter in 1969, the nascent beads of perspiration forming on her upper lip, eyes glowing red through the heavy layers of black mascara, her voice strong and true: "Mr. James, I am the reincarnation of Cleopatra."

After all these years, he still was not sure whether she used this line as some kind of a test or if she was stark raving mad. Whatever it was, he had wisely decided to play along with her and chose the badass warrior, Genghis Khan, as his own reincarnation. She had really loved it when he'd suggested they might even have been contemporaries.

It sounded like the interviewee had also chosen wisely to play along. In a throaty purr with a strong upper-class British accent, she rattled off Helen of Troy, hypnotism, astrology, and magic, all in the same breath.

Brad had to check this out. He stuck his head inside and was rewarded with an overwhelming surprise. There she stood, solemn and shapely, posing and poised. Long, dark hair. A simple black satin dress highlighting the contours of her feminine arcs and curves. In a graceful demi-pirouette, she turned toward the door as Brad entered the room. Under perfectly arched eyebrows, her dark eyes inspected him. There was no emotion. She was sizing him up and he was returning the compliment. The moment was magic and her presence was magnetic.

Devi broke the spell. "Brad, meet Samantha. Samantha, Brad."

Samantha extended a beautifully manicured hand with long, slender, perfectly formed fingers. It looked so delicate. Brad hesitated. Admired it. Took it tenderly into his own.

"Brad," she purred. "My pleasure; Samantha."

He looked at Devi. "Sorry to interrupt. I'll let you ladies get to it."

He didn't see Samantha again until the show was over. The restaurant was full, so Brad let the show go on longer than usual. He was headed for the stairway when she reappeared, gliding gracefully across the dance floor.

"I enjoyed it so much. Your rendition of 'Jody and the Kid' was magic. That song goes great with your style." Her voice was satin, mood music.

"I didn't see you in the room."

"I stayed in the background. Didn't want to make you nervous."

In fact, her presence *would* have made him a little nervous. But there was no way she could know that. She didn't seem the pretentious type. Must have been that magic moment in Devi's office. Maybe he had been too obvious.

"Don't worry. You didn't do anything when we met." She was reading his mind.

Maybe she could read his mind. Brad was going to have to process that. On the one hand, a little mind reading might make his seduction offensive easier. On the other hand, it might turn her off if she saw what he was really thinking.

About to invite her for a drink, she struck again. "There's no time for a drink." Brad squeezed out a lopsided smile replete with a heavy dose of consternation. She moved forward and touched his arm. Her dark, somber gaze was somewhere between tender and affectionate. "I have to run. But I want a raincheck."

That was good enough for Brad. Before he could verbalize his agreement, she broke for the stairway. Stopped suddenly. Turned. "We can talk on the way to my apartment. If you have time. It's only a fifteen-minute walk from here."

Brad decided to forget about being surprised and just roll with the punches. He took her hand. "Okay, let's go." Outside on the street they continued to walk hand in hand. Brad took that as a positive sign. It made him feel good. "How'd it go with Devi?"

"Hard to tell. Devi is secretive. Mysterious. Very profound. How long have you known her?"

"Since 1969 when I came to Paris. She hired me as a 'security agent'—a.k.a. the bouncer—when the Barbary Coast Saloon was called Jacky's Far West Saloon. She's an interesting character. More to her than meets the eye. She was the French Mata Hari of World War II. I think she's still mixed up in the spy world in one way or another."

Samantha stopped dead in her tracks and turned to face him. She squeezed his hand and studied his face. Her dark eyes were somber and searching. For the first time, he had caught *her* off balance. She was so beautiful in this unscripted moment. They stood face to face. She wanted the rest of the story. He wanted to savor the moment, prolong it. So that's what he did.

Her eyes still somber and searching, she purred, "So, tell me about the French Mata Hari."

"It's a long story. I don't know where to start."

"Start at the beginning." Samantha was no longer flirting. Her lips were pursed and her eyebrows knitted together. They continued like that for a short minute while Brad gathered his thoughts. At the boulevard Saint Michel, Samantha pointed across the street. "That's where I live."

Brad walked her to the door. She took her key from her purse and turned to face him. He kissed her on the cheek. She snuggled in and wound her arms around him in a big hug. It was another one of those magic moments. Brad's magic moments meant testosterone up, guard down.

It was the shadow from the streetlamp that warned him. He rolled to the ground with Samantha and just avoided the blow from the metal bar that glanced off his ribcage.

He let his momentum propel him back onto his feet. Two bulky males with billy clubs in their hands and blood in their eyes were bearing down on him.

Chapter 4

Brad's first thought was for Samantha down to his right on her hands and knees. Before he could react, she made an astonishing back vault onto her feet and two even more astonishing backflips to end up several yards behind him.

The bulky boys hesitated. Samantha's acrobatic recovery was not in their playbook. Brad drifted out of range. Their metal billy clubs were about two feet long—mortal weapons in the hands of someone who knew how to use them. Brad could see they did know how to use them. He was worried about Samantha.

"Don't worry about me. I can handle myself." She kept reading his mind.

Bulky Boy Number One moved in on Brad. He was the youngest, the strongest, and the fastest.

Bulky Boy Number Two went after Samantha. It looked like she was going to run for it. She dashed across the street and hand-vaulted over the spiked iron fence that surrounded the park.

Impressive, but she wasn't running for it. She danced around, executing a few perfect cartwheels while she waited, as Number Two hauled his heavy body over the fence. Once he hit the ground huffing and puffing, she took another running vault to the other side of the fence, topped off with a front flip and a cartwheel.

Number Two shook his head in disgust and started climbing back to the other side. He was aggravated and he was frustrated and he was sweating from the exertion. It was a toxic mixture. Hoisting his leg over the metal spikes, his hand slipped and his wrist gave way. He came down hard on the fence, heard a squish, felt the pain. He looked down at a spike penetrating deep into the meat of his thigh. He dropped his club and struggled to free his leg. It wasn't working. His upper body strength was not up to it. The more he struggled, the deeper the spike burrowed into his meaty thigh.

Meanwhile, Number One circled Brad, searching for an opportunity to strike. He was quick and experienced. Brad was faking and feinting, feeling out Number One's moves. Number One was using short strikes, aiming for a hand, a wrist, or a forearm that would weaken his adversary and leave him open for the knockout blow.

Brad faked a left. Number One struck. Brad dodged, moved to the outside, grabbed the metal bar. Number One jerked away. Brad held on, using his momentum to swing inside and headbutt Number One in the face.

Number One fell back. He was dazed, but his instinct allowed him to disengage. Brad followed his retreat, advancing behind a series of left-right punches. The punches missed their mark but made the retreating Number One raise his guard to block them. It opened him up to Brad's long front kick, which caught him full force in the solar plexus. It was Brad's best weapon and would take down most adversaries.

Number One was not most adversaries. He still had his club and started swinging it wildly. The headbutt and front kick had weakened him and, especially, had slowed him down. Brad used this advantage to sweep-kick Number One to the ground. As he went down, Brad grabbed the club and wrenched it from his hand.

Number One rolled to the side and came up with a Bowie knife. Brad landed a glancing blow to Number One's wrist and followed through with full swing to his tibia. Number one screamed. Too much noise. The next blow fell on Number One's head. He screamed no more.

Brad stomped the shoulder of the hand that still held the knife. Then he dragged the unconscious dude between two cars parked on the street.

Across the street stood Samantha. She seemed to be talking to Number Two as she observed his furious efforts to disengage from the spiked fence, but it was to no avail. He didn't have the arm strength to lift his bulky body.

This was good news. It would be easy get some answers from him—if he didn't die first. Blood was everywhere, and it looked to Brad like the artery was blown out. Better hurry.

"Who are you?"

"Help me, man."

"Who are you?"

"I'm John." He could barely get the words out. His voice trailed off; blood spurted all over the place. Then his head slumped forward. The blood stopped. He was dead.

"Rest in peace, John."

The whole scene took less than two minutes, but it seemed like two hours. A couple of cars had passed by, and it was likely someone had alerted the police. Brad did a quick search of Number Two's pockets. Nothing but some bills and coins, a picture of a pretty blonde woman, and a telephone number. No identification, which was suspicious in itself.

They left him hanging by his thigh and went back across the street. Brad frisked Number One and found nothing, not even bills or coins. Brad wiped down the metal club he'd handled and placed it in Number One's hand.

Samantha looked on. Dark and somber. Motionless. No expression. She was a cool number.

"Do you know these guys?" Brad pressed.

Samantha leaned back and raised her eyebrows. "No, do you?"

Her snotty reply surprised him. "No, I don't. I thought you were talking to the dead guy."

She gave him a funny look. Patted his cheek. "Just telling him what I thought of him."

Brad wasn't convinced but let it go at that. The spell was broken. "You better go inside before the cops get here. Do you want me to stay with you?" It was a halfhearted Hail-Mary pass, but what the hell, you never knew. She might ask him to stay.

"Thanks, Brad. You're so gallant. I'll be fine."

"So gallant!" He couldn't argue with that, and it was fine by him.

From what he'd seen tonight, he was convinced she could take care of herself. He was also worried she could take care of him, too. She could read his mind, and within three hours of meeting her, he'd been involved in a life-and-death battle with a pair of gangbangers. He was also certain this was not a random attack. These gangbangers were American, they were pros, and they were out to kill.

The big questions were "who?" and "why?"

In the heat of battle, he'd just assumed he was the target. His past activities had made him enough enemies. It didn't add up, though. His enemies weren't American and probably wouldn't attack him on a main Parisian thoroughfare. Unless, of course, the Papachristou pictures had something to do with it. Maybe someone was trying to keep the existence of the pics secret. Something funny was going on because he was one hundred percent certain that the aggression was not a simple attempted robbery.

Finally, the more he thought about Samantha's reaction, the more intrigued he became. She didn't scream. She didn't cry. She didn't run away. She wasn't paralyzed by fear. She'd backflipped and somersaulted and danced rings around the guy who went after her. Even more puzzling, he was certain she'd been having a discussion with the guy before he died. Like she knew him. Brad needed answers, so he decided to stick around and see how the rest of the evening played out. The bus stop across the street gave him a perfect vantage point.

The commotion in front of Samantha's building was starting to draw a crowd, even at this late hour. There was an ambulance, a *car de police*—a police personnel carrier—and a dozen spectators milling around. When the ambulance team finished strapping the gangbangers' bodies onto gurneys and screamed off, the crowd broke up. One of the spectators in a bathrobe and slippers went back inside Samantha's building. Two bulky, unshaven gangbangers brandishing billy clubs followed close on her heels. Brad had the feeling they were looking for him.

*   *   *

It wasn't really an apartment. It was a seventh-floor maid's room under the roof, thirteen feet long and eight feet wide. Now that live-in maids had disappeared from French family life, these rooms were rented out to university students. This one had a cold-water sink in the corner under a skylight and a Turkish toilet down the hall.

Samantha had rented it for three months, cash in advance. There were still three weeks left on the lease, but she wouldn't be able to take advantage of it. The two gangbangers down on the street suggested that, however unlikely, her cover might have been blown.

She had made no mistakes. Of this, she was certain. The more likely explanation was that Brad was the target. Anyway, she couldn't risk it. The gangbangers were not working alone. John had admitted that before he died. His comrades weren't far away and may have seen her enter the building. If so, they would search it. She was in a hurry.

She stripped off her black-haired wig and shook out a thick mane of medium length, wavy blond hair. She stuffed the wig in her rucksack. A generous dose of cold cream and a couple of Kleenex tissues wiped the swarthy tint from her complexion and the black makeup from her eyebrows. Her dark, somber eyes turned limpid blue when she removed the tinted contacts. She traded her black satin dress and high-heeled pumps for a black T-shirt, black leotards, and black sneakers. A quick look in the cracked mirror above the washbasin confirmed she was no longer Samantha Smith.

Getting back onto the street would be a problem. The sirens and flashing lights outside eliminated the main door as an option. Hiding out in the room was also out of the question. It wouldn't be long before the bad guys were snooping around inside the building. They might go door-to-door. If she was the target, she would be recognized. Her disguise was good, but maybe not that good.

As usual, her escape route had been well-planned in advance. She threw the makeup and change of clothes into the rucksack. There was nothing else. She only used the room to change into

Samantha Smith and back again. It wasn't likely that any fingerprinting would be done, but she wiped down all the surfaces just in case. She strapped on her rucksack and exited the room, careful to lock everything up tight.

Out in the hallway, she headed for the storage closet at the top of the service stairway. She figured time was on her side. The only access to the maid's rooms on the seventh floor was through the service stairway. If anybody was searching, the seventh floor would probably be the last place they checked.

Gruff voices and heavy footsteps in the service stairwell contradicted that analysis. The service stairwell and the seventh floor were going to be the first places they checked. The clock was ticking.

The lock on the closet was one of those primitive mechanisms meant more to dissuade than to protect. There was nothing of value in there, just some cleaning materials, brooms, mops, stools, and a few carpenter's tools. Samantha had already unlocked it many times using her own tools. This time, something was blocking the mechanism.

The voices were already on the fourth floor. She jiggled the tool. The lock gave way. The door cracked open. She slipped into the closet and closed the door.

Now the voices were on the fifth floor. No time to lock it. She grabbed the metal rod attached to the rooftop trapdoor, twisted it to unlatch the lock, and pushed the trap open.

The voices were coming up to the seventh floor. A couple of steps up the ladder and she would be up on the roof. Out of sight. Out of reach.

She looked for the ladder. Not there. Somebody had removed it.

Without the ladder, she couldn't reach the trapdoor. There was a stool in the corner, but even with that, she couldn't reach it. She grabbed the stool anyway and set it carefully under the trapdoor. The voices were on the landing. She rocked back on her heels, shot forward onto the stool, and used it as a trampoline to catapult herself toward the ceiling.

She caught the trapdoor flaps, pulled herself up, and swung onto the roof. Effortlessly, like a trapeze artist. The unlocked door banged open. She shut the trap. It was a tie. They saw nothing; she saw them: two unshaven muscle-bound dudes. They were not cops.

They rustled around in the closet for a few seconds, made sure there was nothing there, then went down the hall to check out the maids' rooms. Samantha breathed a sigh of relief and crept across the rooftops until she got to the building with the fire escape far from the scene. She clambered down and set off on foot. It would be a forty-five-minute walk to her hotel just off the Champs-Elysées.

Chapter 5

Wednesdays could arguably be considered Brad's favorite day of the week. Nothing scheduled in the morning, so he could sleep in. He hadn't heard from Samantha since the attack, but that didn't worry him. He had stuck around long enough to see the gangbangers leave empty-handed and followed them to their car parked two blocks away. Chuck was checking out the license number. Devi told him Samantha had popped by to say hello. No message.

By the time he got to the dojo at 1:00 p.m., morning classes were over and he had the place all to himself. When he finished his workout at 3:00 p.m., he still had enough time to relax and have a snack before his research seminar at the Institut des Hautes Études de l'Amérique Latine over by the Latin Quarter.

The seminar itself was a kick. It was populated by two distinct groups, each of which was indigenous to university life. The first was composed of aspiring academics anxious to showcase their intelligence and share their ideas with anyone willing to listen. The second was a motley crew of wannabe Latin American revolutionaries dedicated to imposing their ideas on anybody within earshot. The members of the first group could generally be described as rational, slightly supercilious, and mostly calm, confident in their intellectual superiority and the undeniable force of their arguments. Members of the second group were generally touchy and aggressive, so certain of their virtue and the purity of their cause that any deviation from the party line was met with verbal abuse and physical threats.

Although different in many ways, both groups had one thing in common: Everything bad in the world was the fault of Uncle Sam. All their competing theories, arguments, and proofs ended with the same conclusion that could be stated in a nutshell. If the United States of America did not exist, all the countries of Central and South America would be flourishing, egalitarian societies of peace on earth and goodwill to men.

As an American, Brad started the seminar with two strikes against him. As someone not necessarily convinced of the prevailing seminar's consensus and perfectly willing to argue the contrary, this was strike three. His presence was taken as an unacceptable affront by most of the other participants. Some had even argued that he should be excluded from the seminar. His supervisor shot that argument down before it even got off the ground. Brad appreciated that. He never missed a class.

Today was his turn to make the presentation, and the seminar had not been much different from the others. He was the odd man out. Truth be told, he kind of enjoyed goading the revolutionaries with logic and facts. Still, logic aside, it was hard for him to understand how they could be outraged so easily by simple statements of fact.

Argentina was the flavor of the day and the subject of his thesis. When he stated that there was only a forty-year difference in the independence of the two countries, 1776 for the U.S. from

England and 1816 for Argentina from Spain, they argued that this was irrelevant—irrelevant to what was not really clear. When he said that in 1923 Argentina had the fifth highest per capita GDP in the world, they were screaming bloody murder—still not clear what they were on about.

That's the way it went until the end of his presentation when his conclusion was that Argentina's current subservient situation as a developing country was the direct consequence of bad economic policy and had absolutely nothing to do with the U.S. By then, they were squirming around in their seats, shaking their heads, slamming their books on their desks, and, if not frothing at the mouth, at least muttering insults. All except for one dude Brad had never seen at the seminar before.

This new dude was out of place in his black motorcycle leathers and slicked-back hair. His chiseled jawline and straight nose clashed with the hint of something soft and perverted lurking behind his hooded eyes and even features. Brad disliked him immediately. His presence attracted some attention when he swaggered in, but the seminar policy was that all were welcome. So nobody said anything.

He sat there expressionless, observing the antics unfolding around Brad's presentation. When it was over, he scooped up his helmet and left without a word. After a short moment of reflection, Brad decided to go after him. He had learned the hard way to beware of coincidences. New Dude's presence was probably not an innocent accident.

Out on the street, New Dude was cranking up his bike. It was a blood-red Harley. Brad hustled around the corner to his Indian Arrow. He was too slow…or New Dude was too fast. He raced off down Saint-Germain and disappeared before Brad had a chance to put on his helmet.

On the outside chance that he could catch him at a stoplight, Brad roared off in pursuit. Slaloming through the heavy traffic, he almost missed it. A flash of red just caught his eye as he blasted past the Drugstore. He hit the brakes. Pulled off to the side. New Dude was parking his bike. Disappeared into the Drugstore.

Brad waited across the street by the newsstand. There were several exits to the Drugstore, but from his position, he could see them all. It was a short wait for a big surprise. Dressed to the nines in a white miniskirt, black spike-heeled thigh-high boots, and an open-knit, ankle-length coat, Madison Samson III exited the Drugstore. She hesitated long enough to get her bearings, then headed straight for the taxi stand. Brad decided to drop New Dude and find out what Madison was up to.

The taxi drove straight to the 16th and stopped in front of an elegant apartment building. Brad recognized it as Papachristou's building. Madison slipped out of the taxi and went inside. The taxi waited.

Brad figured she wouldn't be long if she had the taxi wait. He was right. She was back out and into the taxi in less than five minutes. In a big hurry. Brad let her go and entered the building to find out why.

The answer lay behind a half-open door on the first floor. There was a body in a pool of thick red blood. Brad stepped inside and closed the door with his elbow. Better not to leave any fingerprints. Took a close look at the body. He tensed. It was the elderly gentleman who had left the photos in Chuck's car. A quick search of the spacious apartment confirmed it was empty.

Back in the entry, Brad bent down for a closer look at the wounds. There was one to the chest and— No warning. The body jerked itself upright. Brad threw himself back and crashed against the entry table. His heart pounding, adrenaline pumping, he struggled to stifle his surprise and regain control. The elderly gentleman was trying to speak. His lips were moving, but there was no sound.

Brad took his arm. "Relax. I'll call an ambulance."

The elderly gentleman made an almost imperceptible shake of his head. "Too late. Hurry. They'll be back."

"Who?"

"The Americans. They'll be back."

Brad couldn't believe what he was hearing. "The Americans did this?"

"Yes. Waiting for me when I came in. Tried to capture me. Cut two of 'em, bad, deep. Third guy had a gun. Shot me. They killed Papachristou." The guy was fading fast and the effort wasn't helping to slow him down. "The girl saw it. Gave me the pictures I left in your car. She was there. Filmed it."

"What girl?"

"Pretty girl. Pretty. The other woman wanted to know about the pictures. Asked questions. Lots of questions."

"What woman?"

"She's with the Americans. Just left."

"Who are you?"

"Bodyguard. Personal bodyguard to Madame Papachristou. Hurry. They'll be back to finish me off."

Those were his last words. He was still sitting up, but he was dead.

Sounded like Madison came over to interrogate the old man and left in a hurry when she saw he was too far gone to undergo a proper interrogation.

Footsteps and muffled voices on the landing made the old bodyguard's warning a pounding reality. The bad guys were back. Americans or not, Brad wanted no part of what they were peddling.

The service stairway was not a valid option. If these guys were professionals—and Brad had to assume they were—that exit would be covered. He checked out the back windows. It was only a seven-foot drop into the courtyard.

The apartment door was opening just as he dropped down. He scurried to the edge of the building, found a foothold, and vaulted over the wall into the courtyard next door.

"I saw the motherfucker go into the building. He's in here somewhere. Find him." It was an American accent. The old bodyguard was right.

Hesitation was Brad's worst enemy. He had to act fast. He wouldn't be safe hiding out in the next-door courtyard or building. Flight was the only solution and required that he be gone before they sent someone to patrol the street.

He was in the building, through the lobby, onto the street, and almost to his bike when he heard the footsteps. A quick look back confirmed it was one of the gangbangers trying to run him down. There wouldn't be enough time to get away on his bike, so he slowed down. When the footsteps got close enough, he whipped around to face his pursuer. Caught the gangbanger off guard. The gangbanger skidded to a halt, total confusion deforming his features. He obviously had not thought about what he would do if he caught his quarry.

Brad seized the opportunity and landed a long front kick to the gangbanger's solar plexus. He followed with a left-right combination to the head. As the stunned gangbanger's knees buckled, Brad grabbed his shoulders and pulverized his nose with a textbook headbutt. Gangbanger fell backward. There was a loud pop when the back of his head bounced off the pavement.

The street was deserted, but that wouldn't last long. No time to frisk the guy. Brad hustled to his bike as nonchalantly as possible and cranked up. He was barely halfway down the side street when a group of gangbangers came busting out of the apartment building. They had walkie-talkies and they were calling for help to close the area down.

Chapter 6

Brad didn't accelerate. The street was narrow and cars were parked on the right-hand side all the way down. Chestnut trees lined the other side. No room for maneuver and no other way out. A dark sedan pulled out at the corner and blocked the intersection. In the rearview, Brad could see another dark sedan bearing down from behind. Retreat was no longer an option. At the intersection, three gangbangers stood in front of the sedan. They wouldn't use guns. Guns would draw too much attention. They would use their clubs. One guy had a baseball bat.

Brad rolled slowly toward the intersection. Let the sedan behind close in. Almost to the intersection, he hit the gas, cut to the left, and raised the front wheel in a slow wheelie that kissed off the trunk of the big maple. He threw his weight to the left, kept his momentum, and did a complete 180. It was beautiful. He blasted by the black sedan before the gangbangers could react. At the corner of Papachristou's street, there was no confrontation. The rest of the gang had already vacated the premises.

There was no way they could follow him in a car. It would be a different story if they had motorcycles. He hadn't seen any, but couldn't be sure. As a precaution, he took a roundabout route through the Bois de Boulogne, down some trails and wrong ways on one-way streets. Satisfied he was in the clear, he went straight to Latorre Legal and parked just off the Champs-Elysées.

Chuck was studying his financial statements when Brad came in. His hearty greeting suggested he was ready for a break. "Hey, man, where've you been? I've got work for you."

"That's why I've been avoiding you. Now I've got work for the both of us."

That kind of news was music to Chuck's ears. Action was his thing. He leaned forward, rested his elbows on his desk, and waited for Brad to deliver. By the time Brad finished his account of his afternoon's activities, Chuck was chomping at the bit. "You're telling me that Madison is running a team of gangbangers who killed the elderly gentleman who gave us the pics and then tried to kill you?"

"I didn't say that. I said I followed a suspicious-looking dude on a Harley-Davidson from my seminar to the Drugstore, and Madison exited the Drugstore a few minutes later. She took a taxi to Papachristou's building, went in, and came rushing out less than five minutes after that."

"Any idea who the guy was?"

"No. I think he was probably sent by Madison to check me out. See what I look like so I can be identified if I go snooping around."

"Do you think she killed the old man?"

"No. He said it was 'the Americans.' I think the gangbangers were supposed to neutralize him so that Madison could interrogate him. Or maybe Madison orchestrated the murder and went by to make sure the job was done."

Chuck was getting animated. When he was animated, he was creative. "Think she set you up?"

"She couldn't possibly have known I followed the Harley-Davidson dude. He was long gone before I got on my bike. Blind luck I saw him go into the Drugstore. One thing is for sure. Her behavior is extremely suspicious. Another thing is for sure. The hit team is big, professional, and well equipped. There were four guys after me in the building, four more in the car blocking the intersection, and at least two others in the car chasing me. That's ten guys I saw. There may have been others."

"We've gotta tell Gary, *illico, tout de suite*, right now."

Brad put his hands in the 'stop' position. "Not so fast."

Betty knocked and opened the door. "I thought you might need some of this." She rolled in the serving cart with a steaming pot of arabica, spoons, sugar, and cups. She was right.

Coffee in hand, Brad continued. "We can't tell Gary. He might be involved in some kind of convoluted scheme we're not supposed to know about, and Madison was unequivocal. She does not want us meddling in her investigation. Gary also was unequivocal. He agrees with her."

"So you think we should just sit around and do nothing?"

"I didn't say that. I only said we shouldn't tell Gary. Nothing stopping us from hanging around the Drugstore area and keeping our eyes peeled. I bet Madison and the Harley-Davidson dude will show up sooner rather than later."

"We'll see her for sure. Gary told me she's in a hotel over on the rue Jacob just five minutes from the Drugstore."

"We have to stay away from her. The French are likely to be on her like a blanket if she's registered as official embassy staff. We have to be careful doing anything around there, anyway. The whole area has been crawling with spooks and spies since the Drugstore got bombed out in September. I think the Harley-Davidson dude is our best bet. If he's around, he'll be easy to find. We just look for his bike. Can't miss it. It's a beautiful, bright, blood red."

"Got it," Chuck said. "We don't even have to hang around cafés where we could attract attention. Just walk around the streets in the area and hope to get lucky. Who knows? He might just not be worried about someone spotting his bike. Might even park it in the same place."

"I'll pass by once in the morning and once in the early evening. You take midday and late evening."

Chuck stiffened. "Not too late. I've got an appointment."

"So, Mister Lonely suddenly has an *appointment*. How much do you have to pay for her services?"

"Stuff it, smartass. Nothing like that. I just promised Betty to take her to dinner. Got a reservation at Floquet for 8:30."

Brad was intrigued but could see Chuck was uncomfortable and decided to drop it. He was on his way out when Chuck stopped him.

"What about those gangbangers who tried to mug you the other night? They were American too, weren't they?"

"Yeah. Did you manage to find out anything from the license number or the telephone number?"

"Nothin' yet. My contact is still working on it. He thinks the license plate number might be fake. He'll have an address from the telephone number in a day or two."

Chapter 7

EARLY MAY 1975, PARIS

Brad's hunches tended to cost him dearly. Today was no exception. He had to get up at the crack of dawn and that irritated Veronique, the girl he had been seeing for the last few weeks. She insisted on knowing where he was going so early in the morning and why. Her nose was already out of joint because he had turned down her invitation to spend the weekend with her family in Caen in Normandie. It wasn't that he didn't want to go. He didn't, but even if he did, he couldn't. He had his dinner shows on Friday and Saturday.

He could see their relationship was fast growing dim. She was turning up the heat. Weekends were the new hot topic. They had been on the back burner while she angled for deep, tell-all discussions where he was supposed to pour his heart out and confess to all his sins and fears and regrets. "*Pas de secrets* (No secrets)" was her code word.

He just couldn't get into that. First of all, it was none of her business. Second of all, it would be totally mindless to give her inside information that would fuel her curiosity, tarnish his image, and provide her with chinks in his armor. Third of all, he'd been dealt a pretty good hand and was not willing to start complaining about it. Okay, he had a problem with authority, but it wasn't something he was ashamed of, and he had learned to work around it.

In their heart-to-hearts, he had tried to throw her some red meat—silly fights he'd had in high school, college pranks, too much to drink, things like that. Once, he had the astonishing stupidity to mention Alice, his high-school sweetheart and lifelong soulmate who'd perished in an accident because of him. Big mistake. Veronique could not let that go. Alice entered their relationship and made it a *ménage à trois*—what did he do with Alice, what did he say to Alice, did he share his secrets with Alice, did he spend weekends with Alice, and on and on.

Now Brad could see that weekends together were going to be Veronique's Rubicon. Either he relented or she was gone. She was pretty and cute and smart and sexy. She was also headstrong and power hungry. *C'est la vie.* He was gonna miss her.

He parked his bike by the metro Mabillon and walked over to the Café de Flore. Took a seat on the terrace, ordered a *café crème*, two butter croissants, and a large orange juice. The area was bustling, and the Drugstore was right across the street. The bombing back in September didn't seem to have affected its popularity. If anything, it had increased it.

A careful analysis of the immediate neighborhood suggested the authorities had not forgotten last September 15, even if the customers had. There were three dark Renault station wagons parked in strategic locations on the street around the Drugstore. Each had two occupants keeping a vigilant eye on the surrounding area. The newspaper kiosk had two occupants, one doing the selling and the other watching the street. Brad figured the old man on the terrace in the corner table with a walkie-talkie sticking out of his jacket pocket was a cop as well. He also noticed a man and three women roaming around the area with no apparent destination in mind. Brad recognized the *clochard* (wino) begging on the street from other French stakeouts he'd come across in the past.

All the obvious surveillance, as well as the more discreet surveillance that was surely set up in strategically located apartments around the intersection, meant he and Chuck would not be able to spend much time watching the Drugstore. Even pass-bys would have to be few and far between. Experienced surveillants would spot the suspicious activity in no time. In a way, Brad was reassured by this because he was certain there had been no surveillance on him or Madison's taxi the day he followed her to Papachristou's residence. That meant he was in the clear as far as that episode went.

One of the headlines in the *Herald Tribune* caught his eye: *Senator James 'Jake' Brown accuses CIA*. The Democrat senator from Virginia was a member of a recently formed Senate committee headed by Senator Frank Church to look into abuses by the U.S. intelligence agencies. He had somehow gotten wind of a CIA "security" leak and was demanding to know what secrets had been revealed and who was responsible. From the tone of the article—long on outrage, rhetoric, and speculation, and short on facts—it sounded like he was referring to Madison's Latin American debacle. If he was, Madison was in for a rough ride. Jake Brown was known as a hardline patriot, an implacable foe to anyone or anything threatening the U.S.

His second croissant was half finished when his hunch paid off. There he was, New Dude, the Harley-Davidson guy, crossing Saint-Germain on his way to the Drugstore. He was on foot and his bike was nowhere to be seen. Brad concluded he either lived in the area or had a friend he could stay with who did. Brad doubled down on his attention. He didn't want to lose this guy. The bill was already paid and he was ready to move.

It was a short wait. The Harley guy exited the Drugstore back the way he had come. When he passed the café, Brad noticed he had a copy of the *Herald Tribune* under his arm. Definitely American. Brad let him get a comfortable lead and went after him. It was a straightforward tail job. The guy gave no obvious signs that he was security conscious. He went straight to a hotel on the rue Jacob, the same hotel where Madison was staying.

Brad dropped off at the corner, walked over to Saint Michel, and bought the *Figaro*. The murder of Papachristou's personal bodyguard was reported in a short article on a back page as a robbery gone bad. The victim was a naturalized American citizen from Greece. He was sixty years old and had been living in Paris for the last five years. There was no mention of his relationship with Papachristou.

By now it was 10:30, late enough to make a polite call to Greta Papachristou. If the victim was close to the Papachristou family, as Brad suspected he was, she would probably be needing some support. The call was answered by a nasal male voice with a Spanish accent. "Who is calling?"

"Brad James from Latorre Legal."

"Sorry, Mrs. Papachristou is not available."

There was a short, muffled discussion, then Greta Papachristou's voice came over the line. "Mr. James, how nice of you to call. What can I do for you?"

"I thought I would come by and finish the business we started a few days ago."

The line went silent. More muffled discussion. She came back on. "I would be pleased if you were free to come by this morning."

"I can be there in half an hour."

Brad parked his bike two streets down from Papachristou's and walked the rest of the way. If the building were under surveillance, he would have a better chance of remaining anonymous.

He rang the bell and, after an unpleasantly long wait, was buzzed in. He took the elevator to the top floor and was met by two greasy-looking guards with mustaches. One was skinny. One was fat. As he stepped out of the elevator, the skinny honcho wanted to frisk him. Brad disagreed. He grabbed Brad's shoulder and pushed him into the wall. Brad rolled with the push and used the wall to thrust himself backward, headfirst. His head met skinny honcho's face flush on the nose. Skinny honcho didn't go down, but he was staggering around like a one-legged ass-kicker and his nose was gushing blood.

The fat honcho pulled his club and lunged at Brad. Brad sidestepped the attack and used the fat honcho's momentum to throw him down the stairs. There were fifteen steps to the first landing, and the fat honcho bounced off of every one of them before he came to a stop.

The skinny honcho was coming to his senses, just barely. His pathetic attempt to charge Brad was met by a slap to the side of the head. He stumbled. Brad grabbed him by his coat collar and the seat of his pants, bum-rushed him down the hall, and heaved him down the stairway. He hit halfway down, bounced once, and landed on top of his fat sidekick.

Brad brushed himself off and rang the buzzer. The head honcho from the previous visit opened the door. He threw his head back in surprise at smiling Brad standing there alone. "Where are my men?"

Brad head-signaled the stairway. "They dropped out for a break."

Head Honcho moved to the stairway. Brad brushed by him and went into the apartment. Greta was there, and she looked worse for the wear. Her eyes were still puffy and her nose was still red. Her dress was all wrinkled and her coiffure looked like a rat's nest. In the three seconds between Brad's entry and Head Honcho's *"Parate, cabrón* (Stop, asshole)*!"* Greta had time to mouth, "Not suicide." Brad nodded that he understood

Head Honcho stood there, fists balled up and muscles flexed. Anger and aggression radiated from every inch of his powerful body. He wasn't overly large, 6'1" or 6'2" and 190 pounds, but he was trained, and he was in shape. At 6'2" and 176 pounds, Brad was smaller, but he was trained as well. His muscles were long and lean, and he had half-inch karate knuckles of callus and cartilage on each hand. His biggest asset was his instinct for combat. He had an innate sense of creative tactics and perfect timing that made him a formidable adversary in any situation.

In this situation, Head Honcho had the advantage of three gangbangers with billy clubs to back him up. Brad was reluctant to get involved in a physical altercation with these guys in Greta Papachristou's apartment, but it was looking like he wouldn't have a choice.

That was when Greta Papachristou screamed, "Stop it! Stop it! Stop it!"

That was enough to stop the fight, but not enough to pacify Head Honcho and his men. Head Honcho's eyes were slits and he was snorting like a hog. "You got five seconds to get your white ass out of here, *gringo*."

Brad looked to Greta Papachristou. She was distraught, visibly on the verge of a meltdown. "You'd better go. Everything is fine. Thank you for coming by."

He took her hands into his and gave an understanding squeeze.

"My pleasure, Mrs. Papachristou. I'll leave you with your employees. If you need anything, please don't hesitate to get in touch."

Brad turned to leave. The exit was blocked by Head Honcho and his three flunkies. He motioned them away. After a few face-saving seconds of menacing scowls, they moved aside and Brad exited the apartment. The three flunkies followed. The door closed. Brad checked for the two gangbangers he had thrown down the stairs. They were gone.

The attack he anticipated never came. The three flunkies followed him down the stairs, but stayed far out of range—until the last flight. The door to the apartment on the first floor flew open as they started to close in. The fat gangbanger he had thrown down the stairs came limping out. His left hand held a long knife with a curved blade. His right hand held a billy club.

Chapter 8

Brad got to the bottom of the stairs with the fat gangbanger and his three buddies hot on his heels. Whatever plans they had came to an abrupt halt when another resident entered from outside. Brad said, *"Au revoir"* and left the four flunkies standing there like stupid store mannequins.

The whole Papachristou situation smelled to high heaven. Brad couldn't understand where this overaggressive security was coming from. He wondered who had hired them and why. From what he had seen, these guys were not the sharpest knives in the drawer. The old Papachristou bodyguard was murdered right under their noses. Maybe that's what made them so touchy.

He walked over to a café on the rue de Longchamp, where he ordered a *demi* and thought about Greta Papachristou's message. That she believed her husband did not commit suicide confirmed what Brad had understood from the pictures the now-deceased bodyguard gave him, and it made him even more convinced that the big-haired blonde was the culprit. It also seemed someone wanted to keep Greta Papachristou from getting this message out. Why else would she be kept in virtual isolation by her "bodyguards"? Brad suspected the answer to that question resided with Madison Samson III. However, if Madison was behind it, Brad wondered why she'd chosen to use South American bodyguards to do the dirty work. He also wondered whether she herself was included in "the Americans" the old bodyguard had referred to before he passed away.

The television interrupted his train of thought. It was the afternoon news, and the American Senator Brown from Virginia was being interviewed by a French journalist. The senator was still railing about the security leak and promising he would see to it that heads rolled. In his analysis of the interview, the French journalist argued that the senator would try and ride this issue to run for president. Brad figured that no matter what the senator did, Madison Samson III was extremely unhappy with the publicity her security failure was getting.

A glance at his watch told him it was almost time to make his afternoon pass by the Drugstore. A glance out on the street told him there was a heavy surveillance presence on site. It wasn't there when he entered the café, and he hadn't noticed anything on his way over. He decided to wait and see how things played out.

It was a short wait. Two of the three surveillants Brad had identified out on the street changed positions. They were all intent on the grocery store next door to the café. Sure enough, two of Papachristou's South American bodyguards emerged loaded up with bags full of groceries. They headed back in the direction of the Papachristou residence followed by at least the three surveillants on foot and one on a motorcycle. So! Somebody else was interested in what was going on at the Papachristou's. Once they were out of sight, Brad checked out of the café. It was time to hit the Drugstore.

He parked his bike by the river on the Quai Malaquais and

walked down the rue Bonaparte toward the Café de Flore across from the Drugstore. He stopped on the way for a few seconds at the corner of the rue Jacob and looked around. Nothing to report. When he got to Saint-Germain, however, he got a shock. There, seated face to face on the terrace of the café Les Deux Magots, sat Madison Samson III and the Harley-Davidson dude. Unsurprisingly, he was decked out in black leathers. Surprisingly, so was she.

Looking away from the café, Brad slipped past as fast as he could. He didn't miss the blood-red Harley parked right in front, basking in the admirative stares of anyone who had ever thought about riding a motorcycle.

Brad whipped around the corner and hustled back to his bike parked on the *quai*. If they were going somewhere, he wanted to know where. By the time he got back to Saint-Germain, Madison and Harley Man were getting on the Harley. Brad pulled off to the side to observe the scene. There wasn't any extraordinary activity generated by their departure when they pulled out. They were not targeted. He waited as long as he could to confirm, then he went after them.

The Harley was easy to follow. The placement of the handlebars, high and wide, made it difficult for the Harley dude to squeeze between the car lanes. Brad was able to stay way back, confident he could stay in contact.

They drove straight to a three-story *maison individuelle* (detached house) at the end of a dead-end street in Neuilly-sur-Seine. They parked on the street and entered the property through the open gate. Brad parked his bike across the boulevard Bineau and prepared for a long wait.

They exited the property sooner than he expected and were obviously in a hurry. Brad waited until they were out of sight on their way back toward Paris before crossing the boulevard Bineau on foot to the property on the dead-end street. The gate was still open. He checked for cameras. Rang the bell. There were no cameras and no one answered the bell. He went to the door. Knocked. No answer. Turned the doorknob. The door was unlocked. He went inside.

There was nothing on the first two floors. The third floor was where he found the recently deceased body of a well-groomed man about fifty-five years old sprawled out on the floor. There was an empty syringe in his hand with an empty sachet by his side. There was no sign of a struggle or anything else to contradict the conclusion that the deceased was the victim of an overdose. Brad wondered who had administered the overdose. He also wondered who this guy was.

He put on his motorcycle gloves. They were cumbersome but wouldn't leave any fingerprints, and he didn't have anything else. The billfold on the desk revealed the man's identity: Eric Mittel, fifty-six years old, born in Paris. Documents in the desk showed the man was an investment manager, but nothing linking him to Georges Papachristou. There was nothing of interest in the drawers. He went to the filing cabinets. They were bursting with piles of documents. There was no file for Papachristou. If it ever existed, it was probably in the hands of his predecessors Madison and Harley Man.

Out of curiosity more than hope, Brad rifled through a couple of files labeled *miscellaneous*, looking for he didn't know what. He flashed on an innocuous looking file labeled *segroeg* buried deep in a miscellaneous file. Segroeg is georges—as in Georges Papachristou spelled backwards. You had to be a word weirdo to notice it, but it was Papachristou's file. Brad was betting it was hidden away because it contained secret information.

He followed his intuition and scooped up as many documents in the file as he could pack into his pouch. As he dug deeper into the man's activities, he lost track of the time. Banging on the door brought him back. He had company. The cop kind. He had to get out of there ASAP.

He got only as far as the second floor before the downstairs door opened. *"Monsieur Mittel, vous êtes là* (Mr. Mittel, are you there)?"

The stairway was no longer an option. He ducked into a large room filled with free weights, weight machines, a treadmill—the whole works for a full-scale private gym. The room was wide open and there was no place to hide. The cops would definitely search it on their way to the top floor. The window was open. Too far down to jump. He could reach the branch of the elm tree outside but wasn't sure it would hold his weight. The door opened and he jumped, caught the branch, and swung into the trunk.

Someone was at the window. Brad didn't move. The window closed. He risked a peek. Nothing there. He slid down the tree, crossed the side yard, and slipped across the fence into the front yard of the next-door apartment building.

He was almost to the street behind Mittel's property when a raspy voice rang out. *"Arretez, petit* (Stop there, sonny boy)."

Chapter 9

Brad was ready to run for it when his sixth sense kicked in. The cops were already combing Mittel's property and there was a squad car cruising the street. When he turned, he saw the voice belonged to a gnarled old woman leaning on a wooden walking stick with an ivory handle. She had one of those wise faces that only age, personality, and experience can create.

"*T'es bien pressé, petit* (You're in a big hurry, sonny boy)."

"*J'ai un rendez-vous* (Got a date)."

She had one of those raunchy, titi Parisian accents. Brad could see she wanted some company, and the cops were closing in. Although there was no way they could link him to the deceased, if they stopped him they would get his name and address and who knew what else. He had those documents in his pouch.

She was sizing him up. "Got a cigarette?"

"Black tobacco."

"That's all I smoke, sonny boy. The blond stuff is for pussies."

Brad pulled out his Gitanes sans filtres. She sat down and screwed the cigarette into the corner of her mouth. He lit her up. She took a deep drag and exhaled with the cigarette still dangling between her lips.

After a few puffs, she used her thumb and forefinger to pull the cigarette out of her mouth. "Goddamn daughter doesn't let me smoke in the apartment. Never seen you before, sonny boy. What're you doin' hangin' around here?"

Before he could answer, the gate swung open and two *flics* (cops) stomped in. They were dead serious. "Do you live here?"

The little old lady didn't miss a beat. "Goddamn, son-of-a-bitch. No, sonny, we just sneak in here to smoke so our parents don't catch us. Of course, we live here. What are *you* doin' here?"

The *flics* pulled in their horns. "Excuse us, *Madame*, there has been a problem next door. Have you noticed anything?"

"Not until you came bustin' in."

One of the *flics* was intimidated by this garrulous old gal and her salty lingo. The other, not so much. "Can I see your papers?"

This was not Brad's address. His ID showed it. He was in trouble and he was ready to run. The old gal came to the rescue. "Goddamn, son-of-a-bitch, got nothin' better to do than harass an old woman visitin' peacefully with her grandson. Worse than the goddamn Krautheads. Piss me off! Run upstairs and get the papers, *petit*. Take the back stairs."

Brad was about to move. Once he was behind the building, he would make a run for it and be long gone before the *flics* realized what was happening.

The *flics* hesitated. They were in a hurry and decided there was no money to be made here. "No, that won't be necessary. Sorry to bother you. Carry on. Have a nice evening."

When they got out of earshot, she gave Brad a wink and said, "Now that I saved your hide, you can tell me what you're doin' here. What's your name, *petit?*"

It was crunch time. This crusty old battle-ax wouldn't be taken in by some cock-and-bull story that didn't account for the fact she had seen him coming from next door. He decided for a partial truth. "My name's Brad. Saw some suspicious dudes on a motorcycle casing the place and wanted to see what they were up to."

"It was a dude and a goddamn dame," she corrected him. "You some kind of a friggin' sidewalk superintendent or sumpthin'?"

"They fishtailed me on the boulevard when they turned off. Irritated me."

"There might be some truth to that." She gave him a cagey smile and a wink. "Might also be the mysterious Mittel next door's got your interest. Been a lot of bleedin' traffic over there today."

Brad *was* interested.

"Four bleedin' blockheads were in there this morning. One of them was all dolled up like a goddamn woman."

"How do you know it wasn't a woman?"

She snorted and shook her head. "He had a friggin' Adam's apple and a pecker. Spotted him takin' a leak by the tree over there."

A potential scenario flashed through Brad's imagination: The four "bleedin' blockheads" were part of the "American" gang running around killing people. The cross-dresser was the big-haired blonde. The American gang and the big-haired blonde had murdered Papachristou and two of Papachristou's associates—his Greek bodyguard and Eric Mittel. Madison Samson III, the agent in charge of investigating the security breach, was in cahoots with this gang. If Brad's scenario was on the money, it was no wonder she didn't want him and Chuck snooping around.

Things were calming down next door and the active police search of the area was over. His new girlfriend seemed to be enjoying herself. At the least, she was enjoying the cigarettes. She had already finished three and was working on her fourth. Brad had to admit that the tough old bird was great company. He was getting a charge out of her earthy argot and shrewd observations, but it was time to get going. He was about to say goodbye when she sucked in an oversized lungful of black tobacco smoke that made her voice raspy when she said, *"J'ai le numéro de la putain de plaque* (I got the friggin' license number)."

"De qui (Whose)?"

"Celui du travesti. Il a garé sa putain de caisse devant mon immeuble (The transvestite's. He parked his friggin' wheels in front of my building)."

Brad could see she was pleased with herself. She produced a slip of paper with a series of numbers and letters written neatly in black ink. He wiped his eyes and looked again. Result unchanged. It was the same as the one he'd lifted from the car of the gangbangers who were snooping around Samantha's building the night he and Samantha were attacked. This was a game changer that would require some serious analysis.

She could see he was ready to leave. *"Tu vas te tailler, petit* (You gonna split, sonny)?"

"Oui. C'était un veritable plaisir (It was a real pleasure). *Au revoir, Madame."*

She leaned on the wooden, ivory-handled walking stick to get onto her feet. Her ancient eyes were twinkling. *"Edith. Quand tu veux, petit. Je suis toujours là. Je vois tout* (Whenever you want, sonny boy. I'm always here. Always watching)."

Chapter 10

EARLY MAY 1975, PARIS

The documents Brad brought from Eric Mittel's home were loaded with information. They contained records of hundreds of financial transactions for hundreds of millions of dollars between dozens of companies and a small group of private individuals. The companies were all located in offshore financial centers—Jersey, Guernsey, the Isle of Man, the Bahamas, and Bermuda. The list of private individuals included Georges Papachristou, a mysterious "Mario," an even more mysterious "Junior," and the most mysterious, *"El Gordo* (the Fat One)."

Although it would take a crack team of professional financial experts to determine the details, it looked like the flows originated from three or four companies in Jersey. The chain of command for the outflows was Mario to Papachristou to Mittel, who would log the actual transactions to send the money to their final destination with Junior and El Gordo. Once the funds were transferred, Junior would weave a complex web of transactions among twenty or so offshore institutions.

The takeaway from all this was that Mario was paying El Gordo and Junior for something. They were all going to extreme lengths to keep their transactions secret. The two middlemen, Papachristou and Mittel, were dead. Both deaths had occurred in highly suspicious circumstances. Brad and Chuck agreed that these secret payments and the suspicious deaths were related. If that were the case, the investigation of the CIA security breach should concentrate on the identities of Mario, Junior, and El Gordo.

With Papachristou and Mittel eliminated, the chain was broken. However, Brad figured a thorough search of Papachristou's activities over the past few years would make it possible to determine the identities of Mario and Junior to repair the chain. Brad also figured the person or persons wanting to keep their identities secret—Mario or El Gordo or Junior or all three—would come to the same conclusion. Given that whoever it was was willing to kill to remain anonymous, anyone in a position to supply evidence to repair the chain was in danger of death.

Brad noticed something else. Outflows from Mario's companies ceased in July of last year. Intercompany flows generated by Junior continued until December. The end of July would be a good place to start hunting for Mario. Mario would be someone who Papachristou frequented up until last July. Obtaining info like that would require some detailed analysis of Papachristou's work schedule as well as his social contacts. That was where his wife came in. Brad realized this might explain the tight security around her.

Chuck wanted to go to Gary. "Gary needs to know this."

Brad rubbed his chin and shook his head. "We'll have to put that on the back burner. We'd have to go through the Company to get info like that. First of all, we're not supposed to be nosing around on this. Secondly, any Company involvement would have to include Madison. From what I've seen, Madison is working with the bad guys. She's part of the system, she's got the power, and she would use it to destroy us. Probably already doing it."

"Got any other suggestions, strategy daddy?"

"Yeah, forget about what the Company wants. Let's you and I handle this ourselves. If anybody gets wind of it, we're just investigating the attack on me and Samantha the other night. Nothing else."

"Okay, I'm in. Got any news from her?"

"No. She stopped by the Barbary once, but I wasn't there."

"You and I have to worry. We saw the pics. You've already been attacked for that. Now they know you saw the old man they killed."

Brad had been considering this himself. Seeing the pics wasn't much in and of itself. However, if the bad guys were planning a scorched-earth policy, both he and Chuck were in the line of fire, especially since they knew he had seen the old man they killed.

"I definitely think we do," Brad said. "And I definitely think you are the first target. They know how to find you. Latorre Legal is listed in the directory. Your car is a flashing light. Where is it?"

"I found a place in front of the building. Right down there. Check it out."

There it was, out on the street in full view and almost every passerby took a long look at it.

"Chuck, for the moment, it's probably better to leave the car in the garage. It's too easy to spot and makes you too easy to find."

"You got that right. Let's go down and put it in the garage."

They went down and jumped into the car. Chuck was about to crank it up when Brad stopped him. He and his girlfriend, Veronique, had seen a crime movie the other night, and one of the Mafia's main weapons was the car bomb. Brad didn't really believe there was any possibility of a car bomb, but he thought he could highlight the danger by suggesting there might be one.

Chuck stopped in mid-move. "Shit, you're right. I should've

thought of that." He jumped out of the car and looked underneath. When he came back up, he wasn't smiling, and Brad could see he wasn't playing around.

"There's a freakin'…"

Brad was out of the car before Chuck said "bomb."

Chuck was more nonchalant. "I've seen these things in Nam. Stand back. I'll take care of it."

He went into the trunk of the car and fished around in his toolbox. He found what he wanted and crawled under the car. When he crawled back out, he was holding a bag. There was a bomb in it.

"We'll just hold onto this. Might want to return to sender."

After they parked the car in the garage, Chuck hid the bomb in his office closet and shifted into full-alert mode. That meant minimum exposure. Rather than go home, he would stay in the studio behind his office, which had an exit on the street in the back of the building. No one would know he was there. He also had two unmarked company cars with tinted windows in the garage that would allow him to come and go anonymously. He strapped a bone-handled hunting knife on each ankle and shoulder-holstered his .32 caliber. "Let's go. We've gotta get you squared away."

Brad's bike was parked on the street, not far from where Chuck's car had been parked. After a careful bomb check, they took off for Brad's digs on the rue d'Assas. Brad dropped Chuck off a couple of blocks away from the apartment and drove the bike straight down into the garage. He gave Chuck enough time to get to the building, then called the elevator.

Chuck was waiting for him in front of the apartment door. "All clear."

Once inside, Brad got his Beretta and some extra ammo. "I'm a sitting duck here. I'll have to go to my safe house in Levallois.

Let me set up some decoys to make it look like somebody's still here."

He went into his desk and came up with two timers. One he attached to the light in the living room, the other to a light in the bedroom. He synchronized them so that the living room light came on at 9:00 p.m. and went off at 11:00 p.m. The bedroom light went on at 11:01 p.m., off at midnight, back on at 3:00 a.m., and off again at 3:10 a.m. The 3:00 to 3:10 a.m. light was to ward off anybody planning an early morning surprise.

"Have to leave my bike here. Too distinctive. I can borrow one from the garage in Levallois. Put on this sweatshirt and baseball cap. We're gonna need a little disguise to get out of here unnoticed in case anybody's watching."

Brad led Chuck downstairs into the courtyard behind his building. They scaled the wall and climbed into the parking lot behind the fac. Inside the fac, they integrated with a group of students on the way out. In their sweatshirts and baseball caps, they were unrecognizable. Just to make sure, they took a roundabout route to Levallois with several surveillance checks along the way. They were alone, but they weren't safe. Somebody was out to kill them. Somebody from their own team.

Chapter 11

The safe house atmosphere was electric, like the underdog's locker room five minutes before the championship game. Brad and Chuck were gearing up for a fierce battle.

"How safe are you gonna be here?" Chuck asked. "Madison knows about this place."

"I'll be secure here for at least a week. I can come and go through the tennis club behind the courtyard. Just a question of climbing over the wall. As far as spotting me around the tennis club goes, it's impossible to stake out the place without drawing attention. I'm also gonna wear a disguise."

"Now, we've gotta figure out..." Chuck stopped, closed his eyes, and tapped the side of his head with his forefinger. "Forgot to tell you, I got the feedback on the license number you gave me."

Silence. Chuck was waiting. Smiling. Brad surrendered. "Okay, secret squirrel, like the cornstalk said, I'm all ears."

"There's an address on the rue d'Artois, just behind the Champs-Elysées . It's the same address where the Harley's registered."

"Let's go."

"No, it's just a business service company. Hundreds of small companies are registered there. But I've got a name and a telephone number. My man is working on it."

Something on the TV news caught Brad's attention. It was Senator Brown again railing against traitors and incompetent CIA officials.

Chuck pointed at the TV. "This guy is a security freak. He's got his teeth into the intelligence breach and the traitor in the Russian embassy and won't let go. I bet Madison cringes every time the guy's name is mentioned."

"I read about him in last week's *Time* magazine. He's had quite a life. About fifteen years ago, his two teenage sons were accused of brutally murdering almost an entire family in his neighborhood. Only the ten-year-old daughter escaped.

"Sensational trial. Witnesses recanted. He was confrontational. His sons were arrogant and unremorseful. The first judge recused himself after a series of dubious rulings. The second judge upheld the contested rulings. A mistrial was declared, and the sons went free. He was publicly humiliated by accusations of blackmail, jury tampering, and influence peddling. Played the victim card and somehow got reelected.

"Then everything was roses until about three years ago when his wife was brutally beaten to death in her bedroom. On the way to the funeral, one of the sons had a car accident and was burned alive. A few days later, his other son overdosed on some kind of drug. He was saved in extremis by a good Samaritan who just happened to spot him sprawled out in an alley under a pile of trash. He's a vegetable. Since then, Senator Jake Brown never goes outside alone."

"Jeezus, man, you couldn't make it up!"

"Oh yeah, and the recanting witness and the two judges all met violent ends. The witness was hacked to death in her bedroom with her tongue cut out. The two judges were castrated and had their throats cut."

"Sounds like revenge. What happened to the daughter?"

"She got adopted by an English uncle and disappeared into the UK."

Brad looked at his watch. It was getting dark outside and they had some decisions to make. "Chuck, I don't think we can afford to run and hide. They have City Hall on their side. That's too much firepower. They'll find us eventually, and probably sooner rather than later. We've got enough evidence now. I say let's go to Gary."

Chuck shook his head. "No can do. They called Gary back to Langley. He left this afternoon."

A few resigned goddamn-its later, Brad came to terms with the magnitude of what they were facing. "That's a big monkey wrench in the works. We're on our own. We'll have to go on offense."

"You are a man after my own heart, aggression daddy. We can start with the Harley-Davidson dude. We know where to find him. He can lead us to the other guys, and we can take them out one by one."

"That will be step two. In step one, we need to capture somebody and find out why we're being targeted. The only thing I can imagine is the pics. If it *is* the pics, we have to find out why they're so important. I think the answer lies with the documents I got from Mittel. We've got the names of three survivors—Mario, Junior, and El Gordo—and two cadavers, Mittel and Papachristou. See any link here with the pics?"

Chuck looked sincerely impressed. "Papachristou and the big-haired blonde transvestite! Snoop daddy, you make Dick Tracey look like a rank amateur. Now, let me guess. You're hoping the address we get from the telephone number my friend is investigating will lead us to this dame-dressing dude?”

"Not bad. Call me here tomorrow when you get the info and we can meet in the café by the bridge in Courbevoie.”

Chapter 12

EARLY MAY 1975, COURBEVOIE 92/NEUILLY 92

Brad was partial to this corner café by the Pont de Levallois. The wide-angled view of the intersection and the entire length of the bridge made it almost impossible to access by surprise. In the event that an emergency exit was necessary, there were plenty of options: a front door, doors on either side of the café, and a back door that opened onto a small park.

Traffic was light, most of it flowing toward Levallois and Paris. The park across the street was full of young children romping around under the watchful eyes of their mothers. The sun was up and the only clouds were wispy, white trails streaking through the otherwise clear, blue horizon. Brad ordered an espresso. Chuck ordered a beer.

"Got the name and the address," Chuck said. "It's a bungalow on the Ile de la Jatte, not far from here. It's owned by a company called Atrium, SA. Guess what? Atrium, SA is one of the shell companies named in the Mittel documents."

Brad sipped his espresso and thought it over. "So if the death squad is CIA sanctioned, that means our government is mixed up in the financial shenanigans. If it's a rogue operation, it means

"

Madison is rogue and she's mixed up in the shenanigans."

"It might be one of those bogus 'rogue' deals that gives the government grounds for 'plausible denial.'"

"Whatever it is, it's bad for us. We've gotta find out who we're up against. Let's make a drive-by reconnaissance of the address you've got."

The address turned out to be a detached house on Ile de la Jatte on the Seine near a popular river restaurant called *La Guinguette.* It was on a narrow one-way residential street that opened onto the boulevard Bineau highway. The house had a small dock, and there was a motorboat tied to the dock.

Brad and Chuck agreed. With the resources they had at their disposal, it would be impossible to do any line-of-sight surveillance on the house itself. There was a café at the corner, but with no line of sight to the house. Pedestrian traffic was limited, and most of it came from neighborhood residents of the little Jatte Island. Non-residents drew attention. Since the death squad knew what Brad and Chuck looked like, there was no way for them to conduct discreet surveillance themselves. The best they could do was hang around on the other side of the river from time to time and hope they got lucky.

Chuck interrupted Brad's concentration. "Time is not on our side. We've gotta do something now, in the next day or two, at most."

"Yeah, we can do like we said and try following Madison and the Harley dude and hope they lead us to the big-haired blonde."

"That's a long shot. We've got to take him by surprise, which means alone or almost alone. In other words, we have to know what he does when he's not throwing people off of buildings."

"Wait a minute." Brad's voice jumped an octave. "I've got an idea. Mittel's building is only a few blocks down the street."

"So?"

"Drop me off at the corner. It's only five minutes from where I met Edith, my old lady friend. I've got an idea. I'll meet you back here in fifteen minutes."

*   *   *

She was on the garden bench by the side of the building, sucking on a Gauloise sans filtre.

"*Salut, Edith.*"

"*Salut, petit.*" She patted the seat next to her and Brad sat down. "What was all that rigamarole going on over at Mittel's yesterday?"

Brad pulled out his Gitanes and lit up. "Not sure. You got any ideas?"

Edith cocked her head and squinted through one eye. "Got plenty of ideas. Mittel's a strange SOB—*was* a strange SOB. Whadda you wanna know?"

"I'm more interested in the dude dressed like a woman."

"Not surprised. Saw your interest yesterday. First time I ever saw him. Not many like that runnin' around these parts. My goddamn daughter would have a conniption fit if she found out. She's a friggin' square."

"I need to find out more about this guy. What he does. Where he goes. When he goes. Things like that. He doesn't live far from here, but he knows me. I can't watch him. Thought maybe you could help me out."

Edith was glowing. "Just like the old days with the goddamn Krautheads. We knew every move they made." Suddenly, she was looking cagey. "So, what's in it for Edith?"

This old gal was a real pistol. Brad couldn't help but like her, but he couldn't resist a little payback for all the *petits* and sonny-boys she was tossing his way. "A pack of Gauloises and a book of matches," he deadpanned.

"How about a punch in the nose and a kick in the balls?" She didn't miss a beat. They had a good laugh and decided on a pack of Gauloises, a book of matches, and a hundred francs—per day.

He gave her all the details and made plans to meet the next day. "Leave it to Edith, *petit*. She knows what she's doing."

Brad believed her. He hustled off to meet Chuck. There were some errands to run before his show tonight.

Chapter 13

EARLY MAY 1975, BARBARY COAST SALOON

B rad knew he'd be taking a big risk by doing his show. The death squad stalking him knew how to find him there. Still, if they were going to find him, he preferred that it be on his home turf where he had a logistical advantage. By following his usual routine, he could possibly draw them out on his terms.

The death squad was operating undercover. The attack, when it came, would be designed to preserve its cover. He would, of course, be on his guard at the Barbary Coast Saloon, but he doubted anything would happen there. Too many witnesses. Too much attention. Any attack would more likely come on his way to or from the Barbary. That was where he needed his surveillance.

Since Chuck was a target, his usefulness would be limited, even if he were in disguise. Brad's ace in the hole was Doris, the *de facto* leader of the five middle-aged ladies of the night plying their trade in the area directly around the rue Vavin. Brad liked Doris and her colleagues. They were tough and honest, really nice people—as long as you respected them and their territory. Together with Brad, they had a long history of mutual support against foreign invaders.

They rented the first three floors of the American Hotel on the rue Bréa. Brad found Doris there. He explained the situation to her. She said she would handle it. Brad was confident that with Doris and her colleagues on the case, it would be impossible for any member of any American death squad to sneak into the area unnoticed.

The Barbary was his next stop. The less time spent on the street, the safer he would be. There were some jarhead embassy guards already in the upstairs bar, shooting the breeze, busy razzing one of the guys for his "sexual magnetism."

"Yeah, man. This big guy with long blond hair, high heels, and a short, tight skirt comes into the embassy. Says he has an appointment with one of the consuls upstairs in the secure rooms. While he's sitting there waiting for his appointment, Bobby couldn't stop ogling him. Finally, the guy gets up, minces over to Bobby, and says, 'You free for a drink tonight?' Bobby goes all red and starts trembling, 'No thanks. Can't. Got a date. With a *girl.*' The guy stares at him and shakes his head. Before he can say anything, the consul comes down and they go off together. It was hilarious. Bobby is a sex magnet."

Bobby said, "Fuck you, dork."

Brad was interested. This had to be the big-haired blonde from the death squad meeting openly with one of the embassy spooks. The death squad was looking increasingly like an official operation. His own team trying to take him out.

Brad was about to ask for more info when he heard a throaty purr with a strong, upper-class British accent. "Hi, Brad. I've missed you."

It was Samantha. She was smiling. She was also lovely. Long, dark hair. Perfectly arched eyebrows. Knockout figure and long, comely legs in a short beige skirt. She was smiling at the jarheads.

"Do you mind if I borrow Brad for a while? We have some

catching-up to do."

The jarheads were struck speechless. "Bye, guys." Brad took Samantha downstairs. They had it all to themselves. The restaurant wasn't open yet.

Brad hadn't forgotten Samantha's talent for mind reading. She didn't disappoint him. "You wanted to talk about the confrontation with the muggers the other night." It was a declarative sentence, not a question. She had picked up where they had left off, as if more than a week had not gone by.

Brad relaxed. She was making this easy for him. Brought him back to his time with Alice. Alice had always made him feel the same way. They were adolescent sweethearts and would have been lovers if Brad's resistance to authority had not alienated the father. They became soulmates instead, and would have become lovers in Paris if only…

Brad snapped back to the present. Samantha was waiting patiently for a reply. "A blast from the past, Brad?"

Her insights no longer surprised him. "Yeah, something like that. Any idea what they were after?"

Samantha looked at her hands and leaned forward. "They were after you."

"How do you know?"

"The guy on the fence told me before he died. I asked him why he was after me. He said, 'Not you, him,' and pointed at you. I know I should have told you before, but I needed time to think about it. After I went to my room, two more of those guys came snooping around. I couldn't help but think it was me they were after."

"Why would anyone be after you?"

"Who knows? A young, attractive woman alone in Paris. Maybe they were human traffickers or pimps. I have had the feeling *I'm* being stalked. But why would they be after you?"

Brad lit up a Gitane sans filtre and took a sip of his beer. She was a mind reader, but he had intuition, and his intuition was telling him she might know more than she was letting on. Might as well tell her a partial truth and see how she reacted.

"I think it might be linked to the wife of a suicide victim Latorre Legal is assisting," Brad said. "Latorre Legal is a service company for American expatriates. The proprietor and I were at her apartment, helping her get her affairs in order. Security around her was tight. She seemed intimidated or afraid. When we got back in the car, we found an envelope with pictures in it, pictures taken immediately before the husband jumped to his death from the eighth floor of a building. It was all very strange."

"I don't see the link."

"Chuck—he's the proprietor—and I thought maybe it wasn't a suicide and the pics were some kind of proof. Maybe the killers didn't want the pics to get out. Who knows?"

"Do you still have the pictures?"

It was time to be untruthful. "No, turned them over to the cops. Latorre Legal doesn't do murders. I'm still on alert, though."

"I would love to help you." She had read his mind again. He had been combing his brain trying to figure a way to stay in contact with her. Not because she could help protect him. Rather because she was beautiful and sexy and he wanted to hang out with her.

"Why not? A few cartwheels and backflips would be sure to dazzle the opposition."

She giggled. It was the first time, and it was irresistible. "Oh, that. My uncle owns a circus in France. Ever since I was a little girl, I spent my summers working in the circus. I trained as a gymnast. Those flips were part of my act. I can do the trapeze and tightrope, as well, but I've never worked without a safety net."

"I hope you never do. I would miss you. Seriously, you *can* help. If someone is really targeting me—and I don't believe anyone is—they know they can find me here. Maybe you can check out the audience while I'm doing the show. See if any of the clients look like gangbanger material."

She stuck out her slender hand. "Shake on it."

Brad was congratulating himself on what a smooth operator he was. She would be around till the end of the show, and he had a reason to make another date. On the other hand, he could just go for it and ask her out, but his intuition told him that would be a dead-end street.

"Okay," he said, "see you after the show. We'll compare notes."

The show was over by eleven. Brad joined her at the bar and ordered a beer. She was drinking tap water on the rocks. She hadn't spotted anything suspicious, and neither had he.

"Come on, I'll take you home." Chuck was waiting for him in the company car over by the metro.

Samantha declined. "No, thank you very much, I'll just hop a cab. Come on."

Doris was waiting for him at the corner of Montparnasse. "Hi, Brad, all clear."

"Hi, thanks, Doris. Meet Samantha."

Brad knew Doris well. The sight of Samantha attracted all her attention. She was unusually interested. Studied her closely and hung on every word as they exchanged social pleasantries.

When they parted, Samantha was curious. "Is she what I think she is?"

"Sure is. Great gal. Couldn't do without her."

Samantha gave him a look that was somewhere between curious and admirative. Shrugged it off. At the taxi stand, she gave Brad a big hug and a kiss on the cheek. "I'll be back to help you out." Got into the taxi and away she went.

Brad hustled to where Chuck was parked a few yards from the taxi stand. "Take off, man. We've gotta follow that cab."

It was a short ride. Samantha jumped out of the cab and dashed into the metro at rue du Bac. As much as he wanted to, there was no way Brad could follow her at this time of night. Such strange behavior worried him and made him even more curious. Didn't do anything to diminish his desire, though.

Chapter 14

Brad found Edith on her garden bench, puffing on a Gitane. "Hey, I thought we said Gauloise." Brad was teasing her. Gitanes cost almost twice as much as Gauloises.

"Goddamn foreign clerk couldn't understand French when I said Gauloises. Didn't want to embarrass him. Shit." She didn't miss a beat.

One of those cagey smiles was squirming all over her wrinkled face—the kind that says, "I know something you would love to know." Brad had a feeling she was going to make his day. He decided to tease her a little.

"I suppose you came up empty-handed."

Her face dropped. Smile disappeared. "You guessed it. Goddamn son-of-a-bitch spent the whole afternoon and most of the evenin' drinkin' coffee and smokin' Gitanes. My bladder was bustin' and I could hardly breathe. All for nuthin'."

Now Brad's face dropped. He couldn't believe it. His high hopes were going up in flames.

"Except," Edith continued, "when that huge man with long blond hair came jogging by in a yellow skirt, yellow halter, and

"

yellow sneakers. It was a friggin' freak show. Everybody noticed. One of the regulars told me he comes by every goddamn evenin' on the dot. Wears different outfits, but always at the same time. Goes around the island twice." The smile was back. "Gimme my hundred blades, *petit.*"

"Gave 'em to you yesterday, *grande.*"

"Oh, yeah, forgot. No harm in tryin'."

"Edith, you're the best." Brad meant it sincerely.

The plan was straightforward. He and Chuck would ambush the big-haired blonde on the isolated landfill side of the island, interrogate him, and proceed from there. Brad accessed the island from the Pont de Levallois, Chuck from the Pont de Courbevoie. They reconnoitered at the dump site where it was darkest and the trail curved downhill. This was where they would take him down. If Edith's information was accurate, he should have started his run fifteen minutes ago and would be coming by within the next five minutes. They laid the length of rope across the trail for a classic clothesline takedown and took up their positions on either side.

Brad signaled Chuck when he heard the thump, thump, thump of the runner coming down the trail. They crouched down, out of sight, ready to spring the trap. No warning. A light flashed from behind the dumpster. A voice boomed, "Don't move, motherfucker."

This was a trick play. The big-haired blonde had blockers running interference. Chuck dove to the right; Brad to the left. He rolled down the bank to the water's edge. The buzz of a bullet tore through the bush where he had been standing. Another bullet plowed the ground behind him as he rolled. He scrambled behind an oak tree at the edge and heard a third bullet swish close enough that he felt the breeze. The shooter's concentration on Brad suggested he had not noticed Chuck.

From behind the tree, Brad saw the shooter moving to get an angle. He also saw the big-haired blonde bearing down on him from the other side. His only chance was a dive in the Seine. That was when Chuck exploded from behind the shooter and took him down with a knife-thrust through the kidney. The big-haired blonde hit Brad full speed ahead and knocked him into the water. Then he turned and went for Chuck.

Chuck had his knife, but they needed this guy alive. Chuck backed off. The blonde was on the attack, grunting like a bear. He was fast and aggressive. Brad dragged himself out of the water and crawled back up to the trail. The blonde dropped Chuck and turned to face Brad.

It was dark and difficult to see. He landed a glancing blow to Brad's shoulder, followed with a shot to the head. Brad dodged and slipped. The blonde landed a kick to Brad's ribs and was coming in for the kill. That was when Chuck slipped inside. The blonde swung an elbow to Chuck's head. Too late. Chuck planted his knife in the blonde's buttocks and heaved. Sliced right through the muscle. The blonde went down. He wasn't out. Blood was running like a river, but he still managed to get his teeth into Chuck's leg and chomp. He was spitting out the flesh when Chuck's knife pierced his lung.

His life wasn't over, but he needed emergency treatment if he wanted to remain among the living. He knew it. He wanted to live. "Help me."

Chuck kicked him in his bleeding ass. He moaned. Brad got the flashlight from the dead gangbanger and shone it into the blonde's eyes. "I have questions. I want answers. I will ask only once. If I don't get an acceptable answer, my associate will put you out of your misery. What's your name?"

No hesitation. "Monica."

"Your real name, douchebag."

"Charles Lumbers."

"Who are you working for?"

"Working for Ranger. He's the boss." His voice was muffled by the blood gurgling in his throat. "I'm independent. Just follow orders. Ranger gives the orders. That's all I know. Help me."

"Did you kill the American banker?"

Hesitation. Deliberation. Resignation. "Yeah. He was a traitor."

"Who else are you after?"

Again, the blonde hesitated. Deliberated. It was a battle between professional pride and a chance for life. He chose life. "The Papachristou woman and the Argentine diplomat. Irigoyan."

"Why?"

"Ranger just said 'no witnesses.'"

"Who'd you meet at the embassy?"

"The consul. For Ranger. Help me, man, help me." His voice was trailing off and he was gagging and gurgling.

Chuck tapped Brad's shoulder. "He's a goner. Let's get these guys out of sight in the landfill."

"Hold it," Brad said. "Look."

There was somebody coming down the trail with a flashlight. Voices and another flashlight were coming from the other direction. There was nowhere to hide.

Chapter 15

EARLY MAY 1975, NEUILLY 92

Brad tapped Chuck's shoulder and pointed to the river. On their bellies, they slithered down the riverbank and slipped into the water. They dove deep and let the current sweep them downstream.

The scene they had just vacated was animated by flashing lights and plenty of profanity. Somebody said "in the water," and a group of three gangbangers took off down the riverbank, shining their flashlights, searching for the culprits who had rubbed out their buddies.

Brad and Chuck had a good head start, but the river current was slower than the gangbangers running along the bank. They stayed underwater as much as they could. When they surfaced, they could hear the gangbangers getting closer. Fortunately, the gangbanger progress was slowed by tree trunks and slippery rocks. It was terminated by an iron fence protecting the property of a construction company.

They crawled out of the Seine five hundred yards past the Pont de Courbevoie, where their car was parked. They were wet and cold and happy to be alive, although the gallons of polluted water they swallowed had them worried. They jumped into the car and headed for the highway, wary that the death squad would be on the lookout for cars leaving the island.

They weren't wrong. At the stoplight to the highway, two gangbangers were standing watch. When they saw the car approaching, they stepped into the street and signaled for the car to stop. Chuck slowed down and let them get into the middle of the road—let them think he would stop. When he got within ten yards, he hit the gas.

One dude dove to the right. Too slow. His leg got crushed by the right-front tire. The other dude tried to go over the top. Too low. His knees hit the hood and his face crashed into the windshield. Chuck tapped the brakes and the body flew forward off the hood. Then he hit the gas, rolled over the body, and turned right onto the highway toward Paris.

A glance in the rearview confirmed they were not in the clear. A big black sedan was bearing down on them. By now it was way past 9:00 p.m. and traffic was thinning out. There was no way they could outrun the sedan. The gangbangers had guns and were unafraid to use them—another indication they were a protected species.

Chuck whipped right at the second stoplight, took the next right to a small alleyway, slammed on the brakes, cut off the lights, and turned in, motor still running. The black sedan drove slowly by, spotted the car, and came to a stop at the entrance to the alley. Chuck hit the gas in reverse and smashed into the sedan—dead center—pile-driving it into the line of cars parked on the other side of the street.

The night came alive with car alarms and blinking lights. Chuck shifted into forward and drove prudently back to the highway. Those shitbirds would have some explaining to do.

Back in Chuck's garage, they checked out the damage. One tail light and a banged-up bumper. The windshield wasn't even cracked. The bad news was that this death squad was well organized, well protected, and willing to go to any lengths to accomplish their mission. The good news was that the squad didn't know who had attacked them.

Neither Brad nor Chuck doubted the truthfulness of the big-haired blonde's statements. He'd had nothing to lose, and his delivery was limpid and pure. There were three takeaways. First, Papachristou was murdered, supposedly because he was a traitor. Second, anybody who might know he was murdered was targeted for assassination. Third, an Argentine diplomat named Irigoyen was on the hit list.

The first two takeaways were confirmations of something they already suspected. The third was something new, and, thought Brad, something important. "This Argentine diplomat looks like an important piece of information."

Chuck agreed. "I'm gonna find out who he is first thing in the morning."

"Before I go back to Levallois, I'll stop by Montparnasse and talk to Doris. See if she's noticed anything out of the ordinary."

Doris was deep in negotiations with a client when Brad came by. He kept on going. When he came back, Doris was alone. He was relieved. It might have been a long wait. "Hi, Doris. Any news?"

"Hi, Brad. Nothing around here. But that cute little woman the other night. Samantha. How well do you know her?"

"Not very well. Only seen her twice. What's the problem?"

"I do private parties. Meet a lot of different people." She stopped and stared straight at Brad. "I've seen Samantha several times before. At private receptions and diplomatic cocktail parties.

She's not dark-haired with brown eyes. Her hair is blond and her eyes are blue. She's a jet-setter. Runs with the rich crowd."

"So her name's not Samantha?"

"No. Samantha is the name she goes by. That's how I made the connection."

"You sure?"

Doris cocked her head, gave him the evil eye. "Positive."

Brad thanked Doris and headed off to Levallois. As Gary frequently reminded him and as he had verified through experience, there were no coincidences in this business. Samantha wore a disguise. She appeared, and he was attacked. She disappeared. Chuck was attacked, and she reappeared. She disappeared mysteriously into the metro. What would happen the next time they met?

Chapter 16

Chuck was limping. Rolled up his pantleg and bared the bandage just above his ankle. "It's a bad infection. Gift from pecker-woman's poisonous teeth. No tellin' where that mouth has been. I'm on antibiotics. No alcoholic beverages for two weeks."

"No problem. I'll drink your share. What about the Argentine diplomat?"

"Guy's name is Irigoyen. Mario Irigoyen. He was a big cheese in the government. Here's what's interesting. He left the Argentine embassy in early July. Hasn't been seen since. How does that grab you?"

"Grabs me right where I say this Mario is the Mario mentioned in Mittel's documents. He disappeared when the transfers stopped—or, more precisely, the transfers stopped when he disappeared."

"Got a picture of him and some background info. He was Perón's right-hand man."

Brad thought back to the pictures in Papachristou's living room. "Perón and Papachristou were big friends. I'd say maybe

Papachristou was the traitor getting paid for information he was feeding to Perón through Mario as the intermediary."

"I think you got it, daddy-o."

"Except for one thing. Papachristou passed the money on through Mittel to the final destinations in Junior's shell companies and El Gordo's account. We don't know where the money went after that. Anyway, Gary never raised any questions about Papachristou's loyalty. There's got to be more to it. We need to find this Mario."

Chuck laid out everything he got from the embassy on Mario. Mario was a recognized economist and the chief financial consultant for Juan Perón. All financial decisions were required to have his approval, including international bank loans and negotiations with the World Bank and the International Monetary Fund. He was unmarried and scandal-free but was seen about town with a group of three young Argentine ladies residing at the Georges V hotel: *Mesdemoiselles* Pecchioni, Sabatini, and de la Sarta. He had not been seen since Juan Perón passed away on July 1 of the previous year. He was the object of a manhunt by the Argentine government.

Chuck shook his head. "Mario is going to be hard to find. Maybe one of his girlfriends has some idea of where he is."

"That would be the first thing anybody thought of. Either they don't know anything or they aren't talking. It's the only thing we've got, though. Let's check out the magazines and see what the girls look like and go from there."

There were enough pictures to identify these three lovely ladies and, lo and behold, more than enough to identify one of them as the Samantha he knew. This one was called Samantha de la Sarta. Just as Doris had described her, she was a blue-eyed blonde, even more beautiful than her brown-eyed, brunette alter ego who was hanging around the Barbary Coast Saloon.

Gary's no-coincidence rule struck again. She was somehow mixed up in this ongoing security investigation, and that was why she had been hitting on him. That hurt more than his ego. Chuck noticed, and Brad appreciated the fact he refrained from ragging him about it.

They decided to hang around the area and see if they could find out what she was up to. Brad had rented a Honda 450 from his friend at the garage in Levallois. He had also stopped shaving and washing his hair and started wearing his leathers and motorcycle boots in an effort to pass himself off as one of those rebel bikers. The overall effect was doubtful, but he was difficult to recognize.

Chuck disguised himself as a *chauffeur de grande remise* (chauffeured car driver) complete with the cap and black suit. That made it possible for him to hang around and smoke and shoot the breeze with the stable of drivers waiting for their clients to come out of the hotel.

They were about ready to call it a day when they got lucky. Samantha de la Sarta left the Hotel Georges V dressed for a jog. Black T-shirt, black leotard, black shorts, black sneakers, black rucksack, blond hair pulled back into a neat ponytail. She'd be hard to see at night, but in the daylight, she attracted a lot of attention, most of it masculine.

Chuck signaled Brad and went after her in his car. Brad followed on his motorcycle.

She took her time running down the small backstreets off the Champs-Elysées. Brad knew the area well and managed to stay in contact through anticipation and shortcuts. Chuck followed Brad in the car.

At the Porte Dauphine, she went into the metro. Chuck left his car on the street and followed her in. Brad was right behind him.

He stayed way back and let Chuck move in close.

She didn't know Chuck. Chuck broke off and left Brad alone when she changed at Villiers to line 3. She exited at Malesherbes one stop later and ran the rest of the way to the metro Pereire, where she entered a bourgeois building on the boulevard Pereire. Brad surprised himself and managed to keep up with her.

He made his decision. He would confront her when she came out. It was a short fifteen-minute wait. Dark-haired, dark-eyed, dark-skinned Samantha Smith in tight jeans, blue blazer, and white trainers pranced out onto the sidewalk. Eyes wide, caught by surprise, and clearly distraught, she was not doing any mind reading. "Brad James, what are you doing here?"

"Came by to say hello and ask you a few questions."

There was a moment of tension as she ran through her options. The reel ran out, and she capitulated. "I see. Let's walk while we talk."

Brad got right to the point and asked her what her game was. She told him she was a graduate of Yale Law School with a specialization in international taxation. She was investigating a scandal on behalf of a wealthy client.

"So, what's with the disguise?"

Samantha stopped. Took two baby steps back and fixed Brad with a somber truth-stare. "There was a cocktail party for the '*Tout Paris*'—the Parisian Jet-Set—hosted by the Argentine embassy. Georges Papachristou, vice president of the Crédit Lyonnais and my primary witness, was present. I saw him thrown to his death from the penthouse terrace by a big blond American transvestite. It was murder. At that moment, I knew I needed a new identity if I was going to continue the investigation." She executed a graceful pirouette and took a bow. "And here I am, continuing the investigation."

"What were you doing at the Barbary Coast Saloon?"

"Looking for you. I contacted Papachristou's wife. Told her I had information and pictures. She directed me to her personal security guard. My understanding was that she was under surveillance and couldn't deal directly. I gave him the information and the pictures I took. He gave me the information on you and Latorre Legal."

Brad tapped his head. "Now I understand. You thought you were the object of the attack in front of your apartment."

"Yes, but when my assailant told me you were the target, it confused me. I thought he might just be trying to throw me off guard. I couldn't take any chances and needed time to think. I abandoned that safe house and came here. Then I wanted to find out why they had targeted you."

"Did you figure it out?"

"You tell me."

"My colleague and I think it was the pictures. It looks like a scorched-earth mission to stamp out any possible suggestion that Papachristou was murdered. Somehow, they found out about the pics and that we saw them. But the pics don't really incriminate anybody. So I don't see why anyone would be worried."

Samantha shook her head with a rueful smile. "That crafty old bodyguard didn't give you all the pictures. He must have kept the two where the big blonde is throwing Papachristou overboard. I'll get you copies. Probably thought holding them back would give him some bargaining power."

"He definitely got that wrong, but now I understand why they've been hitting on us. They think we've seen all the pics. How did they find out about them?"

"I think Greta Papachristou showed them to a couple of her bodyguards. Somebody must have blabbed."

Brad feared the answer to his next question, but he had to ask. "Do the bad guys know who you are?"

"They know about this Samantha, not the one in the Hotel Georges V. No pictures. Just secondhand descriptions. Until now, I felt pretty safe in disguise. Not anymore. If an amateur like you can find me, how hard could it be for professionals like them?"

That "amateur" remark kind of hurt. Didn't have time to dwell on it, though. Something had changed. Women waddling around in headscarves and burkas. Men in sandals and robes. This was Muslim land. He was the only blond guy around, and she was without a head covering. They were reaping an abundance of stares.

Given the ongoing racial tensions, Brad was uncomfortable. Samantha reached into her oversized bag and pulled out a colorful headscarf she wound expertly around her head and neck. She was giggling. "You know the old story about the Lone Ranger and Tonto when they got surrounded by the Indians?"

"Very funny. Let's get moving." Chez Tati, the discount department store, was just down the street.

Brad really wanted to trust this exceptionally alluring young woman. Undoubtedly, she was holding back and playing her cards close to the vest—just like he was. Her story, as far as it went, held water. His intuition was telling him to join forces. That was when she read his mind again. "Maybe we can help each other out."

This was the opening he had been waiting for. "How?"

"You have contacts at the embassy. You could help me find the man I'm looking for. I could help you find the man you're looking for."

Brad waited for more. She obliged. "The man I'm looking for is between thirty and thirty-five. Nice-looking, slicked-back hair, strong jaw, straight nose, hooded eyes. Acts like a cool-hand big shot. He has political connections at the embassy. He goes by several aliases, but the one he would use at the embassy is Ranger. I know he's in town."

That was a description of the death squad honcho on the Harley chopper, right down to the name. Without tipping his hand, Brad asked, "Why are you interested in him?"

The question seemed to upset Samantha a little. She clocked a short pause before answering. "He's central to the case I'm working on." Another short pause. "I also think he's involved in the Papachristou murder. That's all I can say for now."

"If that's the case, he's probably involved with those gangbangers who attacked us the other night. So this dude interests me, as well. To be honest, though, the main reason I followed you is because of your relationship with Mario Irigoyen."

She snapped to attention. "What about Mario?"

"His name came up in some financial transactions with Papachristou that require clarification. I need to see him in person."

Her body language said she didn't trust him. Her mouth contradicted her body. "That will be difficult. I haven't heard from him in months." She squeezed her eyes shut and folded her hands. Thinking it over. The decision was made. "Give me twenty-four hours. I'll give it a try and leave a message at Latorre Legal."

"In that case, I think I can help you with Ranger."

Chapter 17

A message straight out of *My Fair Lady*: "The rain in Spain stays mainly in the plain." The word "rain" referred to wealth. The word "plain" referred to the Argentine *pampas*, 463,323 square miles of fertile grasslands. It was a coded reaffirmation of the fact Argentina's wealth depended on the *pampas* in particular and on the agricultural sector in general. Good news for Mario's resistance underground. The meaning was that a major devaluation of the Argentine peso was only a matter of time. The peso was overvalued. An overvalued exchange rate disadvantaged the agricultural sector. A devaluation meant the wealth—the rain—would come back to the agricultural sector—the plain.

Mario sipped his *mate* and reflected on what it meant for his future. Argentina's comparative advantage was the agricultural sector. It was the only sector able compete at the international level. As such, it was the only sector in a position to export profitably. The overvalued exchange rate made it unprofitable for the farmers to export because of the small number of pesos received from each export dollar. Consequently, producers reduced their output and sold locally, thereby reducing the supply of U.S. dollars to purchase the imports of the raw materials, machines, and other intermediate products necessary to keep the rest of the economy running. Up to now, the export shortfall had been compensated by an increase in foreign currency borrowing. There were rumors, however, that the country was reaching the limits of this escape route, which left a major devaluation as the only viable short-term strategy.

For Mario's future, a major devaluation of the Argentine peso would work to the disadvantage of Lopez Rega. Mario had no doubt about that. Food in general and beef in particular represented more than twenty-five percent of the average Argentine budget. The devaluation would cause the price of all agricultural products to soar, especially the price of beef, as agricultural output was diverted from the internal market to the more lucrative export market.

While this would benefit the agricultural sector, it would also cause extreme hardship on the average Argentine household not connected to the agricultural sector. Of course, in the medium term, all sectors would benefit as the agricultural sector ramped up production in response to the market signals. In the short term, however, the person behind the devaluation causing all the hardship and suffering would be in for some intense vilification. Argentina's stop-and-go economic history was testimony to this. Lopez Rega was recognized as that person, the power behind the throne, and he would have a difficult time surviving it.

While Mario's medium-term future was therefore looking pretty promising, it was the present that posed a problem. Ever since he'd escaped from Paris, Rega's army of assassins, the Argentine Anticommunist Alliance—the AAA—had deployed agents all over France, Spain, and the UK actively seeking his whereabouts.

Mario rubbed his forehead and took a deep breath. The intensity of Rega's relentlessness was unexpected. Mario had believed Rega did not do *personal*. Must be the hundred million dollars motivating him.

At least the insurance policy seemed to be working. The word was that he should be brought in *alive*. The problem here was that if he were captured alive, he would inevitably be tortured to find out where the bearer shares were hidden.

He shuddered when he pictured what they could do to him. His ace in the hole was that only he, personally, could retrieve the shares from his lockbox at the Crédit Lyonnais near the Opéra in Paris. So even if he divulged where the shares were located, they could only be accessed if he were alive and healthy enough to retrieve them in person. He fervently hoped Rega would be sensitive to the subtlety involved here.

Mario understood the shares were not a permanent block on the funds. There were legal maneuvers and procedures that could eventually liberate the money. These maneuvers and procedures, however, would be long and drawn out and would leave a trail, a permanent link to the fund's beneficial owner. That would defeat the ultimate objective of anonymity the account was supposed to serve.

He placed his calabash carefully on the end table, got up, and began pacing the room. Outside his small apartment in the center of Valencia, the winter sun flooded his terrace with a cold white light. He stepped out and looked across at the ships docked in the harbor. What a marvelous city! Too bad he had to abandon it. His heavy Argentine accent made him too conspicuous. The gangbangers from the AAA were probably already invading the major Spanish towns looking for a *tio* (a dude) with an Argentine accent. He would be better off back in France or the UK where his Spanish accent would be indistinguishable from any other Spanish speaker's.

There weren't many people left in Argentina he could count on. Rega had wasted no time in rounding up and arresting (or "disappearing") his colleagues on the left of the Perónist movement. Those still around had gone underground. His main support came from those already outside the country. Many were willing to help. The AAA was present, but its actions were limited by what the security forces of the other countries would tolerate. His main problem was figuring out who he could trust.

Mario also had a few cards of his own to play. He had been the financial czar. All financial transactions went through him. Most of them he organized himself. He knew the secrets of everyone in the government. His records were detailed and carefully preserved in a series of lockboxes rented for that purpose. These were bargaining chips. They were protected, and he would know how to use them when the time came.

He reassured himself that up to now he had always been able to come out on top. After he was discovered in a middle-class suburb of Buenos Aires as a child prodigy, it didn't take long for him to realize that his brains were no substitute for power and that he would need power to achieve his goals. His brains would be his ticket to power. The journey would be long and treacherous. He would need protection.

The first leg of the journey was the fast-track trip through university, a master's in physics, and a PhD in finance in the U.S. that left him little time for socializing and personality development. It did provide him with the experience and insight to create the protection required for the rest of the journey. The insight was he could count on no one but himself.

His solution was to create a fake persona he could use as a

decoy, like a lightning rod in a thunderstorm. To make it believable and sheltered from the unguarded moment or inadvertent slip-up, he used his true personality as the model for his fake persona. He hid his duplicity and thirst for power as naïve dedication to his job. He wrapped his cruelty and ruthlessness in the virtuous robes of idealistic purity.

In his early days, he'd come across as a sincere worshipper of Perón. He was known as the pie-in-the-sky dreamer—an overachieving, idealistic intellectual and Perón groupie. By the time Perón got back to Argentina, his political opponents had wiped each other out and there were only two left standing: he and José Lopez Rega. Little by little, he began to imagine a plan that could weaken and perhaps even destroy Rega.

It was the jujitsu strategy. Use the opponent's force against him. Rega's force was his ruthlessness. Any suspected obstacle to his power was immediately destroyed. Mario decided this was the key. He began to target Rega's supporters and identify those not openly hostile to him. He cultivated their cooperation and friendship. Complimented them publicly when he could. Solicited their advice. Did little favors. Rega's ruthless application of the theory that "the friend of my enemy is my enemy" did the rest. It guaranteed that Rega would destroy anyone he suspected of disloyalty.

It worked for a while, but Rega soon caught on and stopped punishing his falsely contaminated supporters. Mario now realized this was good for his survival strategy. Rega would not try to use a third party to pressure Mario. He could never be sure he wasn't doing just what Mario wanted him to do. Mario had no one he was close to, anyway.

Mario's immediate concern was to avoid the AAA gangbangers and endeavor to deprive Lopez Rega of his economic resources by doing everything in his power to close down Argentina's access to foreign bank loans. In his role as financial czar, he knew all the players and he knew where all the bodies were buried. Back in Argentina, his own burial site was already being prepared.

Something changed on the street below. It was a dark limousine with tinted windows. Outside of the occasional spy-movie shoot or diplomatic courtesy visit, nobody drove dark limousines with tinted windows in Valencia.

Four *tíos* exited the vehicle, two on each side. Long hair, unshaven, strutting around in dark suits and cowboy boots, they were not diplomats. There were no cameras rolling. They were not actors.

Mario was prepared, but this would be close. He grabbed his preprepared backpack, closed the door, and hightailed it down the hall to the crosswalk connecting to the twin building next door. The crosswalk was why he chose this hideout. He had an underground parking space where he kept his motorcycle in the twin building. The motorcycle had not been out of the garage since he put it in there. The bike was not in his name. Neither was the parking space. No one knew it existed. By the time anyone figured it out—if they ever did—he would be long gone, and so would the motorcycle.

The door to the crosswalk was always locked. He went to his jacket, where he kept the key. The adrenaline was pumping. Fumbled around. It wasn't there.

Hijo de puta!

Red-light alarm! The elevator clicked on. The *tíos* were on their way up.

The other jacket. He'd changed jackets. The backpack. The jacket was in the backpack. He was in a frenzy. His fingers were stiff and his legs were doing the Elvis it's-alright-mama dance.

Hyperventilating. It felt like a heart attack. He pulled out the jacket. The key was in the pocket. Grabbed it. Stuck it in the door. The elevator ground to a halt. Turned the key, pushed open the door, rushed through, and slammed it shut behind him. He prayed they hadn't noticed.

Out on the crosswalk, he started to relax. He looked down. *Híjole!*

Real trouble. Two of the *tíos* were down there. One was going into the garage. The other one was watching the crosswalk. He couldn't retreat, and there was nowhere to hide.

Chapter 18

Camden Town was for the lost and found. You could get lost there, but you could also easily be found. It was a giant flea market. Everybody went there. Mario's theory was to use crowd cover when doing business and live off the beaten path when not doing business. Non-beaten paths around Camden Town were very dangerous. So that was a problem. Mario solved the problem by moving out of the area to safer digs in Belsize Park. He used the crowd cover of Camden Town for meetings in small restaurants in the tourist area. He came by bus or by underground and used several different disguises. He always left before nightfall. Today, he was wearing a full beard and a black beret and was carrying a guitar he did not know how to play.

His appointment was with Brad James, an American who Samantha said could help him out. He was in London for information on some financial transactions handled by Georges Papachristou. This might be a stroke of luck. If someone else made them public, he could fill in some self-serving background information that would make Rega a threat to the anonymity of Junior and El Gordo. He had copies of the details with him. The originals were hidden back in Valencia.

The thought of Valencia made him shiver. What an escape! Two minutes. It was a matter of two minutes and the vigilance of a paranoid octogenarian that had saved him from a mortal catastrophe. She had spotted what she called a suspicious character entering the underground garage of her building. Called the police. They barreled in, sirens wailing and lights flashing. That was enough to drive off the two *tios* down below the crosswalk where he was trapped. He'd had just enough time to get to the building on the other side of the crosswalk before the other two *tios* broke through the door to the crosswalk behind him. The presence of all the cops down below made them abandon their hunt. They came back later, but by then, he was long gone.

Mario sipped his *mate*. It was homemade. He brought his own *mate*, spices, calabash, and *bombilla*. The restaurant supplied the boiling water. Inconvenient, but there was no other way. Frequenting an establishment that served *mate* was out of the question. These were the first places the AAA checked out for wayward, homesick Argentinians.

The American stared at Mario's beverage. Mario nodded and pushed the calabash forward. "*Mate* should be shared."

The American declined. "I'll stick with coffee. Thanks anyway."

The American took the documents and said he'd get back to him through Samantha. It was time to end the meeting. Mario signaled the waiter and paid in cash with a reasonable tip—just enough, but not too much. *Don't stand out.*

The American disappeared into the crowd. Mario waited and watched. There was nothing to make him suspicious. He exited the restaurant.

Out on the street, he strolled around. Did some routine countersurveillance window-shopping. He relaxed. Nothing there.

Headed for the metro. Glanced into a shop window and froze. Looked again.

Puta madre (Motherfucker)*!*

Behind him stood a terrifying blast from the past. The hooded eyes, the thick meaty lips, the predatory smile. *Cangrejo*, a.k.a. Guillermo Fontanero, the Crab, Rega's enforcer and head of AAA, was watching him. There was nowhere to run.

Cangrejo stood staring through hooded, malevolent eyes. Mario remained motionless, frantically searching for an escape route. Running was not an option. Cangrejo never traveled alone. They'd catch him.

Cangrejo moved forward, still staring intently. Mario moved to the left. Collided with Cangrejo. His guitar fell to the ground. Cangrejo picked it up. Looked him in the eye. Handed it to him.

"Eekskoose me."

What an accent! What a relief! Cangrejo didn't recognize him. "No problem. Thank you." Mario's English was excellent. But it wouldn't be his accent that gave him away. It would be his face.

The hooded eyes locked onto Mario's face, analyzing, searching. Cangrejo nodded, turned, and entered a hardware store. Mario observed three of his men position themselves at the entrance.

As he hustled down the crowded street, Mario's first reaction was an explosion of relief that he hadn't been recognized. By the time he got to the corner, his second reaction kicked in. Knowing the whereabouts of the AAA headquarters would be an amazing coup. His team would be able to discover how many they were, their names, their comings, their goings, and most importantly, where they were vulnerable. However, tailing Cangrejo and his three gangbangers would be extremely difficult and even more than dangerous. Discovery meant torture and death.

His internal struggle between fight and flight was short-lived.

Fight won out. He'd try and follow them to their hideout.

Mario had some surveillance experience. All alone, it would be almost impossible to get in close without getting spotted. He saw that when they moved, Cangrejo had a wingman on either side of him. The third guy hung back ten to fifteen yards as a sweeper. The sweeper was intent on what was between him and Cangrejo, not what was behind him. Mario decided to stick with the sweeper. He'd take him as far as he could

Cangrejo and his men set a fast pace. Mario was wary at first, but after a while it became apparent these guys were oblivious to surveillance. They knew where they were going and wanted to get there as quickly as possible.

They turned left off Gloucester Avenue onto Saint Mark's Cres by Regent's Canal and into a semi-detached house on the water. Mario made it to the corner just in time to see the sweeper go inside.

He hesitated. The temptation to get a closer look at the house was stronger than his sense of self-preservation. He started down the street. A hand gripped his arm, and a gruff voice whispered in his ear.

"*Señor Irigoyen, ven conmigo* (Mr. Irigoyen, come with me)."

Chapter 19

MID MAY 1975, PARIS

His trip to London had taken three days. One day to go over, one day for the meeting, and one day to come back. The Honda 450 he was renting was a good ride, fast and comfortable. He took the hovercraft to cross the Channel. It was more expensive, but much faster than the ferry.

Overall, he was pleased with how things had gone. Mario was wary, but agreed to cooperate when Samantha told him Brad was being hunted by those who had murdered Papachristou. According to Mario, Papachristou was a high-flying financier with strong political contacts. He was especially well-connected in Latin America. He confirmed what Brad had already deduced from the pictures in Papachristou's living room. Papachristou and Perón were thick as flies. As far as Mario was concerned, however, Papachristou's involvement in the financial transactions was limited to his role as a knowledgeable banker serving his client.

Mario confirmed the cash flowing through Papachristou, Mittel, and Junior were payments for financial and political intelligence as well as for access to the U.S. political power grid. He claimed he knew neither who was providing the information and access nor the identities of Junior and El Gordo. He only knew they both represented powerful figures at the top of the U.S. power pyramid.

In the documents he provided, Mario said he'd let his imagination make some plausible deductions. The primary goal of the complicated web of shell companies was to make it impossible to "follow the money" in order to deliver secure payments of laundered cash to the bureaucrats and politicians participating in the information/access network. Some of the documents showed the shell companies were making loans and investments in other companies outside the network that were paying out millions in consulting fees and political lobbying. One of these companies, for example, was run by a former head of the intelligence branch of the FBI. Another was run by a former advisor to Lyndon Johnson. Mario had managed to establish similar relationships with several other shell companies.

In his opinion, El Gordo was an influential politician or bureaucrat who was masterminding the whole operation. Said he couldn't prove it, but had a good idea who it was. When Brad gave him details of the death squad in Paris, Mario was alarmed. Said it tended to confirm his suspicions about El Gordo. His gaze was unblinking and sincere. "If you are right, you are damned. I only have the full might of the Argentine government after me. You have the might of the U.S. government after you."

Brad exposed his scorched-earth theory to Mario and added, "If I'm right, you have both governments after you."

Mario let that sink in for a few moments before replying, "That's the worst news I've heard all year."

Brad believed him. Although he didn't know of Mario's insurance policy in the form of one hundred million dollars' worth of bearer shares of Bellweather SA that would provide him some protection from the Argentine government, he did know Mario had no leverage with those calling the shots in the U.S. Scorched-earth meant the elimination of anyone with the slightest inside knowledge. Mario had extensive inside knowledge. He was a target, and he would be wise to revise his game plan accordingly.

Samantha slid into the booth next to Brad. "How was the trip?"

"It went well. Mario is charming. He gave me some info that confirmed a big chunk of my analysis. But he was holding back. Don't blame him. I think he'll eventually come around. I just hope he does it before the death squad finds him. What about you?"

"Mario contacted me. After meeting you, he said he decided to come back to Paris. Not many details, but he said he almost walked into a trap set by the AAA—Argentine Anticommunist Alliance. They've been hunting him since Lopez Rega took over the government. Fortunately, one of the guys on his countersurveillance team stuck with him after he left you. The guy spotted two dudes following him. It seems Mario himself was following some AAA guys he picked up after he left you. They spotted him and were leading him into a trap. Fast thinking by the countersurveillance guy got him out of there before they could spring it."

Brad didn't know what to think about that. On the one hand, he would be able to get more info from Mario. On the other hand, Mario's presence would draw the AAA gangbangers. Brad was also undecided about what to do with the information he already had. Normally, he would give it to Gary, who would take it from there. But Gary was gone with no way to be contacted, and Brad suspected it was done on purpose so that Brad would have no one to go to. It meant he and Chuck were all alone against some kind of secret government-sponsored black-ops hit squad. If that was the case, they were in it up to their necks and couldn't touch bottom. Those guys would have unlimited resources and total political cover.

He and Chuck had been over this numerous times. Chuck wanted to stay on the offensive and wipe out the opposition. That was a good short-run strategy, but the opposition had an unlimited supply of replacements. Eventually, either the death squad would get them or the French would get them for getting the death squad. This Ranger guy on the Harley chopper Samantha was investigating could be a solution.

"What about Ranger, the Harley-Davidson dude? What's he to you?"

The fleeting expression that flashed across her flawless features was disturbing. "He is the prime witness in a murder for money scheme I'm investigating. It was cooked up by his mentor, a greedy, egotistical sociopath. Ranger is a replica, only worse, the kind of guy who mutilates cats and pulls the wings off flies. Remember this. Never let him get his hands on you. If he ever does, you will spend a long time wishing you were dead."

"Thanks for the warning. What do you plan to do with the uncle when you find him?"

"Bring him to justice."

Chapter 20

The headline on the *Herald Tribune* caught Brad's eye: *Traitor Holds Press Conference in Soviet Embassy.* He purchased the paper and gobbled up the whole article. The press conference was a blockbuster. The traitor admitted to being a CIA agent, but he emphatically denied revealing classified information to anyone outside the agency he constantly referred to as "the Company." The questioning was exceedingly aggressive because the press corps had already concluded he was guilty. Otherwise, why had he fled to the Soviets? His answer was that his life was in danger. Those responsible for the security breach had put a price on his head.

When questioned about who these mysterious characters "responsible for the security breach" were, his answer was straightforward and, if you thought about it, credible. He said the leaked classified information was way above his pay level. He'd received it from one of his informants and passed it on up the chain of command. It could only have come from someone at the very highest level of the CIA directorate. In fact, most of the information—especially the financial information and the names of agents, double-agents, and informers—was not even in the remit of his immediate boss.

He debunked reports he had been under suspicion for a long time by referring to the records showing he was promoted and his security level increased just months before the leak. He also suggested it was suspicious how quickly the holes were plugged. In fact, he claimed he was the first to detect evidence of leaked information. He surmised that the actual leakers never thought the leaks would be detected. When he detected them and the cat was out of the bag, fear of exposure led them to find a scapegoat.

"Who more obvious than the person who discovered the leaks? I am it," he said. His answer to why the Soviets were protecting him was, "You'll have to ask them. I came here because it's the only place in the whole country where I would have the slightest chance of being protected."

The second article below the headline had Senator James "Jake" Brown screaming bloody murder. He was incensed that a proven traitor, someone who was responsible for the deaths of our agents and informers, could hold a press conference in the capital of the United States of America and get away with it.

The press reminded him the embassy was Soviet territory. He was unabashed. Said it was criminal. The traitor should be hanged by the neck, and he intended to see to it that this Benedict Arnold was brought to justice. The integrity of the United States of America was too sacred, and his own patriotism too pure to be sidelined. He would pursue this traitor to the ends of the earth, and he would employ all the government resources at his disposal to do it.

Jake Brown had some heavy artillery to back him up. The second-highest-ranking official of the CIA, the deputy director, Alvin P. Dearman, put out a statement that the traitor and the information he had divulged were responsible for the most serious security threat the United States had faced since the Cuban Missile Crisis.

Even after discounting for political and bureaucratic hyperbole, Brad could only conclude the traitor was in for a long, uncomfortable future. Jake Brown sounded like a tough customer. It was hard to blame old Jake, though. Traitors could not be tolerated. The question here was whether or not this guy was the traitor. The traitor's press conference in Washington and recent death squad activity in Paris was giving Brad some doubts.

Other senators also had some doubts. Clayton Conrad from the great state of New York was criticizing Jake for political showboating. He praised his own experience in Latin America and claimed there was more to the security breach than one relatively low-ranking CIA agent could account for. Winslow from Virginia openly agreed with Conrad and questioned Jake Brown's own patriotism for helping his son dodge the draft. Other senators pointed to Brown's proclivity for self-serving untruths. Since all the doubters were in the opposition, their remarks were taken with a grain of salt.

At the end of the day, it looked like City Hall—as Gary referred to the crushing, complex, symbiotic system of political expediency and bureaucratic authority—was out to destroy anyone and anything threatening its special status of power and privilege. Brad had assumed he and Chuck were members of the City Hall club. Recent events had forced him to call that assumption into question. He and Chuck were now clearly on its destroy list.

Their options were limited. The head-on attack option had already been discarded as impractical. The run-and-hide strategy was also impractical. There wasn't much room to run, and effective hiding places were few and far between—especially if the French got involved. Brad told Chuck he thought it best to play along with City Hall as if they were unaware it was City Hall targeting them. He argued City Hall had no reason to think Brad and Chuck suspected them.

Chuck chewed on that for a long time before asking, "Okay, we play along. And then what?"

"If we play along, they probably won't come at us with their heavy artillery. We can bob and weave. Stay on guard. Make guerilla warfare. Upset their plans. Force them to make mistakes and pull in their horns. For example, we're probably not their most pressing problem. There's Mario, Greta Papachristou, Papachristou's secretary, and the person who took the pictures, to mention only a few."

"Samantha took the pictures."

"Yeah, but they don't know that, and they'll be forced to reveal themselves when they investigate. Look, we don't know who's behind all this. It's someone who's powerful and has influence with City Hall. He has an army on the ground and allies in the Company. But guys like that always have enemies. Someone who wants to take them down and take their place. Maybe we can help the enemies out. Get the bad guys off our back."

"Like how, man?"

"Like fishin'. Throw out the bait. They swallow the hook. We reel 'em in."

"Okay, Ahab, what's the plan?"

Chapter 21

Phase one of Brad's plan was on schedule. Madison Samson III had taken the bait but had still not swallowed the hook. She was back in the uniform she was wearing the last time they met—a gray pantsuit. Her brown hair was teased to get the big, bouffant look. Bright-red lipstick. Dark makeup base. Blue eyeliner. Black mascara. Heavy, black-rimmed glasses. But she had charisma. Brad liked her. She was an ambitious, no-nonsense badass, and she seemed somehow amused sitting there in front of Brad at a back table in an old-fashioned café in the middle of the *Sentier.*

"So, Mr. Brad James, I thought I was pretty clear that you should stay out of this."

"You were, and to be honest, I hadn't given it much thought since we met. Making any progress?"

Madison smiled and shook her head. "It's slow going. I can say it looks like Papachristou's death was just what it seemed—a suicide. He'd been having problems with his job and his wife. There are just a few loose ends we have to tie up before I close the case and go back home. What is this urgent need to meet me all about?"

"Chuck received this at Latorre Legal." He slipped a folded A4 sheet of paper across the table.

Madison began to read. Her smile faded. She squeezed her eyes shut. She was no longer amused. "What is this?"

Brad had given her a copy of one of the documents he had retrieved from Mittel's office. "No idea. Looks like some bank transactions Papachristou handled. Chuck and I thought you should know. Gary's not around, and you're our only contact."

Madison was seriously upset. She tried to hide it but failed. She would need a lot of work if she wanted to go for an Academy Award. "Who else has seen this?"

"Just Chuck and me. There's one in the pipeline for Gary when he gets back. I'd better get a move on. Busy day today."

"Wait. I have to think. Order another round of coffees."

Brad smoked a Gitane. Madison thought. The coffees came. They drank in silence.

Finally, Madison made up her mind. "This looks like blackmail. Someone trying to blackmail Greta Papachristou. Why would they send it to *you*?"

"Not sure. We did some work for her. Her bodyguards were protective—like they were riding herd on her. Maybe they figured she might not get the message if it was sent directly to her. Who knows? Who knows if it's blackmail? Just some numbers and bank accounts with some names penciled in. Why would that be a basis for blackmail? He was a banker. That was his job. Should I deliver this to Mrs. Papachristou?"

"Absolutely not. Top secret. If you receive anything else, get back to me immediately. Use the emergency protocol. I also have to get what you put in Gary's pipeline."

"No can do, Madison. Super secret. He'll decide whether or not to show it to you when he gets back."

Several shades of red, black, and blue flashed across Madison's features, from anger to worry to acceptance. She would be okay with that, and that was Brad's insurance policy—for the moment. He had wanted to stir up the hornet's nest. He could never have imagined the bloodbath the information he had just provided was going to bring on.

Chuck saw it right away when they met. Uncharacteristically departing from his usual down-to-earth self, he waxed philosophical. "You have seeded the wind. Better be ready to reap a big storm."

This philosophical Chuck irritated Brad. "I suppose a wise old Indian said that."

"Naw, it's a French saying I learned from my French teacher."

"That's believable. Anyway, I don't think we'll be directly affected. She'll be afraid of what I put in Gary's pipeline." He stopped, put his hand to his head. "Oh, man, I didn't even think of Gary. I might have put him in the firing line."

Chuck didn't speak. Just shook his head with a wry grin on his face. Stiffened. Frowned. Turned to Brad. "Betty. She opens the mail. I've gotta get back to the office."

By this time, they were almost to the Champs-Elysées. Chuck took off for Latorre Legal. Brad went off to his meeting with Samantha. She was dressed in her dark alter ego and looked as good as ever. Brad had decided to come clean with her about his association with the Company. He presented it as a one-off deal, and she was surprisingly incurious. Just tapped her finger on the table and said, "Yeah, I figured."

Brad summarized the situation for her. Papachristou, the security breach, Madison, Ranger, and the death squad. When he mentioned he and Chuck had taken out the big blond transvestite, she reacted right away. "He goes—went—by the name of Monica. His real name was Charles Lumbers. He and Ranger were very close. Have been since they were teenagers. Very, very close. Ran with a pack of rich kids whose dads worked for the government. Ranger will never forgive you for killing his soulmate. You, Brad James, have made a mortal enemy. He will never rest until he gets revenge."

Samantha was even more worried about the reaction to Brad's info drop on Madison than Chuck was. She agreed the number of potential targets had gone way up. She didn't agree, however, that the info in Gary's pipeline guaranteed any kind of protection. On the contrary! She figured it made him and Chuck even more urgent targets. Madison had time to shut down the pipeline. She didn't have time to keep him and Chuck quiet.

Brad wanted to concentrate on Greta Papachristou and Georges Papachristou's secretary. They were the two most obvious targets. Samantha agreed, but she also wanted to concentrate on Brad's area and the safe house. She was convinced the safe house was not safe. "You can stay in my safe house over by Pereire. I only use it to change into Samantha Smith."

Brad studied her closely before answering. He didn't see any signs of ulterior motives. That disappointed him, but he had the feeling she might have some.

"And don't think I have any ulterior motives." She was reading his mind again. An enigmatic smile played around the edges of her lips for a couple of long Mississippis before she added, "Because I do."

Bullseye. Brad got it right in the heart.

The plan was for Doris the friendly street walker to keep her eye on things around the Barbary. Chuck could handle Latorre Legal. Brad would get Edith to stake out the area around

Papachristou's secretary's apartment in the *Sentier*. Brad would take care of the Drugstore area, where he might be able to catch Madison and/or Ranger going off somewhere.

Samantha said since she was known only through secondhand descriptions, she wouldn't be recognized and could go around to all those places. She was especially interested in the detached house on the Ile de la Jatte.

Brad left the Levallois safe house off the map. He trusted Samantha, but he couldn't be sure his testosterone wasn't affecting his judgement.

She gave Brad the key to her safe house and explained how to disconnect the security. Brad went off to buy some toilet articles and changes of clothes. It wouldn't be wise to risk going back to the apartment.

Chapter 22

Brad had a busy day ahead of him. There was a dress rehearsal before filming the television show programmed for Sunday. He'd be singing "Le Mercénaire" (The Mercenary), the A-side of his new 45 record. There was always a problem with lighting, camera placement, best angles, and things like that. It was customary for him to stay until everyone had done their thing, so it might take a good part of the day. He had a scheduled workout at 4 p.m. with another *karateka* over at la Montagne Sainte-Geneviève and he wanted to be at the Drugstore by 6 p.m. Being seen in the area was not a problem. It was near enough to his class on rue Saint-Guillaume that if Madison spotted him, it wouldn't be suspicious. Nevertheless, he preferred to stay out of her sight.

Before he got started on his busy day, he popped by to recruit Edith to do some surveillance for him. She was stationed in her usual spot under the shade tree smoking a Gitane.

"Hi Edith," Brad said, "what's up?"

"The sky's up, *petit*. So's the sun. What's down?" She was such a smartass.

"You ever heard of the *Sentier*?"

"I was the goddamn queen of the *Sentier*, *petit*. What about it?"

"Need you to do some surveillance for me. Same deal as before."

"You payin' the taxi?"

"Of course."

Brad gave her the money and the address and explained what she should watch for between 6:00 and 8:00 p.m.

"Fingers in the nose"—a French way of saying "easy as pie"—"Those goddamn Krautheads thought they could sneak by us. No way, José. Goddamn blockheads. Spotted 'em every time. Goddamn *ricains* are even worse. No problem. Bang, bang, bang, I gotcha, goddamn son-of-a-bitch."

Always a colorful contact with Edith. "Okay, see you here tomorrow morning."

With that taken care of, he went off to face the day. He was running a little late by the time he rolled up to the Drugstore at 6:10 p.m. and into a wild surprise. The blood-red Harley chopper was parked magnificently on the corner, attracting the usual admirative exclamations. Ranger, the Harley man, was basking in the attention, and Madison Samson III was off to the side in her black leathers, smiling benevolently as she struggled to squeeze her helmet onto her head.

Brad slipped onto the sidewalk and waited. When they vroomed off, he followed. They crossed the river and headed for the *Sentier*. Brad anticipated it would be to where Papachristou's secretary lived. As a security precaution, he took a shortcut and headed them off at the pass. Sure enough, they came roaring by and stopped a block from her building. Madison dismounted and walked off. Harley man stayed in the saddle.

A few minutes later, she strutted around the corner, pushed on her helmet, and jumped on the back of the Harley.

They headed back toward the 16th arrondissement. That was where Papachristou lived. Brad made an educated guess they were headed to Papachristou's, took another shortcut, and waited for them. Right again. This time, they both dismounted and walked around the block. They were in a deep discussion when they came back. Ranger was saying yes. Madison was saying no. Finally, she shrugged her shoulders and climbed back onto the bike.

Brad let them get away. He'd been on them long enough. It was already dark. He left his bike where it was and went to the café around the corner. It was too late for the early crowd and too early for the late crowd, so he had the place all to himself. The table he chose had line-of-sight to Papachristou's street and the grocery store next door. He ordered a *demi* and a *croque monsieur*—a draft beer and a hot ham-and-cheese sandwich. He sat back to wait.

At 10:15 p.m., two muscular, medium-sized honchos swaggered in. Their accents were American. Their size, haircuts, and demeanor suggested they were military, probably Special Forces. Two other similar species waited out on the street while these two purchased cigarettes. There was a walkie-talkie antenna protruding from the pocket of the smallest of the two in the café. Brad thought one of the two out on the street had one as well.

The atmosphere was electric. These guys were radiating pre-battle euphoria. Brad figured there were at least four other honchos out on the street somewhere. Madison had mobilized the troops to eliminate Greta Papachristou in record time. Greta had her small army of bodyguards, but Brad had no confidence in their chances against these military pros.

He went to the barman. *"Un jeton, s'il vous plait* (A telephone token, please)."* He went to the telephone cabin back by the toilets and dialed Greta Papachristou's number. The voice that answered sounded like the Head Honcho's. Brad wasted no time with social pleasantries. "There is a team of Americans preparing to attack you in a few minutes. Prepare yourself." He hung up. Papachristou's defense was warned.

The Americans were gone when Brad came back to the bar. He paid, lit up a Gitane, and strolled outside. It was warm, but he turned up his collar. Checked in his pouch that the Beretta was loaded and ready to shoot. He had nine rounds of ammo in his pocket.

Down Papachristou's street to the left, it was dark. Someone had taken out the streetlight, but he could make out some shadows moving around on the sidewalk. After a few puffs on his Gitane, seven shadows crossed to Papachristou's building. One shadow stayed posted outside.

Brad walked to his bike, cranked up, and sat watching the immobile shadow outside the building. All quiet on all fronts. Suddenly, the shadow dashed toward the building. Lights went on. Three men backed out, firing on automatic. One was limping. Three more struggled out, one carried by the other two. The seventh man crawled out the door to the sidewalk.

The shadow was firing at the top floor. Two men joined him, covering the retreat. He took a bullet in the shoulder, another in the gut. Went down. Staggered across the street and into a van. Bullets rained down from the terrace of the top floor. On the ground, the submachine guns of the retreating soldiers were spitting out bullets as fast as the remaining valid shooters could reload.

It was a total rout and the soldiers were on the run until a dark sedan careened around the corner, screeched to a halt. Three gangbangers jumped out and trained the full firepower of their submachine guns on terrace above. It was enough to get the troops into the van and make their getaway.

Brad cruised after them with his lights off. He had a good idea of where they were headed, but he wanted to be sure. The wild-west shootout back there was something that never happened in France, especially in the chic 16th arrondissement of Paris. It would be interesting to see how the newspapers handled it.

He could just see the taillights of the sedan turn onto the *Périphérique* when he heard a loud pop and the zing of a bullet whiz by. In the rearview, he saw a motorcycle bearing down on him. The pilot was brandishing a .45 automatic. The American gangbangers were all ahead of him.

So, it was the Papachristou pistoleros mistaking him for a gangbanger. Who would believe that crew of losers could get organized so quickly? *Wonders never cease.*

Nowhere to turn, he was going full speed, and he could not outrun the hail of bullets forever.

Chapter 23

Brad slammed on the back brakes, controlled his skid, hit the front brake. The rear wheel lifted. He threw his hip and rotated the handlebars; did a 180. The pursuing motorcycle flew by on the left. The passenger with the gun slipped off the bike trying to get a shot off just as the driver braked. Brad was long gone in the opposite direction by the time the other motorcycle stopped, got turned around, and picked up the fallen shooter. It was a close call—irrefutable proof that the Papachristou guards were well prepared. They were starting to look more competent and more committed than he thought. Gave Brad an idea on how he might be able to take advantage of their professionalism and commitment.

He hit the gas and shot down the boulevard de Lannes to the *Périphérique.* Several turns later, he determined he was in the clear. By the time he got within sight of the gangbangers' hideout on the Ile de la Jatte, the van was just pulling away. He tensed up to follow but relaxed when it only went as far as the other side of the highway and parked. The driver walked back to the house.

Brad packed it in and went back to Samantha's digs, very

relieved he had a safe place to stay, and hoping secretly she would be there. She wasn't, but he got a good night's sleep. The next morning after he showered and dressed, his first stop was the *marchand de journaux* (newspaper stand) on the Place, where he purchased the *Herald Tribune* and the *Figaro*. His second stop was the café across the street.

Over a *café crème* and two croissants, he searched through the *Herald Tribune*. There was never much local news in the *Herald*, and today was no exception. So the gunfight was not going to be international news. Brad half expected to find a big story on it in the *Figaro*. He was disappointed. The only mention was a back-page, ten-line report of an attempted robbery in the 16th where some gunshots were heard. No names. Nobody wounded. Nobody apprehended. It appeared as if the French were putting a lid on this, which would confirm Brad's conviction the U.S. government was involved, even if it wasn't pulling all the strings.

By the time he got to Edith's, she was chomping at the bit. "Hey, *petit*, you take the mornin' off?"

Brad saw a pile of Gitane butts by her feet. She must have been sitting there for a couple of hours. "Had some errands to run. How was your evening?"

That opened the floodgates. "Goddamn, son-of-a-bitch, was a long evenin'. Checkin' out the broads and the *baba-cools* chasin' 'em. Gotta know the neighborhood. Sat there and sat there. Needed a couple'a wines to keep me alert. It's on the bill. Worse than the Krautheads, *ricains* stand out. Two bleedin' bully boys all dressed up for the dance. Along comes the broad with the big tits in motorcycle gear. Gives 'em the secret high sign. Struts off. Bleedin' bully boys drink their beers, cross the street, go in the building. I'm friggin' countin'. Got to five hundred. Bully boys come stompin' out, smilin'. I'm waitin'. Had another wine. Here come the cops.

She's dead, the secretary. Bully boys killed her."

Edith finally took a breath, and Brad got to ask, "What did the guys look like?"

"Typical American. Like you, *petit*." She stopped.

"That's all?"

"Goddamn right. That's a lot." She gave him the evil eye. Then she winked. "Got pictures, too." She pulled a roll of film out of her purse. "Didn't have time to get it developed. Thought you'd get your ass out of bed on time and do it for me."

Hard evidence. There was no doubt Edith knew what she was doing. He could see she was pleased with herself. "So, Edith, you ready for another mission?"

"Goddamn right. But I'm pretty busy these days, *petit*. Money's tight. High-quality professional help is hard to find."

"You're coming through loud and clear, Edith. I'll be back later."

Chuck was uncharacteristically curt when Brad called in from a public phone. "Get over here ASAP, to the studio."

Brad eschewed the elevator for the stairway and walked up the six flights to Chuck's studio. He knocked. Waited. Knocked again. The door finally opened onto little Betty standing there in a bathrobe and slippers.

"I didn't hear the elevator. The peephole is too high. I had to get a chair. And don't try to act surprised, Brad James. You know Chuck and I have been an item for a long time—even if he tries to hide it."

Chuck came out of the bathroom, shaved and dressed. His usual unflappable demeanor was stretched thin this morning. "We've gotta move fast. Caught Betty before she left last night. Took her here and passed by her place. There was a team staked out there. She's a target."

"Good thing you kept her here." Brad went on to describe his late-night adventure and Edith's account of her evening.

Chuck whistled through his teeth. "Jesus F. Christ! This is war."

"Yeah, we can't afford to make a mistake. They've got seemingly unlimited resources and firepower. I guess stirring up the hornet's nest was a higher-risk proposition than we counted on."

"You can say that again, brain daddy. First on my list is to get Betty to safety. I've got a place on the Costa Brava in Spain. She'll be safe there."

Chuck with a vacation house in Spain! Unbelievable! He'd have to dig into that. "Right on. We are in one of those rocky, hard places. We have to decide on what to do for ourselves. Now we're high-profile targets." Brad took his time lighting a cigarette and blowing a few perfect smoke rings before he continued.

"Basically, there's nowhere for us to run. Uncle Sam's City Hall is everywhere. Direct conflict is out of the question and always has been. But I'm seriously doubting we're fighting the entire City Hall. Otherwise, we'd have the French on our ass. Maybe we can recruit the other part of City Hall to notice and help us out."

Chuck's body language was negative. "That's the same argument that got us into this shit-creek dilemma."

"Yeah, strong proof it's working. There was some desperation in what they did. Admit it. Shooting up the 16th in Paris, France, smells of panic. Let's go underground for a few days. Disappear. Keep our ear to the ground. Get Betty to Spain. You're safe here. I've got Samantha's place. This Mario guy is coming in tonight. I'm convinced he's got some solid proof tucked away for a rainy day. With Samantha's pictures and Edith's pictures, so do we. We can put it together and go to Gary. I've got his number in Washington. Already warned him about the situation here and the danger he's in." There was a noise out on the landing. Brad put his finger to his lips and squinted through the peephole. "Relax, it's just the cleaning service. They'll be gone in a few minutes."

Chuck was surprisingly nervous. Betty was surprisingly calm. "Don't worry, Chuckie, I'll be fine down in Spain. I'll bring copies of the files with me and keep things going. I'll need something to keep me busy with you gone anyway."

Brad couldn't believe his ears. Chuckie! She called him Chuckie and he didn't even flinch. Man! "Okay, Chuck, I've got a meeting with Samantha about Mario. I'll call you at this number when I get the info." Brad thought about throwing a "Chuckie" in there but wisely decided against it.

Samantha was waiting for him when he got back to her safe house. She was in her blonde Samantha de la Sarta costume. Even more beautiful than her Samantha Smith alter ego. He could see she was excited, but she played it cool. "Any news?"

Brad proceeded to brief her on what had gone down last evening, leaving out the names and descriptions of Edith, Betty, and Madison. One of his mottos was "Trust, but beware." In spite of the growing bond between the two of them, Brad's experience had taught him to employ a high discount factor to his trust in the opposite sex.

Samantha agreed the shootout in the 16th was a sign of weakness, but she said Ranger was a wild card, fearless and unpredictable. Nothing he did would surprise her. She was anxious to tell Brad about Mario.

Brad looked around the studio. It was pretty bare but still had a feminine touch to it. He had carefully made the bed before he left. It wasn't something he usually did, but he figured it would win him some brownie points.

She read his mind. "Thanks for making the bed. I hate

disorder." She curled her bare feet under her legs and leaned back in the armchair. Her eyes were sparkling. "Mario's in town. He wants to meet. I think he wants to join forces."

"What can he bring to the table?"

She leaned forward with her hands under her chin. She had a cute way of pursing her lips when she wanted to make a point. "He has hundreds of millions of dollars and the backing of the Montoneros and the Argentine left. They have a big network in Spain, France, and the UK."

"He told me he's being hunted by his government."

"He is. But they want him alive. We are meeting him tonight."

Chapter 24

MID MAY 1975, VERSAILLES TO THE ISLAND OF JERSEY

It was a short wait. Mario arrived at the secluded park on the outskirts of Versailles accompanied by two bodyguards. Brad had noticed several others rustling around in the trees before he actually showed up. Mario's voice was soft and slow in perfectly accented English. Although he showed no nervous tics, he was obviously in a hurry. Pleasantries were kept to a minimum. No hard feelings on either side.

"My information is limited to transactions with Papachristou. I know the names 'Junior' and 'El Gordo,' but nothing more." He held up his hand before Brad could react. "However, I have made some inquiries. There is someone who can give you more information. His name is Adam Crowcroft. He is at the head of the biggest, most reputable law firm on the island of Jersey. He has been contacted and after some deep discussion has graciously agreed to collaborate. Given the high stakes and risk, his price is also high—one hundred thousand U.S. dollars in cash."

Brad tried to intervene, but again Mario held up his hand.

"My understanding with Samantha is that you are rogue actors on the run, just like me."

"That would be an accurate description of our situation," Brad said.

"But unlike me, you have no money."

"Right again."

Mario paused for effect. Waved to his bodyguard, who came forward with a gym bag. Placed it in front of Brad. Mario pointed to the bag. "There is one hundred and eleven thousand U.S. dollars in there. Ten thousand for the round-trip boat trip to Jersey, one thousand for the man who will guide you to and from the meeting with Crowcroft, and one hundred thousand for Crowcroft. The guide is to be paid after he has brought you back to the boat. The captain of the boat is to be paid after he brings you back to Saint Malo. I know the captain well and can vouch for him. This is the first time I have dealt directly with Crowcroft, but he has a sound reputation."

Brad was gathering his thoughts before he nodded toward the bag. "You know, Mario, I'll never be able to pay you back."

Smanatha stepped in. "Don't worry about that. It's taken care of. I am fronting the money."

Brad was only mildly surprised. He knew Samantha de la Sarta was a rich heiress. He still wanted to know why Mario was doing this. "What's in this for you?"

"It's an investment. I'm in a very precarious predicament for the time being. I may need a favor sometime."

"Message received, Mario. We'll be in touch. It's been a pleasure. *Au revoir.*"

"Instructions, names, and addresses are in the bag. If you leave now, you can be in Saint Malo before 1:00 a.m. The boat trip is about ninety minutes. The meeting with Crowcroft will be short and sweet. You can imagine that with all the confidential information he has at his disposal, he is heavily protected. He is also under constant surveillance by those with whom he shares secrets. *Au revoir.*"

The air was warm, late-evening traffic was thin, and there was no radar. They were at the Saint Malo port by thirty minutes past midnight. Mario's instructions were detailed and precise. It took only a few minutes before they were standing in front of a medium-sized fishing boat and a huge mountain of a bearded man wearing what was once a beautifully embroidered blue gentleman's jacket. He looked like the reincarnation of Black Bart, the buccaneer, without the eye patch and three-cornered hat. His voice was deep and gruff. "Ahoy, matey. Am I lookin' at Brad James and his woman?" His accent was somewhat Irish and his manner surprisingly friendly.

"Indeed. This is Samantha."

Samantha gave him a funny look before she said hello. The giant beamed an admirative smile and tenderly took her small hand into his gnarled paw. "It is such a pleasure to meet such a lovely young lady, *mademoiselle*. I am Blackie." A short bow. "At your service." Samantha loved it. This man was a charm machine.

The lights from the boat were winking on the wavelets of the incoming tide, the first increments of the larger waves they would face when they got out on the sea. Brad wasn't looking forward to the sea voyage. He was a landlubber at heart and would be glad when it was over. Blackie ushered them onto the boat, gave the signal to his matelots, and they weighed anchor.

The sea was relatively calm and the firmament was bright with stars and a shining moon. In another context, it would have been romantic. Even in the current context, Brad was enjoying it. He was not susceptible to seasickness. The same could not be said for Samantha. She was getting a little green around the gills and trying unsuccessfully to hide it. Finally, she disappeared around the other side of the boat. She was looking better when she returned.

When the lights of Saint Helier appeared, Blackie called them into the cabin. "We'll be landing soon. You'll be going ashore in an isolated spot. It's rarely patrolled. I have no contraband or anything illegal, so I can wait until you get back. But be quick, matey."

They landed in a tiny cove with a small strip of sand to the right of the dock. Brad grabbed the bag and jumped onto the dock. Samantha followed. There was no sign of their guide, but they were running thirty minutes early for the exchange. Still, Brad had a bad feeling. It was too quiet. Something was off-key.

He reached into the bag and extracted his Beretta. Stuck it in his belt. They crossed the sandy strip and stopped at the edge of the tree line, listening, searching for their contact. A rustling sound behind a big boulder made Samantha back off. Brad advanced.

The beam of a powerful spotlight captured Brad moving forward and momentarily blinded him. He shielded his eyes and attempted to disengage. A glancing blow from some kind of a club took him down. He rolled to the right, but the dry sand slowed his safety roll.

Another blow caught him on the leg. There were two of them. The second gangbanger was coming in for the kill when Samantha rushed forward, executed a flying front flip, and came down feetfirst on his back. He dropped.

She came up on her feet and cartwheeled into the first gangbanger, who was momentarily surprised by the fate of his accomplice. The heel of her rotating right foot connected with his neck, and he fell into the sand.

Brad jumped to his feet, out of the light. A third gangbanger was rushing forward swinging a sickle.

Friggin' farmers!

Brad dove to the right, rolled forward, and came up on his feet. The sickle swinger was hot on his tail. Brad dodged behind a tree, grabbed his Beretta. The sickle blade slashed through the air. Brad ducked, pumped out three bullets to the head—all bullseyes. The sickle slasher fell on his back. The top of his head was blown away.

Brad looked to the beach. One gangbanger lay motionless in the sand. The other was running around trying fruitlessly to corner Samantha, who was literally dancing rings around him. Brad ended the chase with a series of left-right combinations that left the gangbanger moaning in the sand. He really wanted to destroy the guy, but needed him for some answers. It looked like Crowcroft had attempted to double-cross them.

"Why did you attack us?"

"Fuck you."

The guy was going to play hero, and there was no time for that. Brad seized the gangbanger's elbow and wrist. With all his strength, he brought the forearm down on his knee. The bone exploded, and the gangbanger passed out. Some saltwater and a kick in the head brought him back to his senses.

"Last chance. Why did you attack us?"

The gangbanger was perspiring profusely, and in the moonlight his face was ghost-white. "The money. We keep half the money."

"What money?"

"Your money. The money you're launderin'. Mate, mate, I'm sorry. Really sorry."

"You work for Crowcroft?"

"Crowcroft. No. Don't know him. We got a tip that a boat was headin' this way."

Brad figured the tip had come from Crowcroft but didn't have time to try and prove it. Samantha tapped Brad's shoulder. "Headlights."

Brad nudged the gangbanger. "Don't make a sound."

Samantha was behind the boulder. Brad was in the woods. Headlights went out. Doors closed. Muffled voices. Footsteps. Two men casually dressed came to a stop before the two bodies in the sand. Brad stepped out. "Mr. Crowcroft?"

The taller of the two waved toward the two gangbangers in the sand. "Mr. James. It seems you have found the poachers for us. They have been very troublesome. They poach our clients' money and poison the business environment." This Crowcroft was a smooth operator.

"There's another one by the tree. He has a head injury."

"No problem. I'll handle it. In these circumstances, it is preferable that we accelerate the transaction. Here is the information you are seeking." Unflappable Englishness.

"Thank you. Here's the money." Brad reached into the bag and withdrew two packets of five thousand dollars. He handed the bag to the shorter of the two. "There's one thousand for the guide in there, and your one hundred thousand."

"Thank you. Now, if you will excuse me, we have some loose ends to clean up here. So nice to meet you. You as well, young lady."

Back on the boat away from the island, Brad breathed a sigh of relief and took a look at the documents Crowcroft had delivered. He couldn't believe what he was reading.

Chapter 25

Two weeks. It had been two weeks since Gary had started pussyfooting around Langley. This was an extremely long time for a station chief to be absent from his station, especially in the exceptional circumstances currently prevailing in Paris. Gary had been around the block too many times to swallow the party line of an urgent need to debrief him on industrial espionage by the Soviet Union in France. That took all of one afternoon and stretched into three more follow-up meetings on trumped-up requests for clarification.

He was being sidelined on purpose. That could only happen on orders from the top of the pyramid. Gary was not a mathematician, but he did know two plus two makes four. He also knew Madison Samson III had overseen a colossal security breach. She survived that. The security breach metastasized to Paris. She survived that, as well, and then was given the responsibility of fixing the leak and solving the problem—something completely contrary to Company protocol.

Put it all together with the common knowledge that Madison Samson III was the personal protégé of Alvin P. Dearman, the deputy director of the CIA. The mathematical conclusion here was that Dearman was either protecting her or using her in some kind of complicated foreign flag operation. Gary would leave the analysis of the what's, why's, and wherefore's of Dearman's behavior to the psychologists. What he wanted to know was why he, the station chief, was being excluded from the operation.

As he entered the office, something told him he was about to get an answer to that. "Hello, Martha."

"Hello, Gary. Mr. Dearman is waiting for you."

Gary knocked once and entered. The social pleasantries were short and sweet. Gary was fine. Dearman was fine. Everybody was fine, thanks for asking.

Dearman looked down at the papers on his desk. Signaled for Gary to sit down. Put his hands together and sighed. "I need your help, Gary. We have a problem in Brussels."

Full alert. Alvin Dearman was like the spot on the horse where the sun rarely shines. When it does open up and the sun comes in, a big load of stinky stuff is about to come out.

"Alvin, when you called me back to Langley, my deputy took over. I've been in constant contact with him. Everything is rocking along. The only red flags are linked to the top secret security breach Madison is handling."

"She has run into some dangerous and unexpected opposition. A band of renegades. Nothing she can't handle. There will be an important meeting of the European foreign ministers in Brussels next month. We're shorthanded. I need you there to coordinate things."

Gary took his time before answering. This conversation was in coded bureaucratese. He was being demoted. It was only temporary, but Alvin Dearman was demoting him. No shoulders, pot belly, bald head, and a facial expression somewhere between squinting into the sun and sniffing a stinking sewer pipe, Alvin P.

Dearman was beyond physically disgusting. He was known as a cruel, ambitious, pathological liar. He began his career in the ranks of the administrative hierarchy of the OSS—the Office of Strategic Services—that morphed into the CIA after the war. He was a long-serving company man who had manipulated, cheated, and schemed his way to the second-highest-ranked position in the Company. He stayed and he ruled. His memory was long and self-serving. The people below him knew it, and if push came to shove, his word would be law.

"Alvin, you know you can count on me. What is it you want me to do?"

"I want you in Brussels in ten days. Use that time to secure everything in Paris while you are gone. Count on being there for a month."

Back in his office, Gary fired up the coffee machine, cooked up a pot of pure Costa Rican arabica, and poured himself an oversized mugful. He added three sugar cubes and stirred. Before he sipped, he took a fourth sugar cube, dipped it in the coffee, and ate it like candy. When he was upset, coffee-dipped sugar cubes were his go-to analgesic. Today was an exceptionally bad day, so he decided to have two.

Dearman gave him no details on the Brussels deal. He would be briefed when he arrived. This sudden special assignment was so exceptional Gary could hardly believe it was happening. His information set was incomplete, but there was enough in there to convince him it was directly related to Madison and her investigation into Papachristou's death. Brad's call had been short and cryptic. Basically, Brad had told him in their agreed code that he and Chuck had uncovered some important information that made them assassination targets of the *home team*. When he got the message, he was skeptical. The meeting with Alvin P. Dearman confirmed not only that Brad's claim was credible, but that the order was coming from the highest echelon of the Company. It looked like Dearman did not want him interfering.

His first act would be to do the old CYA—cover your ass— trick. He typed a dated memo with three carbon copies to Alvin P. Dearman, where he detailed the meeting that had just gone down. He wax-sealed the original in a dated envelope he gave to his secretary and told her to hold it for him. A second copy he stuffed into an envelope addressed to himself at his mother's address. The third copy he would have notarized and sent to himself at his brother's address.

Thus prepared, he was ready to do battle. He had ten days to get the situation in Paris straightened out. Once he was gone, there was no telling what would happen. Whatever did happen, it would not be good for him or his team. Brad's message made that clear.

The evening news didn't do anything to help his distress. There was that insufferable windbag, Jake Brown, ranting on about the traitor holed up in the Soviet embassy. He was still incensed a proven traitor with blood on his hands could hold a press conference in the capital of the United States of America and get away with it.

When he was reminded there had been no proof of the traitor's guilt outside of a statement by the deputy director of the CIA, he questioned the journalist's patriotism. According to Jake, questioning the CIA was tantamount to spreading traitorous propaganda. Jake Brown doubled down on his patriotism and love of the United States that mandated he see to it this traitor be jailed and executed.

The traitor should be hanged by the neck, and he intended to see to it that this Benedict Arnold was brought to justice. The integrity of the United States of America was too sacred and his own patriotism too pure to be sidelined. He would pursue this traitor to the ends of the earth and would employ all the government resources at his disposal to do it. And on and on and on.

As a seasoned intel analyst, Gary was sensitive to what was said as well as what was not said. So far, the accusations were devoid of facts about what exactly had been leaked to our adversaries. There was nothing specific, just some vague statements about classified information. Gary had learned some of the information was financial in nature and had caused the deaths of some of our undercover assets. Beyond that, he had nothing precise. It was Madison who was holding all those cards.

Chapter 26

From their parking spot on the boulevard Bineau, they sat for a while to get a feel for their surroundings. Traffic across the bridge was starting to pick up. Across the river, there were a few lunch stragglers on the terrace of *La Guinguette*. The gangbangers' hideout next door was quiet. If he didn't know better, Brad would say it was empty. He wondered what the gangbangers did when they weren't out killing people.

Time to stretch his legs. "Let's take a walk, Chuck." Out on the street the air was warm, but there was a sting of pollution in it. Brad rubbed his eyes. "Did you get Betty squared away?"

"Yeah, she's all set. Apartment overlooking the beach. Beautiful weather. I'll pop down to see her every chance I get."

"What's your take on the info I got from Crowcroft?"

"The major takeaway is we have the account details of those doing business with the accounts we found in the Mittel documents. From this we can put names to these accounts. The next step is to find the beneficial owners of the accounts. I was surprised Junior and El Gordo are not people. They're companies. Georges Papachristou was funneling the money Mario Irigoyen was paying for the intelligence into these companies. Do you think the Company knew about this?"

"That's a good question," Brad said. "Gary obviously had no idea. But Papachristou must have known. That's why he was killed. There's no evidence he was benefitting personally. He was probably just passing the information on the payments up the chain of command in the Company. In any case, it got me thinking. His wife's security detail was always a big question for me. Why does she need that level of security? Why does she continue to hang around Paris after her husband is dead and buried? What does she know that would warrant a military-style Special Forces attack on her apartment in the richest neighborhood of Paris?"

Chuck nodded emphatically. "What about this? Where does her security detail come from? They took out a well-armed, well-planned assault by well-trained professional soldiers. How could she assemble a team like that? More importantly, why would she even imagine she would need one?"

Over across the river, there was some movement in the gangbangers' hideout. A couple of guys came out onto the dock and started smoking. A third guy with bandages on his head and arm came out and laid down on a deck chair.

Brad and Chuck went back to their car. Brad lit up and blew a lungful of smoke at his sidekick. "Got an idea. Let's go." At the Porte Maillot, Brad spotted an operational telephone cabin. "Stop here."

He put some coins in the phone and dialed a number. The conversation took less than a minute. Back in the car, Chuck was curious. "What was that all about, mystery man?"

"Called Greta Papachristou's. Talked with Head Honcho. Gave him the gangbangers' address. I'm betting he would like some revenge on the gangbangers who sneak-attacked him."

The smile on Chuck's face said it all. He was impressed. "Brilliant, brain daddy. Let's secure a ringside seat."

"Papachristou's pistoleros will probably do some serious reconnaissance before they act. I'm gonna get Edith to keep an eye on the neighborhood this evening. You and I can come back tonight to observe the fireworks. How much you wanna bet they won't waste any time?"

Edith jumped at the chance to spend an evening spying on the gangbangers, drinking wine, and smoking Gitanes. Brad met her at 10:00 p.m. on her way back to her apartment. She looked tired and seemed to be relying more than usual on her ivory-handled walking stick. Still had her spirit, though.

"Four of 'em. Four goddamn spics prowlin' around the gangbangers' hideout. Rode in on motorcycles. Left two of 'em sittin' on the opposite side of the goddamn highway. Friggin' greasy-lookin' grifters. Shifty SOBs. *Putain de merde.*"

"Did you see any gangbangers?"

"No."

Brad said goodbye and hustled up the boulevard to join Chuck, who was parked in sight of the hideout across the river. "Something's going down. Two spics are on their motorcycle ready to take off. Two gangbangers just got into the black sedan."

The sedan pulled slowly away from the curb, crossed the bridge onto the quai toward Clichy. The motorcycle followed discreetly, followed discreetly in turn by Brad and Chuck. At the next bridge, the sedan caught the stoplight. The motorcycle pulled alongside. The passenger looked into the car and knocked on the window. The irritated gangbanger rolled it down and cursed. They were his last words.

The motorcycle passenger pumped two shots into the car, one at the driver, the other at the passenger—both headshot bullseyes.

He dismounted, opened the car door, pushed the dead driver onto the dead passenger, put the car in gear, and drove off when the light turned green. The motorcycle followed.

Brad and Chuck broke off toward Courbevoie. They were impressed. But before they could verbalize their admiration for the smoothest hit job either of them had ever seen, a motorcycle pulled abreast.

Chuck had a flash. He hit the brakes. The driver was shooting as the motorcycle flew by. Thanks to Chuck's quick reaction, the shots went wild.

The motorcycle spun around to make another pass. Brad jumped out of the car, Beretta in hand. He got off two shots. They may have missed. Maybe not. The motorcycle spun away. Brad jumped back into the car as Chuck U-turned on the bridge back toward Paris.

Chuck checked the rearview. "We've got company. Looks like the gangbangers."

Brad looked back at a dark sedan bearing down on them. It was a gangbanger sedan. Chuck hit the gas. He made the first light at sixty-five, the second at eighty, the sedan gaining ground. The third light was going red and Chuck was going ninety. He hit the brakes and slid into a perfectly controlled turn down the side alley. The sedan was not so lucky. It flashed across the intersection, collided with a garbage truck, and was catapulted into a line of parked cars, where it exploded in flames. No one exited the burning vehicle.

Chuck cut down the alley to the next boulevard, back down another side street, back to the next boulevard. Brad was scouring their trail looking for anything resembling a tail. After fifteen minutes of this, they concluded they were clean and let themselves relax.

It was a sobering experience. Chuck was the first to break the silence. "Those pistoleros from Papachristou are professional badasses. They must have spotted us following and sent that motorcycle to take us out. You were lucky to chase them off with your peashooter."

"I don't think they were afraid of my peashooter. I think they spotted the gangbangers' sedan that chased us. Probably thought we were together. Think anybody got the license number?"

"Don't care. Changed plates with another car like this one. I'll change 'em back when I get home."

"Drop me at the metro. I'll see you tomorrow." Tomorrow's meeting with Mario had him worried.

Chapter 27

Brad was feeling pretty good about the previous evening's activities. The gangbangers lost two vehicles and at least four men. Unless one of Papachristou's pistoleros got hit by one of Brad's bullets, these guys came out unscathed. Luckily, so did Brad and Chuck. There was also no way to link them to the attacks.

When Brad briefed Samantha, she was less than thrilled. It was Ranger's reaction that had her worried. She said Ranger was a psychopath who could not accept defeat. He would go after anyone and anything he suspected, either rightly or wrongly, of opposing him. That included indirect opposition, such as being a friend or relative or even a neighbor of someone he suspected. The wide net meant both Brad and Chuck were on the firing line, along with anybody they spent more than five minutes talking to.

Brad was convinced attacking Ranger and his minions head-on was the way to go. He figured running and hiding was a losing strategy that would only encourage Ranger if he had nothing to fear. Samantha was convinced Brad did not have the firepower to worry Ranger or his operations. Ranger was backed by a part of the enormous U.S. government. She compared Brad to the ant on a men's room toilet seat.

When they got that out of the way, Samantha took Brad to meet Mario in a detached house in Antony, south of Paris. Mario sided with Samantha when they told him about Ranger's losses. His analysis was even more negative than Samantha's.

"Brad," Mario said, "you've weakened my position and put Samantha in danger. Up to now, I was a short-term enemy for Ranger, and Samantha was probably not on his radar. I just needed to hold out until Rega falls. It's only a matter of time. Argentina is almost out of foreign currency reserves and can't borrow. Rega's taking the heat. Once he's gone, I'll be back in. Ranger doesn't know who's responsible for the attack, so he'll be targeting anything and everything. I'm on that list. You found me through Samantha. No reason why Ranger won't do the same. It's what he does to her when he finds her that has me worried."

That made sense to Brad, and he was starting to feel bad, but not bad enough to regret what he had done. He was glad to see those worthless gangbangers go down in flames. "You seem pretty well protected."

"I've got the Resistance on my side, but as long as Rega's in power, we're considered outlaws by the other countries. I have no official cover, and Rega's AAA is out to capture me."

"Not kill you?"

"No, I have something he thinks is his: one hundred million dollars in a company called Bellweather SA. He wants it back. If they do capture me, I'll probably wish I was dead. But still, it's much more difficult to capture someone than it is to kill them. I can also count on the AAA to protect me from someone trying to kill me, at least until Rega gets back what he wants."

Samantha was in a hurry. "What is it you wanted to tell us?"

Mario clasped his hands and looked down. He spoke slowly and chose his words carefully. "There is a CIA agent in the Soviet embassy accused of being a spy." Full stop. Five Mississippis. "He is innocent."

"How can you possibly know that?"

Mario's smile was somewhere between sarcasm and a smirk. "Because the information he reported to his boss came from the person who paid for it: me. I was the person who paid for it. I gave it to him. He's just the scapegoat. Unfortunately, I don't know who the originator of the information is. I only know it comes from a CIA mole delivered through a political connection."

"Got any proof?"

"I do. I have all the proof you need." Mario nodded. He was confident. "When the time comes, I will produce it." There was a slight hesitation, then he added, "And I think if you find out who Ranger is working for, you will also have found the mole."

On the ride back to Paris, Brad was deep in thought. Mario's analysis made sense, and Brad suspected he knew more than he was letting on. If Mario was right, the stakes were much higher than simply cleaning up the mess of a security breach. There was a mole in the system, and the mole had control of the CIA resources to undermine the U.S. and to protect himself. That meant he and Chuck were nothing more than Samantha's toilet seat ants—which made Brad very, very angry.

Back at her flat, Samantha broke the silence. "I might have to spend more time over here if things look too dangerous."

For once, Brad's mind was faster than his mouth. He took a long look. Samantha wasn't smiling, but there was a mischievous twinkle in her otherwise innocent eyes. He stifled his automatic reflex for a smartass one-liner and let his true thought come through. "I think I can get used to that."

It was a bullseye. Samantha stepped forward, and Brad gathered her in his arms. Their lips met. They held each other for many Mississippis, sharing the moment, exploring their intimacy.

Chapter 28

MID MAY 1975, MONTPARNASSE

Samantha was in the restaurant, dressed as her dark-haired, dark-eyed, dark-skinned alter ego. Chuck was in the upstairs bar, dressed as himself. They were on the lookout for gangbangers. Doris and her colleagues were keeping an eye on the street. Brad didn't really believe Ranger would try anything in the Barbary Coast Saloon, but it was better to be safe than sorry. Ranger's reputation as a loose cannon and his military attack on Greta Papachristou was proof he was capable of anything.

Brad finished off his show with a rendition of "Girl of Mine" especially for Samantha, but he didn't go join her when he got offstage. They had decided it was more prudent to keep their intimate relationship under wraps as long as Ranger and his gangbangers were on the loose. Gary was there, anyway, and wanted to talk to him.

He was sitting alone, finishing his coffee, when Brad came over. Just off the long flight from Washington, his eyes were set deep in their sockets rimmed by dark-gray circles, and his shoulders were slumped. He wasn't smiling and didn't show any enthusiasm when Brad sat down. "Long time, no see, *amigo*."

"Hi, Brad. Good show." Normally, Gary would make a joke about Brad getting a day job. That wouldn't happen tonight. Tonight, Gary had other things on his mind. He was worried. "I spoke with Madison today. She's unhappy with how things are going. She complained explicitly about you. Said you were interfering in the investigation. I thought I told you to stay out of it."

Brad wasn't ready for this kind of aggressive attitude from Gary, especially after it had been so long since they'd met and compared notes. He controlled the urge to blow him off. Instead, he asked, "What exactly did she say?"

"She said you dug up some old offshore bank records that mentioned Papachristou. Made it sound like blackmail."

Madison's portrayal of the bank records as "old" and "blackmail" was a blatant attempt to disguise their importance. "Gary, we have three names associated with those bank records. The first is Mario Irigoyan, the Argentine agent who admits to receiving the classified intelligence and paying for it. The second is Georges Papachristou, a senior CIA agent, who was murdered. The third is Eric Mittel, a financial advisor who was also murdered. Some entries are as recent as last July. So they're definitely not old, there is nothing in them to implicate Greta Papachristou in a blackmail scheme, and most importantly, the two murders are linked directly to the gang Madison is currently running with."

Brad decided it was time to come clean with Gary. He sat back, took out his Gitanes, and lit up.

"Madison is right," he continued. "We have interfered in her investigation. What she told you is just the tip of the iceberg. Here are the facts, and you should be worried."

Brad proceeded to brief Gary on everything that had gone down since Gary disappeared back to Washington. He started with the attack by the gangbangers the night he met Samantha. He detailed Madison's relationship with Ranger. How he followed Madison to Papachristou's, where he found the dying bodyguard who blamed "the Americans" and told him about the pics of big blonde killing Papachristou. How the "American hit team" came after him. The tight security on Greta. How he followed Madison and Ranger to Mittel's house, where he found Mittel's murdered body and the financial info. He didn't mention Samantha.

The more Brad talked, the more Gary looked puzzled. "This makes no sense. How can Madison be doing all this?"

"I think it's more than a scorched-earth reaction to the pictures of Papachristou's murder. And it's not just Madison. The Company's in this up to its ears."

"How did you get the pictures of the murder?"

"It's a long story." Actually, it was a short story. It was Samantha as a guest at the reception who had taken the pictures, and it was she who had delivered them to Greta Papachristou's bodyguard. When Brad mentioned to her the pictures of the murder were missing, she gave him copies. In any case, it was too early to tell Gary about Samantha.

Gary's jet lag was making him impatient and cantankerous. "So what else is there?"

"They put a bomb on Chuck's car. We wanted to tell you, but you had already gone back to the U.S. Anyway, we discovered where they were hiding out and decided to go on offense."

Gary shook his head. "How did you discover that?"

"Chuck traced a license plate to a detached house on the Ile de la Jatte. It's owned by Atrium SA, one of the shell companies named in the Mittel documents."

"I'm afraid to ask, but how exactly did you go on offense?"

Before answering, Brad took a big hit on his Gitane. He wanted to gather his thoughts. "First, we tried to capture Big Blonde, but that didn't work out and we had to kill him. By the way, Big Blonde is friendly with one of the consuls at the embassy. Anyway, all the evidence suggested Madison was in cahoots with the American gangbangers, so I gave her the information she told you about. Wanted to see if that would get a reaction. The reaction was even more spectacular than anything I could have imagined. The American gangbangers launched a full-scale military attack on Greta Papachristou's apartment."

Gary snapped to attention. His surprise was surprising. He wanted all the details. As a frontline spectator, Brad gave him everything he needed to know, including his role in tipping off the pistoleros. Gary was gobsmacked. None of this had come through to him. When Brad recounted the pistoleros' counterattack, Gary just sat there, incredulous. Finally, he said, "Do you have any paperwork?"

"In the usual pipeline. It's all there. You just have to retrieve it. I have also been informed the 'traitor' is telling the truth. My informant tells me there's a mole in the Company. The mole was selling the classified information he had access to—secret operations, strategies, plans, names of agents and informants, military intel, the whole shebang. One of the accused traitor's informants acquired the classified information and transmitted it to him. The accused traitor passed the information on up the chain of command. My informant assured me he has the proof he will produce when he feels the time is right. The 'traitor' is the scapegoat." Brad stopped, stared hard into Gary, and added, "I think we have enough to go after Madison, the mole, and his minions."

Gary rocked slowly back and forth. He was thinking it over and liking it less and less. "This is explosive stuff. It could blow us all out of the water. Regular channels are not going to work. I need the detailed bank records to get the names. I also need the 'proof' of the leak from your informant. I also need time, and I don't have any. I have to be in Brussels by the end of next week."

It was Brad's turn to be gobsmacked. "Why? For how long?"

"Deputy director has a special mission for me for a month or so. Don't say anything. I know it smells bad."

Brad's smile was condescending. "Once you're gone, the game is over. There will be no place for us to hide, and no one for us to go to. That leaves us less than two weeks. Madison probably knows the timeline. She doesn't know all the evidence we've collected—lucky for you. If she did, you would be a target, if you're not already."

"I need proof of Madison's guilt."

"Besides myself, I've got an eyewitness."

"Credible?"

"Very." Brad was sure Edith would dazzle them in a court of law. "And try and get the skinny on this Ranger dude."

"You get me the proof about the traitor. I'll get the info on Ranger. The names behind bank records you've put in the pipeline will be more difficult. Regular, legal channels are a dead end. I'll have to go around them. I know somebody who owes me one. But can't promise anything."

"Chuck and I have moved to new hideouts for the time being. Here's his telephone number. Use the code to set up a meeting. We'll do the same with your number."

Chuck was the first to leave the Barbary. Outside, Doris gave him the thumbs-up. Samantha went upstairs to the bar, where she flirted with the jarheads until it was time for her to leave. When it was Brad's turn to leave, Doris was at the door, shooting the breeze with Jackie. She gave him the "no" look so he went into the bar, where the group of eight jarheads was getting ready to head for Pigalle. Brad joined them.

They were goofing around and laughing as they made their way to the metro. Brad tried to stay in the middle. At the corner, he spotted two gangbangers lounging around trying to look inconspicuous. Good luck with that, ploughboys!

Brad noticed a table on the café terrace with two more gangbangers drinking coffee. He didn't feel in any immediate danger. There was no way these guys would go after a party of eight U.S. Marines. That was what he thought until the two guys at the table got up and the two on the corner plunged headfirst into the unsuspecting group.

The jarheads recovered fast, but they had been drinking. The four gangbangers were former Green Berets. The question now was whether eight inebriated marines could overcome four sober former Green Berets. The answer was yes, with a little help from a fast-moving Brad James.

He stopped the first gangbanger knifing into the group with a perfectly timed front kick to the solar plexus. The guy's momentum against the force of Brad's kick sent him rolling to the ground choking on a half-swallowed tongue.

The second gangbanger following behind the first collided with Brad and knocked him into a car parked on the street. Brad bounced off and dodged a powerful right hook that glanced off his shoulder. The gangbanger charged again with an onslaught of rights and lefts and a couple of weak kicks. Brad weaved away to the left and countered with two body shots to the ribs. No visible effect.

Marine Sergeant Tommy Tucker came out of nowhere and delivered an explosive right to the face that stunned the gangbanger. Brad's uppercut to the jaw destroyed his upper row of teeth and took him down. Brad kicked him in the head and went through his pockets. Nothing. The other gangbanger was still rolling around on the ground, choking. Brad kicked him in the stomach. That dislodged his tongue and knocked him unconscious. Brad went through his pockets. Nothing.

Meanwhile, the other two gangbangers were trying to get away from seven marines chasing them down the street. A dark sedan suddenly pulled up, they jumped in, and it pulled away. By then, a crowd was starting to gather. Good Samaritans who had absolutely no idea of how the altercation began were ministering to the fallen gangbangers and casting dark glances at the burr-headed, English-speaking barbarians who had taken them down. The gangbangers were wounded, but they had enough presence of mind to disengage and jump into the dark sedan that pulled up alongside. Brad got the license number as it sped away.

It looked like the gangbangers had planned to kidnap him. Four guys to neutralize him and get him into the car. They hadn't counted on the contingent of U.S. Marines. Brad looked at Tommy Tucker. "Hey, Tommy. Thanks for the hand."

"Yeah, no problem. I think it's broken."

"It was for a worthy cause. Next beer's on me."

The marines were already high on alcohol. The adrenaline made them exuberant. They were high-fiving and chest-banging and laughing and bragging. Brad said goodnight and got out of there as fast as he could. He had a Beretta in his pouch and did not want an encounter with the French police.

He was almost to the metro when Chuck stepped out. "What took you so long?"

"Four gangbangers." Brad went on to describe the encounter.

Chuck was proud of his brother jarheads. "You can always count on the United States Marines."

"Can't deny that. It's hard to believe you were once a member. Anyway, I've got some important info. Let's walk for a while."

As they walked down boulevard Raspail, Brad filled Chuck in on his meeting with Gary. Chuck agreed they had to get rid of Ranger and the gangbangers before Gary transferred out. They were both surprised Gary had no knowledge of the events that had taken place on his home turf. He had purposely been kept out of the loop. It was clear to them somebody highly placed in the CIA was in cahoots with the gangbangers.

Brad summed it up. "We've gotta figure out who's behind Ranger and his gangbangers. We should find out something if Gary gets the details from the names and documents I gave him. I personally think Mario's 'proof' about the traitor being innocent is the key."

"Why do you say that?"

"Because if it's real proof, it will finger the person or persons who actually outed the information."

Chuck nodded. "That makes sense." Then he did something out of character. He got personal. "Let me ask you something, Brad. I don't want you to be offended."

An introduction like that from former Marine Sargent Charles "Chuck" Hall captured Brad's full attention. "No problem. What's up?"

"How much confidence do you have in Samantha? I mean, what do you know about her?"

Brad's knee-jerk reaction was aggressive defensive, but he knew Chuck wouldn't ask if there wasn't a serious reason. He put that on the back burner and thought it over. Actually, he knew next to nothing about her except she was beautiful and mysterious, a great acrobat with two identities—one as a blonde millionairess, the other as a brunette legal detective. She had appeared about the same time as Ranger and the gangbangers, and it just so happened that she was a close friend of Mario, the guy with the financial contacts and the "proof" of the traitor's innocence.

"Any particular reason why you would ask me that question?"

"Yeah, I ran a check on her 'de la Sarta' name. Her uncle raised her, she's a millionairess, great student, great athlete, went to Yale, etc. She travels the world as a philanthropist with a focus on crime victims. Everything checks out, except for one thing. Her past stops when she was ten years old. Absolutely nothing before that. I find that strange."

Brad had to admit it was very strange. Too strange to be left unanswered.

Chapter 29

Back at her safe house, blonde Samantha was curled up on the sofa with a balloon glass of red wine. An imperceptible sigh of relief escaped her lips when Brad walked in. "I was starting to get worried."

"Met up with Chuck after I left the Barbary. Also had a run-in with some of Ranger's gangbangers."

More worried frowns. "What happened?" After a detailed description of the evening's events, Samantha could not hide her concern. "Brad, you can't continue with business as usual. I already told you, Ranger is a psychopath. You have crossed him and he will do anything to get even. You were lucky tonight. You won't always be lucky. You have to lie low. Let things calm down."

It was Brad's turn to be concerned. "I hear you, Samantha, and I see where you're coming from. But that's not the way to handle psychopaths. I'll never have any peace as long as this psycho is alive and kicking. He's got to go."

That was the end of the discussion, but he knew Samantha was upset. It upset him as well, but it also pleased him in an egotistical sort of way. She was upset because she was worried about him, just like Alice used to be when he went off on one of his adventures. In fact, Samantha's presence increasingly created an atmosphere around him reminiscent of the Alice days, the best days of his life—except at the end. He would never forgive himself for the end. He still had not come to grips with that.

The next morning, Samantha went out as her dark alter ego. Brad used a mini-disguise of slicked-back hair and motorcycle attire. He was on his way to meet up with Mario. Gary wanted the evidence the "traitor" in the Soviet embassy was telling the truth.

On his way out the door, Brad was about to turn off the morning news when last evening's interview with the "traitor" came on. "It is impossible for me to be responsible for the security breach. Besides financial information on some of our government officials, the information I discovered was top secret. It included photographs of transcripts of cabinet meetings, meetings in the Oval Office with the secretary of state, and private meetings with the president and foreign leaders. People at my clearance level do *not* have access to that kind of information. The number of people with that clearance level could be counted on a normal man's fingers and toes. I am responsible only for uncovering the espionage. The true traitor is trying to frame me to save himself. The true traitor is one of the few officials with access to the top secret information."

Convincing words and a convincing delivery. It was hard not to believe him. The interview was followed by an irate Senator Jake Brown spewing an unvarnished invective worthy of Adolph. Wrapped in his self-described, unapologetic patriotism, he called the traitor everything in the book and accused him of almost every crime mentioned in the Old Testament—and then some. He vowed to hold a hearing and have this traitorous turncoat exposed and condemned. Nothing short of death would do. Brad had to admit old Jake was extremely convincing. It didn't look to Brad like the traitor holed up in the Soviet embassy stood much of a chance.

Brad was meeting Mario at a brand-new luxury apartment building overlooking the Seine. The security was impressive. After passing through two armored doors, there was a receptionist behind a massive desk flanked by an armed guard on either side.

Brad gave the name of the apartment owner, Amanda Guglielmi, and was told to take a seat. A short phone conversation later, the receptionist directed Brad to the elevator. It stopped on the twelfth floor, where he was met by a Claudia Cardinale look-alike. She escorted Brad to another elevator she activated with a key and sent Brad down to the fourth level of the underground parking garage, where he was met by two rangy pistoleros similar in appearance and behavior to those protecting Greta Papachristou.

After a short walk down the driveway between the enclosed parking places, they stopped and frisked Brad. The taller of the two pushed a button that activated a metal door. It opened to reveal a parking garage large enough for four full-sized autos. Only one was present, parked on the left. The rest of the garage was organized into a comfortable studio apartment complete with a private bathroom with shower at the back and a small kitchen. The sitting room occupied the full width of the parking places next to the parked automobile. Mario sat back and motioned for Brad to join him.

When he entered, the garage door closed behind him. The soft hum of an air conditioner served as background music. Brad was impressed. "Nice setup."

"Thanks. It gets a little tiresome down here. We're the only ones on this level, but we're still careful with noise. Don't want anybody getting suspicious and come snooping around. I spend most of my time in Amanda's apartment on the twelfth floor. Sleep down here. No one has access to this level. I have the only key."

"How do you get out if there's a fire?"

Mario shot him a puzzled sidelong glance. "What do you mean?"

"I mean even rats don't let themselves get trapped in places with only one exit."

The reply seemed to relax Mario. "I see what you mean. There's a stairway. It's locked at level 3. Only I have the key. There's the car ramp blocked by a locked metal door. Only I have the keys. There are also other options. I'm safe down here."

Mario opened the mini-fridge and pulled out an ice-cold Stella. "They tell me you're a beer man."

"Thanks. Excellent intelligence."

A short pause marked the transition into the motive for the meeting as Mario sipped his *mate*. "I asked you to come because I've got the American gangbangers breathing down my neck. Somehow, they traced me to this area. Don't ask me how, because I have no idea. But they don't know my address. They only know the general area. They probably managed to trail one of my men who live around here. Anyway, I want them off my back. They attracted the AAA to the area. I am target number one for the AAA."

"Where do I come in?"

Mario drew a long, thin cigar from a lacquered box on the end table, manipulated it carefully, and lit up. He offered the box to Brad. Brad declined and lit up a Gitane. "Brad, you might remember I mentioned proof that the accused traitor is innocent?"

"Yeah."

"The proof is all the intelligence I paid for over the last five years. It includes information the accused traitor could not have known or had access to—things like transcripts from cabinet meetings, diplomatic exchanges, military plans, etc. This kind of info is way above his pay grade. Once this information is made public, it will be obvious the accused traitor could not possibly be the one selling this kind of info. Then the mole will become the object of a hunt for the real culprit."

Brad nodded in agreement. "Can't argue with that."

Mario continued. "The Americans are after me primarily because they know I have this proof and want to keep me from making it public. When I say 'Americans,' I mean the ones working to protect the mole. You are in a much better position than I am to get the proof into the right hands. So I'm going to turn it over to you and let you handle it. That should take some pressure off me as a target for the *gringos*. Once the *gringos* know the information is out there with somebody else, I won't be such an important target."

"Let me get this straight. You're telling me this information is the information the supposed traitor revealed?"

Mario finger-gunned Brad. "Yes, I am."

"How do you know?"

"Because, as I told you before, I was the one who received the documents and paid for them. I was the one who delivered them to Papachristou. He turned them over to the 'traitor.'"

Brad was gobsmacked. That was the key to finding the true traitor, the mole. "My friend, this is huge. All I need is the proof you turned this info over to Papachristou."

A hint of amusement danced around the corners of Mario's lips. "Of course. I have photos, a 'receipt' signed by Georges Papachristou, and my own personal testimony signed before a notary and two witnesses. I will make this proof available to you when the time is right. For now, you'll have to be content with the documents."

The full impact of what Mario was proposing took a couple of seconds before it hit home. It explained why the Americans were so focused on Greta Papachristou. They were afraid she had the information and knew how it originated. It also explained why if he took it, it would put him on the firing line.

Brad snarked out a crooked smile. "That's gonna put a lot of pressure on me as a target."

Mario shook his head and made no attempt to mask his insincerity. "Yeah, I know. Sorry about that."

"Okay, show me what you got."

He had a lot. He produced a fat folder full of photographs of official documents emanating right from the very bowels of the government of the Unites States of America. Some of the documents were policy analyses, some were analyses of foreign leaders, some were transcripts of cabinet meetings, and some were transcripts of private meetings in the Oval Office. Some were unsigned, some were signed by anonymous bureaucrats, some were signed by known bureaucrats, some were signed by the secretary of state, Henry Kissinger, and some were signed by the president, Gerald Ford. All were marked *top secret*. The most explosive documents contained the names of our undercover agents, double-agents, and informers. It was this information that had generated the murders of individuals and even entire families.

Even from the quick look Brad had at the folder's contents, he could see it was dynamite on steroids. What an intelligence failure! The fallout, if this information were made public, was mind-boggling. No wonder there was so much frenetic activity going on.

However, he could see the threat was not so much from foreign adversaries using the information against the interests of the U.S.

Those actions would be costly in the short run but could eventually be countered or eliminated as the situation evolved. The threat was to the reputations and careers of those bureaucrats and politicians mentioned in the documents, and to those who were responsible for letting this information get out.

And herein lay Brad's dilemma. If he accepted these documents, he was putting a huge target on his back. He would become threat number one to the organisms thriving in the bowels of the U.S. government. One and all, they would stop at nothing to destroy the threat to their perks, their power, and their personal prosperity.

Brad had to admit he would love to give these guys a kick in the balls. But he was starting to feel there might be limits on how far he would go.

Gary's wise words echoed through the rocky canyons of his mind. "You can't fight City Hall."

"How exactly, did you get these documents? What was the system?"

"It was straightforward. Using a prearranged code, I would meet my contact in a hotel room. He would give me the documents, and I would give him the cashier's check for the agreed amount in U.S. dollars. There was no chitchat, no discussion, no pleasantries. It was slam, bam, thank you ma'am, and he was gone."

"Always the same guy?"

"Always the same. About thirty-five, slicked-back hair, nice-looking. Chiseled jawline. Thin, straight nose. Hooded eyes. Looked like a pervert to me. Pictures of him in there."

Brad took a look. It was Ranger. He studied the ceiling. Stroked his chin. Lit up a Gitane. Sipped his beer. Mario understood the stakes. He sat back and sipped his *mate*. He was not going anywhere, and he was not in a hurry.

Brad made his decision. Maybe he could go around City Hall.

"I'll need two copies of everything, one to deliver and the other to use as insurance."

Mario was no stranger to the importance of insurance. "No problem."

Brad left the high-rise the same way he came in, through the front door. Two folders full of documents were stashed away in his soft leather pouch. He realized these documents were dynamite, but he also realized they would cause no damage to those responsible for leaking them unless the chain of transmission was established. Mario was well aware of that. Brad would have to find out why Mario refused to provide the necessary proof.

Chapter 30

Brad purchased a copy of the *Herald Tribune* at the kiosk before entering the café at the Porte de Champerret. He took a table in the corner and started reading. Two stories on page 2 caught his eye. The first story was about the aftermath of Nixon's resignation last August. It argued that the government had been wreaking revenge on the lower-level officials who had helped bring him down. The story was full of details on the number of witnesses, journalists, and collaborators with the prosecution who had been targeted by IRS audits and DOJ lawsuits since the resignation. The conclusion was if you dare to cross City Hall, City Hall will come for you and make you pay.

Senator Jake Brown was the subject of the second article. He still had a knot in his knickers about the traitor in the Soviet embassy. He claimed to have come into possession of the classified information the traitor had supposedly sold to our enemies, and none of it was above the traitor's security level. Jake was using this to prove the traitor's defense argument was false and he was guilty as charged.

Brad was unimpressed. The information provided consisted of

more or less innocuous excerpts from the actual documents in Brad's possession that contained the highly classified material. In other words, it was a cheap trick designed to hide the truth and railroad the traitor. Brad had admired Jake's hardline patriotism. Now he was revealing himself as just another mealymouthed political hack.

These two stories highlighted Brad's dilemma. Nobody was really interested in the truth. Different factions would latch onto the specific aspects of the story that would reinforce or coincide with the narrative they were defending. They would mercilessly attack the aspects that diverged or contradicted it. Unfortunately, the unvarnished truth was compatible with a very narrow narrative that was usually held by such a small faction it would never see the light of day.

Brad was not certain the information he was bringing to the table was one hundred percent accurate, but he was one hundred percent certain it diverged from the narratives of most of the shadowy factions he had been dealing with up to now. The question was how to use his information. His adolescent black-and-white knee-jerk personality told him to jump on his stallion and charge headlong into the fray. His mature adult personality told him this strategy would get both him and his stallion killed. It also told him it was too late to forget the whole thing. He had the information, and the other factions knew or suspected he had it. He should have taken Gary's advice up front and stayed out of it. That left his gut feeling. His gut feeling was to concentrate on self-preservation. It was decided. His first priority was to overcome Ranger and his group of gangbangers.

When Chuck came in, Brad briefed him on the meeting with Mario and the proof he had provided that the "traitor" was innocent. Chuck wondered why Mario had leaked the documents back to the CIA in the first place. Brad explained that Mario told him he did it to protect himself. Said he figured if the CIA already knew of the espionage, he would no longer be a target of the spy trying to keep the espionage secret.

"That holds water," Chuck said. "Does he have any ideas on why it didn't work?"

"He thinks that for some reason, someone in the CIA is using the traitor story to cover for the real spy. So somewhere along the line, there are CIA agents complicit in the cover-up. He says since he's the only one who can prove the story false, he's target number one for whoever he or they are."

It was an epiphany. Chuck sat back in his chair and folded his hands in front of his face. "Now *you* also have the information to prove the story false. *You* are also target number one. You're toxic, man."

"Also, contagious. It's nice to have company. No reason to panic, though. Nobody but Mario knows I have the info. No sense goin' around braggin' about it. Let's just sit on it and see how things play out."

"What about Gary?"

"He's been benched. He'd have to turn the info over to his superiors, dudes who might not have our best interests at heart. He's trying to find a way to get back into the game. If and when he does, we can reconsider it. For the moment, we have to identify our immediate threats and go after them."

"I'm thinking Madison is in cahoots with the Harley dude and his gangbangers."

"Me too. She was responsible for security when the leak was discovered. She immediately accused the 'traitor' when he was the one who discovered the leak. She's making the investigation over here a secretive affair. She's helping the Harley dude eliminate the witnesses, including us."

Chuck's hand slapped down hard on the table. "We've gotta take her out."

Brad shook his head. "She's got the whole Company behind her. If we do that, we'll have the whole Company after us. The hole will be so deep we'll have to dig until we get to China if we want to get out. Ranger and his gangbangers are not government men. They're mercenaries working *with* the government, not *for* the government. My guess is they're working for the dudes in the CIA trying to railroad the 'traitor.' The government doesn't care about them and won't hold it against us. They're also our most immediate threat. Let's go after them."

"Got a plan?"

Brad's smile made Chuck wary. "I do. It's the crafty old Cassius Clay entomological insect strategy."

Chuck just sat there expressionless, looking off into space. He was not about to bite on that one. It was a long wait. Finally, he couldn't stand it anymore. "Okay, I think I have heard this one, but I'll bite. What's the crafty old Cassius Clay entomological insect strategy?"

"'Float like a butterfly, sting like a bee.' Won the World Heavyweight Championship with it. We stay out of sight. We anticipate their moves. We wait for an opportunity. We strike and we disappear."

"What about your friend Samantha?"

Chuck was obviously underwhelmed by Samantha and overtly suspicious. Brad's testosterone was telling him Chuck was being ridiculous. There was nothing to suspect. Brad's brain was telling him Chuck had a point. Brad wasn't a blonde, so it would be brains over emotions.

"Let's keep her in the dark as much as we can. Mario has

obviously told her about the info and is probably waiting for her to confirm it's gone out. I'm going to tell her the info is with Gary."

Chuck seemed relieved. "Ten-four, Kemosabe."

"We start tonight. Besides their hideout on the Jatte, the gangbangers are surveilling Greta Papachristou around the clock. I've seen them. I think they're planning to pick off Papachristou's pistoleros one by one. Let's go for them there."

Chapter 31

The sun was disappearing behind the trees in the Bois de Boulogne when the taxi pulled up and Edith began her painful extraction from the back seat. First came the ivory-handled walking cane, then a leg, then another leg, then an arm, and finally, a gray head. Brad and Chuck were observing the show from the terrace of the café. She was huffing and puffing and cursing under her breath. The taxi driver was attempting to assist, but she kept waving him off. When she finally got onto the sidewalk, she gave the guy a friendly pat on the back and dragged herself over to the café.

"It's a goddamn proven fact. You ain't old if you can crawl out of a taxi on your own. Son-of-a-bitch! A friggin' red wine would grease up my gills and get me talkin'."

Brad ordered a house red for Edith and took a sip of his *demi*. "I suppose you were unable to identify the gangbangers." He had found that a little teasing brought out the best in Edith.

Her derisive snort was masterful theater. "Listen, *petit*, I was runnin' rings around the goddamn Krautheads before you were even kickin' the slats in your cradle. Got 'em comin'. Got 'em goin'.

There's at least six of 'em."

Her house red arrived, and she knocked back a heathy swig.

"They use the café next to the grocery store, a black sedan with tinted windows, and a gray van. The van has two bully boys inside with line of sight to the building. The other four are paired up. They hang out in the café and wander around the neighborhood on foot. One pair of bully boys uses the sedan to ride around the neighborhood."

"That's all?" Brad knew the best was yet to come.

"That's all? Goddamn, son-of-a-bitch, that's plenty for a measly hundred francs and a pack of Gitanes."

Her wrinkled face was all screwed up, and her eyes were burning holes in his face. She held it for a while, then softened up and let a crafty smile creep into her frown.

"They rotate every two hours," she continued. "Goddamn gray van drives off, and another takes its place. Two bully boys get out and go into the back. Black sedan drives off and picks up the two guys on foot. Another sedan pulls up, drops off two dudes, and parks down the street."

Brad was impressed. This was a full-court press. It looked like he was onto something. It was a cinch the gangbangers were not spending all that time and energy as a long-term strategy. "Not bad, Edith. Congratulations. You really outdid yourself. You don't think they noticed you, do you?"

"Hey, *petit*, of course, they noticed me. Every man's head swivels round when I prance by. Impossible to miss me." Three Mississippis. "Goddamn stupid question. Nobody notices an old lady with a cane hobblin' down the street."

Chuck wanted to know if Edith had seen Papachristou's pistoleros. Brad could tell Edith liked Chuck. She gave him a big smile. "Son-of-a-bitch. Finally, somebody with a sensible question.

The pistoleros have a guard on the terrace. Every hour or so, a pair of pistoleros comes out and walks around the block. The street at the end of the block is torn up. I think some of the pistoleros are pretending to work on it."

"Thanks, Edith. Great job. See you tomorrow." She was beaming.

Chuck was driving in his chauffeur outfit. Brad was in the back with his hair slicked back, in a dark-blue suit with a red power tie and a black briefcase. The plan was to take out the two gangbangers in the van.

Brad exited the car near the café. Saw that two gangbangers were at a table having a snack at the same time the two gangbangers on foot set out on their tour of the neighborhood. Consequently, Brad and Chuck would have about fifteen minutes to take care of the van.

Brad gave Chuck the thumbs-up signal and circled down the street behind where the van was parked. Chuck circled the block, stopped next to the van, cut the engine, and got out of the car as if he were waiting for his client. The car was blocking the van's line of sight to the Papachristou building. The gangbangers wouldn't tolerate that for long.

He adjusted his chauffeur's cap, lit up a cigarette, and started puffing away. Brad was positioned on the sidewalk behind a big maple tree. The minutes ticked on. Brad began to worry the gangbangers wouldn't react. A car came by and passed easily between Chuck's sedan and the row of parked cars on the other side of the street. No reason for him to move the car.

That must have triggered the gangbangers. The back of the van opened, and a wiry dude jumped out. He was agitated and not trying to hide it. "You can't stay there." The voice was sharp and irritating. The accent was American.

Chuck studied the guy for a couple of Mississippis, took a long drag on his cigarette, and answered in French. *"Pourquoi (Why)?"*

The guy was holding a tire iron. "Because I said so, asshole."

Chuck shot him the bird. In the same motion, he ripped the tire iron from the guy's hand. In a second motion, drove it through his chin into his head. The guy was dead before he hit the ground.

The second gangbanger, who had been observing the confrontation from inside the van, jumped out with a gun in his hand. "Don't move, motherfucker."

That was when Brad grabbed him from behind and wrang his neck.

The whole scene lasted no longer than ten seconds. They loaded the bodies into the van. Brad jumped behind the wheel and followed Chuck's sedan down the street. They arrived at the Ile de la Jatte without incident, where they backed into the landfill at the end of the island.

Chuck removed the cadavers, and Brad drove off in search of a parking place. He found one not far from the hideout, in fact, a little too close for his liking. He locked up the van and headed back to the landfill, where Chuck was just pushing the bodies into the current of the Seine.

They jumped into the car and drove off toward Paris. Chuck was snickering. "That should give them some food for thought."

"Yeah, they're gonna figure the pistoleros are sending them a message. Betcha diamonds to doughnuts they're gonna go after some pistolero ass tomorrow."

"Think we should warn them?"

"We're Christians, aren't we?"

Chapter 32

Samantha was unhappy. It wasn't anything she said, or even the silent treatment. She wasn't sulking or pouting. Nevertheless, she was somehow communicating her displeasure. This was a situation Brad had experienced with his girlfriends many times before, and still he could not comprehend how they did it. Women seemed to have some kind of secret power that enabled them to send subliminal messages. He had learned, however, that responding to these subliminal messages directly was a surefire way to start an argument you had no chance of winning. So he played it cool, feigned ignorance, and pretended everything was hunky-dory.

She sat next to him and smiled. He put his arm around her. She leaned into him, and her sadness seeped through like the dampness on a wall. He pulled her closer and she cuddled up, but the sadness was intensifying. Suddenly, she pulled away and took his hand. "Can I ask you something?"

"Of course." He was dreading it.

"Do you trust me?" Her gaze was straight and true.

He returned it unflinchingly. "Yes. Totally. Why?"

She held her gaze, and he didn't blink. He counted more than ten Mississippis. The barrage of subliminal messaging suddenly ceased. She leaned forward and kissed him on the cheek. "Just wondering. How about a coffee?"

Now that they were back on the same wavelength, Brad wanted to talk. He gave her a blow-by-blow description of what went down the night before. When he finished, her face was flushed with emotion. "Amazing" was all she said, but he could see she was sincere. "Ranger will not let that go unpunished."

Brad launched a full-throated laugh. "That's exactly what we're counting on. We're planning on stopping by this evening to see if he tries something. Wanna come?"

She gave him a big hug. "Wouldn't miss it for the world. By the way, how did it go with Mario?"

"Short and sweet. He gave me a file of documents he says will prove the 'traitor's' innocence. I put it in the pipeline to Gary." He hated to have to lie, but as any suitor or surviving soldier knows, all's fair in love and war. "Let's go meet Chuck."

Brad spotted a functioning telephone cabin when they exited the metro at Argentine. He dialed Papachristou's number. Head Honcho answered on the third ring. Brad gave him details on the surveillance and told him to be on alert for a violent attack.

"Who is this?"

Brad hung up.

*   *   *

Chuck pulled up in a black Renault with tinted windows. He was in his chauffeur outfit and signaled Samantha and Brad to get in the back. It was already dark as they drove toward Papachristou's apartment. They passed two *cars de flics* (cop transporters) parked near the *Périphérique*. Slightly unusual. The 16th arrondissement was the richest area in the city, and it was the most protected. A constant game of cops and robbers, but usually the cops were more discreet. A drive by the café confirmed what Brad had expected. Ranger had already deployed his men.

When they drove past the apartment, it was clear Ranger was planning on making a definitive power statement. Two of his vans were already in place in front of the apartment building, and there were two more dark sedan support cars located around the corner.

Chuck pulled into a driveway three blocks down the street and cut the lights. Brad and Samantha got out, stationed themselves where they could see the building's main door, and started canoodling like a couple of teenagers.

They didn't have long to wait. Two gangbangers came down the street from the left. Two from the right. They smashed the door and rushed into the vestibule, arms extended, guns at the fore jerking right to left, just like in the movies. They crept Indian file up the stairs. Meanwhile, the back doors on the vans slid back. Four gangbangers armed with machine guns slipped out and took up positions where they could target the sixth-floor terrace. The drivers stayed in the vans.

Samantha was excited. "It is really gonna blow."

It did, but not the way she thought. Suddenly, there were the *wah-ouh* sirens of the cop cars wailing, spot lights beaming, and loudspeakers blasting, "Drop your guns! Put up your hands!"

There were two helicopters buzzing around, and at least thirty CRS soldiers (Compagnies Républicaines de Sécurity) armed to the teeth. All the streets were being blocked by the arriving troop carriers and military vehicles.

Brad and Samantha saw the approaching troops and were able to retreat back to the car from where they witnessed the faceoff.

The gangbangers were in a lose-lose situation. A firefight meant certain annihilation. Surrender meant capture, humiliation, and a long vacation in a French penitentiary. They were pros, and they realized the magnitude of their uncomfortable situation. The warm summer air was heavy with silence as the French waited for their next move.

Chuck cranked up the car and prepared to move out. The CRS on the right flank moved forward behind their shields. They stopped. The CRS on the left flank followed suit. There was movement from the vans. Front doors opened and the drivers crawled out, hands in the air. Then the frontline gangbangers stood, hands in the air. A team of six CRS herded the gangbangers to the sidewalk and held them on their knees.

A second team entered the building. Disappeared up the stairs. Ten Mississippis of silence. A shot rang out, followed immediately by fifteen seconds of uninterrupted machine-gun fire.

Silence.

A CRS exited the building and made a signal. He was followed by his five comrades dragging four bodies behind them.

It was over in a flash. The dead bodies were loaded into one troop carrier and the prisoners into another. The commander gave a signal, and the helicopter peeled off. A second signal and the CRS climbed into their vehicles and melted back into the night.

Chapter 33

"Four dead Americans, six arrested, all of them with firearms in France on tourist visas. It looks like a Mafia hit squad. The embassy is being overwhelmed by French diplomatic outrage. You wouldn't have anything to do with this, would you?" Gary's face was flushed, and he was sporting the raccoon eyes reserved for his most stressful moments.

Brad leaned forward and rubbed his chin. "What happened?"

Gary spoke slowly, choosing his words carefully. "After the shootout at Papachristou's the other day, the French put an around the clock, full-court press on the area—agents, vehicles, electronics, everything they had. They knew the gangbangers were coming and set up an ambush. My problem, the embassy's problem, is that officially we have no idea who these guys are and what they were up to. Unofficially, because of you, I have a good idea of what they were up to. What do you know about it?"

Brad summarized what had gone down over the last two weeks and what his investigation had revealed, studiously omitting any mention of Samantha and his role in provoking Ranger and his gangbangers.

He reached into his pouch and produced the envelope with the documents Mario had given him. It contained all the intelligence Mario had paid for over the last five years.

"My conclusion," Brad said, "is that Ranger is the bagman and enforcer for whoever the mole is. The accused traitor is a smoke screen to protect the real traitor. In the documents I've given you, you'll see the information goes way above anything the accused traitor had any access to. Mario Irigoyen claims he delivered these documents to Georges Papachristou, who passed them on to the accused traitor."

Gary jerked himself upright. "If that's true, it means the accused traitor is innocent. I'll need proof Papachristou did receive these documents. Solid proof. Papachristou was one of our most trusted agents. He would most certainly have told us if…"

"If he hadn't been assassinated."

The intensity of Gary's excitement filtered into his voice. "Exactly. I need that proof. What is it?"

"Irigoyen says he has photos, a 'receipt' signed by Georges Papachristou, and his own personal testimony signed before a notary and two witnesses. He says he will produce it when the time is right. It looks like there was a conscious decision made by the Company somewhere along the line to sacrifice the agent who brought the info and just shut the matter down. Who knows why? Maybe one of those complicated counter-counterspy disinformation deals."

"This proof of delivery to Papachristou is indispensable. Our case will be airtight. You've got to get it for me."

The table waitress came over. "You okay, Brad?"

"Hit me again with another Heineken."

Gary waved her off. "I'm okay, thanks." Back to Brad, he said, "You were wondering about the security surrounding Greta

Papachristou. Interesting story. She's one of the Sacasa sisters from Nicaragua. Big mysterious political family. Wealthy beyond your wildest imagination. She owns the building in the 16th. Owns real estate all over London and New York. Her son's family lives in a penthouse apartment overlooking Central Park. Her father is a security freak. He does not allow anyone in his family to be photographed."

rad interrupted, "That would explain why there were no photos of her in their apartment in the 16th. I always wondered about that."

"Yeah, the old man has to be on high alert at all times. His family has been a frequent target of kidnapping and assassination. He recruits and pays for the security detail on her and her family. These guys are the elite of the elite of the Special Forces in all of Latin America. They have all undergone intense training in the Special Forces of France, the UK, or the U.S. They all finished in the top of their class and spent years in the field. They are all unscrupulous mercenaries bought and owned by the Sacasas."

Brad chortled, "That would explain why they chewed up Ranger's men. Her family's political connections go a long way to explaining the French effort to shut those guys down, as well."

"She's on her way back to London."

"So anyway, Gary, we've got this Ranger and his gang running around Paris trying to assassinate anybody and everybody who could provide proof the 'traitor narrative in the Soviet embassy' is false. By the way, have you been able to find out who Ranger is?"

"Name is Ranger Wilde. He's a rich playboy, an accomplished athlete, and a financial genius. Cornell undergraduate. Went to Cambridge for a year. Did a master's at the University of Chicago. Became the youngest partner ever at Suivest Consultants and then struck out on his own. His preference zone is Latin America. He has highly placed clients in many if not most countries in the region."

Brad snorted. "Doesn't sound like the description of a guy cruising around Paris on a chopped Harley at the head of a murderous gang."

"He rarely rides. Most of his time is spent in banks on the Champs-Elysées or around the Bourse."

Brad could tell Gary felt on the defensive. It was understandable. His authority at the embassy was being undermined by his own superiors. He was also upset he and Chuck had gone out on their own against his strict orders not to do so.

"Look," Brad said, "Chuck and I got sucked into this in spite of ourselves. We became unwitting targets when you sent us over to help Papachristou's widow. It's more than just a traitor and some intel. Think of it. A group of Americans running around murdering people and shooting up Paris. The French break out a battalion of CRS to shut them down. Wild stuff, man. Madison Samson III is intimately involved in all this, and you're being sidelined to Brussels."

Gary relaxed a little. Sipped his beer. Gazed at the couples on the dance floor. "You're right. I've got a bad feeling about it. Let's go with your take. The accused traitor is a smoke screen to protect the real traitor, who Ranger's working for." He raised his eyebrows and shook his head in reluctant acquiescence. "All this is unofficial. It goes against my principles. You're on your own, but I'll do what I can. By the way, Madison has been summoned back to Langley. She came by to see me before she left. She is seething. Says she has been setup to protect the real mole or maybe a double agent. In any case, her blossoming career is over. She's on her way to jail at worst or a plea deal at best."

"Too bad. I kinda liked her." Brad wasn't convinced she would be that easy to dispose of.

*   *   *

Samantha was relieved. "Thank you, Brad, for not outing me. I want to stay as far away from the CIA as I can. It's like a wild beast. You never know when it will turn on you." She caressed his cheek.

He took her hand. "Did you know Ranger was a well-connected financial consultant?"

He had dreaded asking the question and wasn't surprised when she jerked to attention. "What do you mean?"

"I mean he's important to your investigation and you seem to know a lot about his personality, but you never ever even suggested that he was anything other than a criminal gang leader. Gary told me he has a star-studded resumé and spends most of his time in banks."

Samantha looked down and studied her folded hands. She was doing battle. Her internal conflict was clearly a painful experience that registered as a series of shudders and facial tics.

She heaved a deep sigh, looked up, and said, "I do know him well. I have been following him for many years. He is like a chameleon, morphing from one character into another. Extremely talented. Handsome, intelligent, athletic, charming. He excels at everything he does. But he is a psychopath. He gets off on hurting people, physically, financially, emotionally. It makes no difference."

"So why are you interested in him?"

"My client's family was massacred some years ago. He has reason to believe Ranger was involved. Ranger was never suspected or accused, but a reliable witness put him at the scene. We know who ordered the massacre. He is very powerful and has managed to avoid being implicated. We know who executed it. They and their accomplices have been taken care of. Ranger is the link between the person who ordered the massacre and those who carried it out. I want to use Ranger to get to the person behind the crime."

Samantha's emotional delivery made her story all the more convincing. Still, he wasn't convinced. "Why have you been holding back on me?"

"I'm building a case against him. A financial fraud case, something completely different from what he's doing with you. I didn't see any sense in muddying the waters. For your investigation, he's a bloodthirsty gangbanger. For mine, he's a smooth financial fraudster. He's about to rip off a group of investors for millions of dollars."

Brad was having trouble coming to terms with Samantha's story. "How did you get information like that?"

Samantha was relaxed, back in control. She smiled and took his hand. "When I'm not Samantha Smith, I'm Samantha de la Sarta, a wealthy philanthropist. My world is populated by these people, and I court them to help fund my charitable endeavors. They talk to me. It doesn't hurt that some of them find me attractive."

"You mean all the normally constituted males?" Brad couldn't resist the opportunity to score a few flattery points.

A squeeze on the hand communicated her appreciation. "For example, I have organized a conference next week on victims of violent crime. All the top people in the field, including scientists, politicians, caregivers, et cetera, will be there." There was a mischievous light in her eyes. "Let me check my diary. Yes, just as I thought. Ranger is on the list."

"How about me?"

"I'll see what I can do."

She was laughing. Brad was in an emotional tailspin. What else was Samantha hiding?

Chapter 34

MID MAY 1975, PARIS SUBURB

The demise of Ranger's mercenaries wasn't enough for Chuck to let his guard down. Ranger was still on the loose, and who knew how many men he still had? Samantha swore he took everything personal and would never rest until he got revenge. That meant Brad stayed with Samantha, Betty stayed in Spain, and Chuck continued operating out of the studio behind his office.

Brad took the usual precautions on the way to Chuck's place. He was pleased Mario had agreed to turn over the paperwork proving it was he who had delivered the five years' worth of intelligence documents to Georges Papachristou. Gary was adamant that this proof was indispensable to overcoming the mole's protection. Mario had communicated a rendezvous point where he would deliver the promised proof.

Brad wanted to touch base with Chuck about how to proceed once he got the info. Chuck was uncharacteristically philosophical. "We'll have to see how the cookie crumbles." Translated, that meant Chuck had no confidence it would change anything at all for them. Gary would have to do some strenuous bureaucratic infighting to convince the Company hierarchy the "traitor" was innocent. That, of course, would be easier than convincing them they should publicly admit they had made a mistake and the real traitor was unknown, on the loose, and still slithering around. They might be able to pin it all on Madison. There was enough proof of her tooling around Paris eliminating potential witnesses. But there was no proof she had come by the information other than from the innocent "traitor." Worst of all, Chuck knew they could not relax until Ranger was out of the way.

"Where's the meeting?" Chuck asked.

"Rue de Pressbourg by l'Etoile. I'm gonna walk up there now."

Traffic was heavy for this late in the evening. Tourists were thicker than flies. Brad melted right in, keeping his eyes peeled. A group of teenage boys from Italy were flirting with a group of teenage girls from America. The boys were strutting around showing off. The girls were screeching and laughing. There was a group of middle-aged American women with puzzled expressions looking around and studying a map. They had attracted the attention of a couple of swarthy predators in hoodies and tennis shoes lurking around looking for a vulnerable victim. A short guy with an Errol Flynn moustache chomping on a baguette sandwich was having an animated discussion with another short guy with a handlebar moustache and beard. Everyone else was just passing through.

A Renault van pulled over and stopped. The driver looked at Brad and gave him the thumbs-up. Brad went to the van. The short man with the Errol Flynn stopped arguing and stepped behind him. His hand held a cattle prod that he jammed into the small of Brad's back.

The jolt jerked Brad backward. Tried to react. The second jolt paralyzed him. A third jolt to the neck finished him off. Brad stumbled, clutched his neck. The door to the van slid open. The second short man with the handlebar moustache caught the slumping Brad and stuffed him inside. The door slid closed, and the van pulled away.

Consciousness dawned slowly on a foul breeze blowing across Brad's face. He looked. Hooded eyes, thick, meaty lips, a malevolent, predatory smile on a big, round face stationed inches from his nose met him head-on. But it was the breath. Smelled like the guy had been eating rotten bodies.

Brad was tied to a metal chair in the middle of what looked like a giant warehouse furnished as a dormitory for a small army. He recalled the van and the excruciating pain before the lights went out. In front of him sat the man with the rotten breath. Next to him sat a short man with an Errol Flynn moustache holding a black metal box with wires coming out of it. He could see another six men stationed around the warehouse. They were all armed with some type of machine gun.

Brad's back and neck were killing him. He would have given anything for a thorough massage. Didn't look like that was going to happen anytime soon. He tested the bonds on his hands. Sloppy job. There was some play there. Evidence these guys were not Ranger's men. Otherwise, everything else was looking bad. Had to find out what was going on.

"Who are you?"

A humble nod of the head. A self-deprecating smile. "I am *Cangrejo* (the Crab)." The accent was Spanish. The guys looked South American. "Let me introduce you to *Chispa* (Sparky)." Cangrejo motioned to the short man with the Errol Flynn seated next to him.

Brad noticed the wires running from Chispa's metal box were attached to his own fingers. Before he could process that, Chispa's hand tapped the box and Brad went rigid. Twenty milliamps were coursing through his body. He was paralyzed for ten seconds. When it stopped, many doubts had been erased. This was not going to end well. He started working on the ropes tying his wrists.

Cangrejo adopted a sorrowful expression. "I am so sorry, *Señor Gringo*, but it was necessary to communicate the *importancia* of our conversation. I need something from you."

Cangrejo was still in his face. The electroshock had done nothing to impair Brad's sense of smell, nor had it improved Cangrejo's breath. Brad was going to lose his lunch. Cangrejo raised his finger. Chispa hit the switch. Thirty milliamps blasted through Brad's body. Brad didn't pass out, but he wished he had.

"Now, *Señor Gringo*," Cangrejo said, rubbing his hands together, "I think we understand each other. *Mi paisano, Señor* Irigoyen, has given you some very important documents. These documents cannot go to the *gringos*. I want them."

Cangrejo's use of *paisano* meant they were Argentines. For the first time since he came to his senses, Brad could relax a little. These guys had nothing to do with Ranger. That was a relief. Returning those documents Mario had given him would be no problem. One set had already been given to Gary.

Brad nodded. "You are so persuasive. I'll be more than happy to make you a gift of those documents."

"I want the documents you received yesterday, the ones that you will hold until *Señor* Irigoyen gives you the green light to release them."

Brad drew a blank. Something was very wrong here. There were no documents delivered yesterday. This could be a trap to test his sincerity. If he pretended that the documents existed and they didn't, they would know he was lying. As punishment, Sparky would give him a few shock treatments.

On the other hand, Mario might have lied to them about their existence for some reason. If that were the case, and they believed those documents did exist, Brad was going to be hurtin' for certain because there was no way, no matter how many shocks, that he could produce what did not exist.

It was a no-brainer. He'd go for scenario number one. At the worst, he'd get a few extra shock treatments before handing over the documents he really had. Meanwhile, he'd have to try and find a way to turn the tables on these lowlifes.

Brad nodded. "No problem. Let's go."

That got a big laugh from death-breath Cangrejo. "You goin' nowhere, *gringo*. Where are the *documentos*?"

Brad sighed and tried to appear frustrated. Sparky hit the switch on the metal box and sent Brad into a paroxysm of pain. "In my locker at the karate club. 34 rue de la Montagne Sainte-Geneviève. Locker number 50."

"Key?"

"In my gym bag in my apartment. Just use a screwdriver."

Death-breath thought that over. Motioned to a guard at the back of the warehouse. The guard lumbered over. The closer he got, the bigger he got. He was massive. Not tall, massive. His head was the size and shape of a mature watermelon. No neck, huge traps, lats like a stingray, but it was the shoulders and arms, gigantic mounds of muscle and meat. This guy could kick sand in Charles Atlas's face. "*Piccolo* (Tiny) will take care of you while we are gone."

Brad's chances were getting slimmer by the minute. Piccolo was going to be a major impediment to his escape plans. Brad figured he had about an hour and a half to two hours before Death-Breath and Sparky got back with the unfortunate news there were no documents to be found. He would have to be gone before then.

He managed to loosen his right wrist enough so that he would be able to free his arm. That left the other wrist, his ankles, and Piccolo. He was working on his left wrist and both ankles when he heard it: the burpy rumble of a Harley chopper. The warehouse door opened and in walked Ranger Wilde. Brad just could not catch a break.

Black motorcycle leathers, slicked-back hair, chiseled jawline, and straight nose, he swaggered over to the middle of the room. He was a good-looking dude. His hooded eyes glowed through the warehouse shadows and highlighted the perversion lurking behind his even features. It was impossible for Brad to like this guy. Samantha's words were ringing in his ears. "Never let him get his hands on you. If he ever does, you will spend a long time wishing you were dead."

Ranger spotted Sparky's metal box. "What's this?" He hit the button and shot Brad a message of thirty milliamps. Brad jerked and shook. Ranger was pleased. "Very interesting. I'll remember this. It might come in handy. Meanwhile, I'll just cut things short. We can start with the toes." He snickered and extracted a set of bone saws, scalpels, pliers, and knives from his rucksack.

He motioned to Piccolo, who untied Brad's ankles and began to remove his boots. Brad saw Ranger was holding a cigar snipper in his right hand.

*   *   *

Chuck observed Brad from his car on the rue de Pressbourg. He'd had a hunch and decided to monitor how the document transfer went down. Nothing out of the ordinary. Plenty of tourists running around, some teenagers goofing off, a group of women map-reading, and two guys arguing. Looked like he was wrong.

A Renault van pulled up in front of Brad. Blocked Chuck's

view. Drove off. Brad was gone. So were the two guys arguing. Chuck's hunch had paid off. He cranked up the car and drove after the van.

The van took the avenue de la Grande Armée and headed straight out of town. After about twenty minutes, it crossed the Seine and turned down a side road to a large warehouse beside a small rock quarry. Two other Renault vans were parked outside.

Chuck pulled over to the side and observed as four dudes dragged Brad out of the van into the warehouse. Chuck could see that Brad was having a bad day. He went to the glove compartment and grabbed his binoculars. Studied the area inch by inch. There was only one way to approach the warehouse unseen.

It took him the better part of twenty minutes to access the back of the warehouse. Through the air vent, he saw Brad tied to a metal chair in the middle of the spacious warehouse. Two men were seated in front of him. One was talking, and one was fondling a metal box. There were six other men with machine guns stationed strategically around the warehouse.

Chuck slipped back to his car. Went into the trunk for his 12-gauge pump. Back in the car, he watched as two dudes climbed into the van and drove off. That left six in the warehouse. His pump held five shells. That might be a problem.

He was about to make his way to the back of the warehouse when he heard the singular sound of a Harley chopper coming down the pike. He wasn't surprised when it turned into the warehouse driveway. He also wasn't surprised when he saw Ranger Wilde dismount and enter the warehouse. No time to waste.

*   *   *

The last electro-jolt wasn't as bad as the first two. Brad relaxed his body and played possum. When Piccolo freed the last ankle, he sprang to his feet.

Piccolo fell back in surprise. Brad jerked his right wrist free and swung the metal chair still attached to his left wrist into Ranger. Two swings. Ranger went down and the left wrist slipped free.

Piccolo was struggling to get back on his feet. Brad smashed the metal chair into his face, whipped around, and caught Ranger's head with a chair leg. Ranger was out. The other guards were watching, but not moving. Piccolo was on his feet. He would handle it.

He was a raging bull. Bobbing and weaving, he charged behind a barrage of right hooks, left hooks, uppercuts, and jabs. Brad had never experienced anything like it and had no answer for it except to retreat. Unfortunately, Piccolo could go forward faster than Brad could go backward. A right hook to the shoulder slammed Brad to the left, and a left hook to the ribs sent him back to the right—just enough to avoid the vicious uppercut that would have ended his day.

Piccolo was moving in for the kill when the warehouse door flew open and the blast from Chuck's 12-gauge blew off the right half of his face. Chuck turned on the guard nearest the door and took him down. Brad ran for the closest guard and grabbed his gun.

The other four guards recovered from the shock of what was going down and began to spray the warehouse indiscriminately. Brad got off a burst. One of the guards screamed. The others started ducking.

Chuck took one last shot and slipped outside. Brad dashed for the door, saw the guards come up for air, and hit the dirt. Just in time. The salvos from three machine guns exploded into the wall above his head. He dived for the door and rolled outside.

Brad ran behind the van where Chuck was positioned. Chuck raised three fingers. Mississippi one, Mississippi two, Mississippi three.

The warehouse door flew open. The first guard out caught the buckshot in the chest. The other guards dodged back inside and slammed the door.

Brad and Chuck scrambled up the hill to Chuck's car. They heard the Harley come to life.

Chapter 35

Mario sits back in his bunker and sips his *mate*. He has a lot to be thankful for. Although Rega still reigns supreme in Argentina, his power is slipping away. The economy is failing and Rega is getting the blame. It is just a short matter of time before the economy crashes and the peso is devalued. When that happens, Rega will be deposed and Mario will be back in business.

Meanwhile, the destruction of the American gangbangers was a godsend that eliminated them as a personal threat. Most importantly, their boss in Washington, the mole, decided a deal with Rega would allow him to continue his activities and give him the cover he requires.

The deal involves bringing Mario into the fold. For the mole, it's business as usual. Rega replaces Mario as the intermediary. As such, Rega guarantees the mole's anonymity. To ensure Mario will not collaborate in the effort to absolve the designated "traitor" in the Russian embassy and relaunch the search for the real traitor, Rega offers Mario an olive branch. Rega will call off the AAA and guarantee Mario's security. In return, Mario agrees to end his collaboration with the Paris investigation. As a token of good faith, Mario agrees to deliver the one hundred million dollars' worth of bearer shares for Bellweather SA at the end of three months in return for a ten million dollar cash payment from Rega. He will also act as middleman between Rega and the client intelligence agencies in Latin America who pay for the mole's information.

Of course, Mario doesn't have unlimited faith in Rega's word. Still, he feels pretty confident that the deal for the bearer shares will keep him safe for the next three months, or at least until Rega works out who Mario's client contacts are. It's the longer term that has him worried. Rega's deal with the mole depends on the "traitor" being convicted, and the search for the mole ending. If the "traitor" is determined to be innocent, the mole's activities will be short-circuited.

The proof of the designated traitor's innocence depends on two things: the documents, and the proof of how they were delivered. The proof of delivery involves photos, the "receipt" signed by Papachristou, and Mario's personal signed testimony—none of which he has delivered. Only Mario can validate the authenticity of the delivery.

Mario invented the story of having delivered this information to Brad because if Rega thinks the info is out there somewhere and might reappear, he'll have Mario to deny its authenticity. Mario figures this is reason enough to keep him alive and happy.

Mario feels bad about Brad James. James is going to be in a world of hurt before he gives up the ghost. He likes the guy, but you know what they say in France. Anyway, Mario concludes it's a small price to pay for a few months of relative security. Furthermore, Rega doesn't do "personal." At least that's what he's always been led to believe.

*　　　　　*　　　　　*

LANGLEY, VIRGINIA, USA

Madison Samson III is a woman. She has been seduced, used, betrayed, and sold down the river. She knows it, and she knows who is responsible. Her scorn for the disgusting little shit before her is infinite. Narrow, rounded shoulders, pot belly, shiny bald head, face like a sick owl, he sits there with the supercilious expression of a contented cartoon character.

Her dispassionate demeanor conceals the smoldering inferno burning deep within her soul. She is on the warpath, painted for war. Bright-red lipstick. Dark makeup base. Blue eyeliner. Black mascara. Heavy black-rimmed glasses. She has teased her hair for the big bouffant look. Her black sheath dress accentuates the arcs and curves of a sensuous female on the make. Madison Samson III has arrived.

Alvin P. Dearman is looking forward to this. He delights in his reputation as a cruel, avaricious psychopath. This will be another feather in his cap. "Madison, I think you know why I have summoned you."

Silence. Madison Samson III smiles the icy smile of disinterest and impatience. Alvin P. Dearman waits. In vain. Madison continues to smile, accentuating her disinterest and impatience.

Alvin blinks. "Okay, Madison, that's how you want to play it? Do you know why I have summoned you?"

Madison speaks through her smile. "Why don't you tell me, Alvin?"

Alvin does not understand her attitude, and he does not appreciate it. He is used to making big men cry. He expects nothing less from little women. "You have been the object of an internal investigation. I am disappointed in you, Madison. You lied about your knowledge of the traitor's activities to protect your own guilt. In Paris, you collaborated with a gang of assassins to eliminate any and all who could testify to your guilt. We have the proof."

Madison does not react. This is not going the way Alvin planned it.

"You will be convicted and incarcerated," he says. "You are going to jail, and they will throw away the key."

"Bullshit."

Alvin jerks himself upright. This is not in the script. "What do you mean, 'bullshit'?"

"Look it up in the dictionary, Alvin. You're talking pure, unadulterated bullshit. It was you who modified my report. It was you who ordered me to collaborate with the gang of assassins."

Alvin lets a triumphant sneer break out on his twisted owl beak. "That would be very difficult to prove, since it is totally untrue."

Madison lets a ray of confidence escape from her otherwise expressionless face. "Have you ever seen those miniature recorders we are issued?"

Alvin jumps to his feet. "Empty your purse."

Madison smiles. It worked.

Her purse is small. She pours the contents onto Alvin's desk. He verifies there is no miniature recorder. He also knows she would never have mentioned a recorder if she had one in her purse.

"So, Madison, you are trying to blackmail me?"

Madison understands that it is Alvin who is recording this conversation. She is not intimidated. On the contrary. "Alvin, you and I both know the truth."

Alvin has had enough of Madison's impertinence. "This meeting is over. You are on paid leave pending a decision by the board."

Madison is reassured by that. If she's really as guilty as Alvin is pretending, she would be suspended, not put on paid leave, and the decision would already have been taken. Alvin is fishing.

She decides to push him a little further. "While I was in Paris, I got to know Ranger Wilde very well. You know him, don't you?"

"I know the name, of course, not the man."

Madison giggles. It's a feminine giggle, something she knows annoys Alvin. "He told me that he had worked closely with you in the past. He has some good stories. Oh well, who cares? I have to run, Alvin. Important appointment. I am looking forward to my paid vacation, as well as my full reinstatement in the briefest delay."

Madison gathers her affairs and exits triumphantly. Alvin Picks up the phone. He knows what has to be done.

Chapter 36

By the time Samantha came in, Brad was feeling pretty chipper. He had some burns from the cattle prod on his back and his neck and some bruises from Piccolo's blows to his shoulder and ribs. And Ranger had gotten away. Other than that and a bruised ego, he felt pretty good—physically. Mentally, he was at war with himself.

Mario had double-crossed him. Mario was Samantha's big friend and intermediary. Samantha was a mysterious, unknown quantity. In spite of himself and all his feelings, Brad had to admit she was a shady little lady with two distinct identities: de la Sarta and Smith. Socialite philanthropist. Certified lawyer. Aggressive investigator. Accomplished gymnast. No childhood.

"You're wondering who I am." She'd read his mind again. How she managed that was another mystery he had to come to grips with. He nodded. She smiled. "I'll tell you. You deserve to know."

She curled up on the sofa. Gathered her thoughts. Brad braced for what was to come.

"It was a warm summer evening in Georgetown. I was ten years old. My mother, my father, my younger brother, and I were enjoying a Saturday night barbeque on the terrace by the swimming pool. Dad was doing the cooking. Mom was setting the table. My brother was in the pool. I was in the garage getting some games to play after dinner."

Samantha's voice was soft. She was reliving the scene.

"I heard some strange voices outside. I went to the window. There were three young men. Two of them were in the light, confronting my father. I knew them as our neighbors from down the street. The third stayed back in the shadows. I couldn't see him well enough to recognize him, but he was encouraging and directing the other two."

Samantha stopped to gather her composure. Her eyes misted over.

"My father ordered them to leave. One man slammed my father with a baseball bat. Dad went down. The other grabbed my mother. The man with the bat proceeded to beat my father's head into mush. He kept repeating 'You like that, motherfucker? You want some more?' My mother tried to scream. The man punched her in the gut. They ripped her clothes off and stood there ogling her, laughing and poking her with their bats. My little brother in the pool started to cry. The younger of the two men pulled him out. Told him to stop crying. When he couldn't stop, the man started banging his head on the edge of the pool. Cracked his head wide open and threw him back in the water like a dead fish."

Samantha was rocking back and forth. Tears were streaming down her cheeks. She soldiered on.

"They gave my mother an order. She refused. A coal from the fire on her breast changed her mind. She performed fellatio on the younger man. The older one watched and cheered her on. They switched places. Hot coals on her buttocks motivated her when they were dissatisfied with her performance. They took turns raping her. Before they ended her life with a blow to the head, they violated her anus with a hot poker." Samantha paused. Clasped her hands. "Can you get me some water, please?"

Brad was having trouble keeping calm. All kinds of emotions were churning around in his head. "Sure. Look, Samantha, you don't have to go on. It's too painful."

"No, I have to finish. This is the first time I've spoken about this since the trial."

Brad fetched the water. Samantha took a healthy sip and took up where she left off.

"When they finished, the third man in the shadows said, 'Let's find the daughter and see what she's made of.' I ran to my secret hiding place between the walls. They searched and searched, but never found me. I stayed hidden until I heard the police come in the next day. When I came out, I was a different person."

Brad could only nod.

"It was a sensational trial. There were other witnesses, but our next-door neighbor and I were the main ones. I was only ten years old. I recounted the entire incident in detail, exactly like I just did. They tried everything to discredit my testimony, but I was unshakable. The other witness corroborated the main points of my testimony. There was other proof that placed the culprits at the scene of the crime. It looked like a slam dunk.

"Not to be. The culprits were the sons of a U.S. senator. He was confrontational, claiming that this was a politically motivated accusation. His sons were arrogant and unremorseful. Things started to change. The first judge made a series of dubious rulings blocking certain pieces of key evidence. Then he recused himself. The second judge upheld the contested rulings. The other key witness recanted and changed her testimony. It became a total three-ring circus. A mistrial was declared, and the sons went free.

The senator was publicly humiliated by accusations of blackmail, jury tampering, and influence peddling. He stonewalled. Played the political victim card, was not charged, and somehow got reelected."

Brad had to have a cigarette. He was moved. "What happened to you?"

"I was ten years old. My father was a multimillionaire and left everything to me. My mother's brother adopted me. Changed my name from Smith to de la Sarta, my mother's maiden name. I went to live with my uncle in the UK. He saw to it that my inheritance was wisely invested. I went to the best boarding schools in Europe. I'm fluent in English, French, German, Spanish, and Italian. My uncle owned a circus in France. My passion was the circus. I spent my summers performing with the circus on the trapeze and doing acrobatic tricks. My obsession was to avenge my parents. I spent my spare time honing my acrobatic dancing skills, training in small weapons and hand-to-hand combat. I studied criminal law. Graduated summa cum laude from Yale."

What a story! Brad wanted to do something to show his empathy. But nothing seemed appropriate. The best he could do was to squeeze out a question he already knew the answer to. "Who was the senator?"

"James Brown from Virginia."

"He's the one so obsessed with the 'traitor.' I remember reading that he has had some recent bad luck. His wife was brutally beaten to death in her bedroom. One of the sons had a car accident and burned alive. His other son overdosed on some kind of drug that reduced him to the state of a vegetable."

There was no smile on her face. Her voice was hard. "Don't forget the recanting witness who was hacked to death in her bedroom with her tongue cut out, and the two judges who were castrated and had their throats slit."

The tension was sucked right out of the room. The cards were on the table. Brad now understood what he was up against. Samantha was after Jake Brown. He had one more question, but he thought he had the answer to that one as well. "Any idea who the third guy was?"

"I think you already know it's Ranger. The story goes that Ranger was orphaned at an early age. For reasons that no one knows, Brown took responsibility and mentored him. Some gossiped he was Brown's illegitimate child. They say he liked Ranger better than his own kids. He and Ranger have worked hand in glove ever since Ranger finished his university studies. My uncle is Argentinian. He was a high-level intelligence agent for many years. He knows all the actors well. Senator James Brown was close to Juan Perón. Ranger was the bagman."

Brad flashed back to the photos he'd seen in Papachristou's apartment. The trio: Papachristou, Perón, and the tall balding gentleman with thick, shaggy eyebrows and a crooked, slapstick smile. Now he recognized him. Senator Jake Brown. Samantha had provided the link to Ranger's activities in the pictures, dates, times, and places Mario had given him. Senator Jake Brown, the traitor crusader, was the mole.

"What's your real relationship to Mario?" Brad asked.

"My uncle was very anxious to help me approach Ranger and Brown. As a senior intelligence operative, he was familiar with all the politicians. He introduced me to Mario for that reason. That's why I know him, and that's why I'm here."

On the one hand, Brad was relieved. Samantha was not an enemy. On the other hand, her goals were not aligned one hundred percent with his own. Brad wanted to smoke out the mole and his network. She wanted to kill Brown and Ranger. At the end of the day, since Brown was the mole and Ranger was an integral part of his network, their goals were not necessarily contradictory.

Samantha was struggling to control the emotions of reliving her nightmare. Brad sensed her hesitation. He took her hand and pulled her close.

It started with a few tears. Then she began to sob. Brad looked down when her sobbing ceased. She was asleep. He was alone with his thoughts and dreading what he would have to do.

Chapter 37

Madison had always wanted to be a blonde. She opened her eyes and looked in the salon's wall mirror. Golden, wavy locks framed her face. She was blonde. She liked it. Set off the deep blue of her tinted contacts and complemented her new sexy fashion statement. Tight top, hip huggers, stilettos. She paid in cash.

Groovy's New and Used was two blocks down the street. She picked the red Mustang. Paid cash. The Company had supplied her with two alternative identities. She'd had the good sense to take them with her when she left her apartment. The Company would assume she was using them for cover and dash off on a wild goose chase. She would not use them. She would use the identity she'd created for herself, Madelyn Salmon. She'd chosen the name carefully to be close enough to her real name on the off chance she'd run into someone she knew. She had a driver's license, passport, and credit card in that name. On the identity pictures, she had blonde hair and heavy makeup—more like Madelyn Salmon than Madison Samson III.

She jumped in her Mustang and took the interstate due south.

Time was not on her side. Alvin Dearman was already facing a huge scandal with the "traitor" claiming his innocence and providing some believable proof.

If events in Paris got linked to the traitor snafu, his career would be on the line. He needed a scapegoat. In fact, she now understood he'd always known he might need one and chose the overachieving Madison Samson III as the perfect candidate.

She'd played *his* hand so cleverly, and never missed a cue. She winced at the thought of her naivety. But then came hand two. She'd gotten some cards of her own and raised the stakes. Now she could serve as a scapegoat only if she was dead. A living Madison would take him out. He knew that, too.

*   *   *

PARIS

Brad had Chuck's full attention. "Here's what we're up against. The mole we're looking for is none other than James 'Jake' Brown, the senior senator from the great state of Virginia. He was big friends with Juan Perón, Argentina's president. Perón was buying intelligence from Brown and selling it on to other Latin American governments. Mario was the intermediary for Perón, and Ranger was Brown's bagman."

Chuck nodded in agreement. "Sounds plausible. So why all the killing?"

"When Perón died, Mario lost his power and became a target of the new regime. Because he knew the mole's identity, he also represented a threat to the mole. To protect himself from the mole, he gave Papachristou some proof incriminating Brown. He thought once the information was out there, he would no longer be deemed a threat. He was wrong. Papachristou turned the information over to the CIA agent, who turned it over to Madison. Madison and her superiors decided that the agent was the mole trying to protect himself."

Chuck said, "Papachristou was a senior agent. All they had to do was ask him. The supposed traitor surely told them how he got the info."

"That's what has me stumped. It looks like they were covering up for Brown and never asked him. Maybe because he's a senator. In any case, they accused the agent of being a traitor. They tipped Brown off and Brown's big-haired blonde killed Papachristou. His death eliminated the 'traitor's' alibi. Then, Madison came over to help them wipe out anybody who could possibly link Brown's men to the murder. She got called back to Langley, and her head's on the chopping block."

"Well, they forgot about Mario."

Brad guffawed. "That they did. It looks like they patched that hole, though. He really tried to screw us."

Chuck's eyes sparkled. "Yeah, you were really shocked by that, *n'est-ce pas, amigo?*"

Brad laughed in spite of himself. Then he turned serious. "Ranger's back in business."

They both knew this was their immediate problem. "Yeah, we can deal with Mario later. This Ranger dude is dangerous. He's also got this bunch of Argentine Anticommunist Association gangbangers to run around with."

The setting sun was painting the sky in shades of blue, yellow, and pink. Brad admired the scene long enough to make his decision. "We're gonna have to take the battle to them. We can't hide forever. Anyway, these guys are nowhere near the caliber of Ranger's group. We know where they're headquartered. Let's go in there and take them out. I've got a plan."

Chuck didn't have to speak. The ear-to-ear smile on his face said it all. "When?"

"Tonight."

*   *   *

CARRIERES-SUR-SEINE 78

There were lights in the warehouse by the quarry. Brad parked his bike in a lane off the road. They walked a hundred yards to the warehouse beside the quarry, where they reconnoitered behind a gigantic machine. Everything was quiet. No guards or security were in evidence. Part one of the plan was to take possession of the entrance to the warehouse.

They waited and watched for the next twenty minutes. Nothing. Brad signaled he was ready to move. Chuck held up his hand. Went into his backpack and pulled out his night goggles. After five minutes of careful scrutiny, he held up four fingers. He pointed to the front of the building and held up two fingers. Pointed to the back and held up two more. Whispered, "They're hiding in foxholes. Picked 'em up on the infrared. Start at the back."

The wooded hill behind the warehouse provided the cover they needed to approach the two men in the foxholes guarding the back of the building. They would have to overcome them and then go for the guards at the front of the warehouse.

From the edge of the woods, Chuck used his night goggles to observe the two guards ten meters away. They weren't moving. A sharp grunt suggested the one closest was napping. He signaled Brad to stay put. He moved cautiously out of the woods Vietnam-style, slithering along like a snake.

Almost to the foxhole, the napping guard snorted and launched into a coughing fit. The guard at the other corner jumped up. *"He, che, que pasa* (Hey, pal, what's happenin')?"

Chuck froze. The guard climbed out of his foxhole and started toward his noisy *compañero*. Chuck's knife glinting in the moonlight gave him away. The guard jumped back.

"Hijo de…"

Brad broke cover. Charged the guard fumbling for his gun. A shoulder to the gut took him down. A knife to the throat left him gagging his last breaths. Meanwhile, the sleeping guard had only enough time to feel Chuck's arms close around his head before his neck snapped and his life ended.

That was too noisy. A walkie-talkie started crackling. They stepped back, looked at each other. Brad made a snap decision. He reached down and picked up the walkie-talkie. Clicked the *speak* button.

"Si."

A stream of rapid-fire Spanish came through. Brad didn't understand a word. He decided on "yes" as the most likely correct answer.

"Si."

The crackling stopped and the apparatus went silent. Chuck showed his concern with the "let's vamoose" sign.

Brad raised his hand. "Let's see what happens."

There was movement along the side of the warehouse. Brad checked the other side. Movement there, too. He signaled Chuck to jump in the foxhole with the dead guard. He dumped his own dead guard in the other foxhole and jumped in on top of him.

They waited. A bearded face peeked around the corner of the warehouse. Spotted Brad in the foxhole. Brad sat hunched down and motionless. The bearded guy was fooled. He relaxed.

"He, cabrón, porqué no me contestas (Hey, asshole, why aren't you answering me)?"

By the time he got in close enough and realized his mistake, it was too late. Brad used his nunchakus to stun the guy. A kick to the balls and a left-right to the head took him down. A stomp to the neck ended his resistance.

Brad looked to Chuck. He was at the corner of the warehouse, back to the wall, waiting. The other guard must have been alerted when the bearded guard's question got no reply. He was taking his time.

The silencer on the barrel of a .45ACP machine gun poked around the corner. Chuck grabbed the silencer, jerked it forward, and sliced down on the wrist of the hand that held it. Blood was spurting everywhere, but the guy got a one-word expletive out before Chuck's blade ended his life. That expletive alerted the gangbangers inside that something was amiss.

The coast to the entrance was now clear. Brad and Chuck scooped up two .45ACPs and all the magazines they could carry. They hotfooted it to the front of the warehouse. Part two of their plan depended on the reactivity of the French police and the fact that access to the warehouse was limited to the front.

They positioned themselves thirty yards from the warehouse. Chuck was on the left behind a car. Brad on the right behind a tree. They unscrewed the silencers from the rifles in order to make as much noise as possible.

The door to the warehouse banged open. Two gangbangers stepped out. Brad and Chuck opened fire. The din of the detonations destroyed the nocturnal calm in a spectacular series of bullets and bangs.

One gangbanger went down. The other ducked back into the warehouse. Pandemonium exploded inside. Screaming and yelling. Furniture moving. Gangbangers running around.

Silence. Slowly, the door began to open. Brad and Chuck

opened fire again. The gangbangers attempted to return fire but had to slam the door shut in the face of the firepower concentrated on the small door.

More screaming and yelling, orders and arguments. Silence again, followed by the squeaks and creaks of the loading door rolling up. This was a surprise twist that called for some improvisation. The gangbangers were going to attempt a breakout through the large loading door.

Brad pointed to it. Chuck was in a better position to cover that exit. Brad took the pedestrian entrance.

The small door flew open and two gangbangers burst out. Four gangbangers rushed out simultaneously from the loading door. Brad's fusillade drove the two from the pedestrian entrance back inside. Chuck pinned down three of the gangbangers from the loading door at the edge of the entrance. The fourth one had managed to get around the corner of the warehouse and was firing away at Chuck's position. The corner shielded him from Chuck, but he was a sitting duck for Brad. Brad took him down.

Brad cocked his ear. All quiet. It had been more than twenty minutes since they'd started their assault. There was no way the gunfire could be construed as anything but gunfire. Brad was counting on the French cops reacting to it quickly. There was a commissariat not more than two kilometers away, and the sound of the shots would be resonating in its walls. Neighborhood residents would be reporting the gunfire as well. Now it was a question of time. The cops had to get there before the gangbangers broke out. There were too many of them to be held off much longer.

The gangbangers were massing for an offensive. It would be impossible for Brad and Chuck to stop them all. Brad signaled Chuck it was time to run for their lives.

Then they heard it. At first, it could have been wishful thinking, but it quickly became the distinctive moaning *wahou-wahou* of a police siren.

They trained their guns on the doors and began firing away. The gangbangers swarmed out like an army of ants and began to advance. Brad and Chuck continued to fire as they initiated their retreat.

The *wahou-wahou* and the flashing lights of the cop cars at the entrance to the quarry announced the arrival of the cavalry. The gangbangers ceased fire and began to run for the hills. Brad and Chuck slipped off down their planned route to their vehicle stationed strategically for a speedy, surreptitious exit. The cops would take care of what was left of the AAA gang.

Brad and Chuck had not expected the gangbangers to fight the French cops. According to Mario, their presence was semiofficial, and as long as they caused no trouble in the French community, they would be tolerated. The sustained gunfire back at the warehouse suggested the tacit truce had been broken.

This was good news and bad news. The good news was that rather than a straightforward expulsion of some of the gangbangers if they simply surrendered, a firefight and French casualties meant that the AAA would be eradicated from the country. Brad, Chuck, Samantha, and even Mario's security would be substantially improved. The bad news was that a firefight and French casualties would cause the French to cast a wide net and throw all their resources into the effort of apprehending the perpetrators. Brad and Chuck had too far to go before the French got organized—unless they broke through before the dragnet got set up.

The cops had come in from the north. Brad and Chuck saw the gangbangers fleeing to the south and scattering to the east and west. Brad pointed north. Chuck nodded his agreement.

Brad cranked up the bike. Cut down the lane to the highway. Flashing lights and wailing sirens were coming from the east. Brad killed the headlight. Shot across the highway down a sharp embankment. He almost lost it before he skidded to a stop. It looked like nothing but bushes and trees that they would not be able to navigate in the moonlight.

Chuck donned his goggles and studied the terrain. "There's a break over there."

They pushed the bike through the underbrush to a narrow trail. Lights and voices from the road. Military commands. The French were setting up the dragnet. Brad and Chuck had made it by the skin of their teeth.

They pushed the bike down the trail for thirty minutes. Stopped and took their bearings. Cars were passing by on a road thirty meters away. Chuck crept to the edge of the woods. There was no obvious police presence, but the irregular behavior of car headlights coming from the northeast made him wary.

"I think there's a roadblock down to the right. Let's stay on the trail."

They pushed the bike across the road and cranked it up. Chuck lent Brad his goggles, and they rolled along at a snail's pace for another twenty minutes. They came out on a residential street that took them to the highway. An hour later, they were back in Paris, headed for the Champs-Elysées. That was when the spotlights went on and the cops pulled them over.

Chapter 38

The *Herald Tribune* had a scoop. After a ferocious gun battle, a South American gang of hoodlums headquartered in Les Yvelines had been broken up and arrested last night. Details were sketchy, but the French authorities confirmed that a major police action had taken place. Several French police officers were wounded, and several members of the gang had been killed. Most of the other hoodlums had been rounded up and taken into custody. There was an intense manhunt underway to locate and detain those few who had managed to escape.

That would explain why the cops at the roadblock last night had lost interest in Brad and Chuck when they found out they were American. They were looking for the remnants of the South American AAA.

It was late by the time Brad dropped Chuck off at the Etoile. Samantha wasn't at the apartment when he got in, so he managed to get a good night's sleep.

He knew he was going to need it. He and Chuck had decided that the next step in their strategy was to eliminate Ranger. His intuition told him that this was going to be a problem for

Samantha. Something about revenge. He could sympathize with her, but he couldn't wait around for her to spring her trap. Ranger was gunning for him and Chuck, especially him, and he knew how to find them both. The same could not be said for Ranger. His headquarters were still a mystery.

Brad was wrestling with his problem when blonde Samantha de la Sarta opened the door and paraded into the apartment. Suddenly, the atmosphere was electric. Her subliminal communication system was working overtime. She was so graceful, so feminine, so irresistible.

"Oh, Brad, I was so worried." The catch in her voice betrayed her emotion. "Are you alright? I came as soon as I heard. You didn't tell me. I didn't know. How did you do it?"

Those five short sentences had it all: concern, support, reproach, question. Brad played for time. "What do you mean?"

She took his hand. Studied his features. "You attacked and destroyed the Argentine Anticommunist Alliance's forces in France. Why?"

Samantha's messaging was becoming less subliminal and more accusing. It surprised him, and he wanted to understand why. Sensing the sensitivity of the moment, Brad chose his words carefully. "I think it's obvious, Samantha, don't you? They tried to kill me. They had to go. Where's the problem?"

Brad saw she realized she had overplayed her hand. Pulled in her horns. Went for the heartstrings. "You should have confided in me. I care about you."

"I care about you, as well. Don't want you to worry. But since we're laying our cards on the table, you might as well know that Mario and Ranger are on my hitlist."

"I figured as much. They will be difficult. Mario is holed up in his bunker. Ranger left town for London." She studied her hands for a few seconds. When she looked up, she was sincere. "Can we work together on these two? I need them alive for a while in order to complete my investigation."

Brad understood and decided to go along with her. "Okay, what's the plan?"

"Mario and Ranger are working together with Rega and the AAA. I don't want to upset that relationship until after my conference next week."

Brad nodded his agreement. Next week was a long way away.

*   *   *

Gary was mildly pessimistic. He was convinced that the evidence was convincing. But the guilty parties were in the upper crust of the crushing, complex, symbiotic system of political expediency and bureaucratic authority that would destroy anyone and anything that threatened its special status of power and privilege.

"Let's look at the facts," he said. "Top secret intelligence was being leaked to a foreign power over a long period. It caused the death of some of our best agents and assets in Latin America. Who knows how much other damage it caused in economic, military, diplomatic, and reputational losses? When the security breach was discovered, the investigation concluded that the trusted ranking agent for the region was a double agent working for our enemies. Although this 'traitor' escaped to the Soviet embassy before he could be arrested, it looked like the security breach had been repaired. Then Georges Papachristou, one of our most senior operatives, turned up dead in suspicious circumstances. That's when the trouble started."

Brad and Chuck nodded appreciatively. Gary continued. "Then

you two guys got involved. You found out that Papachristou was murdered by a blonde transvestite and have pictures to prove it. He belonged to a gang of Americans who went around killing anyone with knowledge of the murder. You have eyewitnesses that the agent sent to investigate Papachristou's murder, Madison Samson III, was a member of this murderous gang."

Again, Brad and Chuck nodded appreciatively. Chuck chimed in, "We also have the bank records from Mittel that Papachristou was laundering the money paid to the mole for the intelligence he was selling."

Gary downed a coffee-soaked sugar cube. "Let's don't get ahead of ourselves. The money went from this Mario to Papachristou to Mittel to two accounts, Junior and El Gordo." He stopped, stared intently at his two listeners. "We don't know where the money from the El Gordo accounts ended up, but we know that the money in the Junior accounts ended up in accounts for James 'Jake' Brown and his family members."

The bombshell. Neither Brad nor Chuck reacted right away. They were processing the information, making sure that they had understood correctly.

Gary interrupted their thoughts. "You heard correctly. My friend got me the info on the bank accounts. James 'Jake' Brown, the senior senator from the great state of Virginia and self-appointed traitor crusader, and his family were the recipients of the spy money. It's the smoking gun. He's the mole."

Brad took out his Gitanes. Chuck said, "Gimme one of those." They lit up and sat there puffing away, each in his own thoughts. Gary couldn't hide his satisfaction.

Finally, Brad said, "We've got the backup proof that Ranger Wilde was the bagman for the spy money as well as the head of the American assassination squad. He has also worked for Jake Brown since he was a teenager."

Gary glanced at his watch. "Gotta run. Let me put all this together in a report and see how it looks. I think we have enough to take it to the hierarchy. If we do, there will be a huge blowback. Brown is a big dog and a ruthless infighter. He has influence. People owe him. He can do favors for them. Company careers are on the line. These guys hate each other internally, but when an outside threat arises, they close ranks and kill in cold blood. Still want to go through with it?"

For Brad, it was a no-brainer. For Chuck, it was a stupid question. Gary was less enthusiastic. He knew he didn't have all his ducks in a row. The missing link was the proof that Mario Irigoyen had delivered the leaked intelligence documents to Georges Papachristou. Without that, it was a jump into the unknown. His years of experience were screaming for him to back off.

Chapter 39

Gary's legs were all cramped up from the flight to Washington in economy class. Inexplicably, there were no seats in business, and the Company would not pay first class prices. He'd had to settle for economy, since the "urgency" of the meeting required him to take the first plane with an available seat.

The "urgent" meeting with Dearman hadn't surprised him after the report he sent in. Dearman had upped the ante on urgency by instructing him to come to Langley directly from the airport. It was an old psychological trick highlighted in the instruction manual to put your adversary at a disadvantage. However, since Gary had read the manual as well, it had the opposite effect. Dearman didn't need an extra psychological advantage unless he felt vulnerable. He was already the big cheese.

As he entered the office, Gary knew he was about to get an answer to that. "Hello, Martha."

She didn't look up. "Hello, Gary. Mr. Dearman is waiting for you."

Gary knocked once and entered. The social pleasantries were

short and sweet. Dearman was grim and curt. He motioned to the wooden chair positioned far from his desk in the center of the room, directly under the naked ceiling light. The staging was reminiscent of hostile interrogation scenes. Dearman was pulling out all the stops on psychological bullying. He looked down at what Gary surmised was the report he had sent in. Put his hands together and sighed.

Gary took the measure of the man. No shoulders, pot belly, no hair, big round-rimmed glasses, and a beaky nose, Dearman was perched in the chair he had jacked up as high as it would go. Reminded Gary of a disgusting evil owl he once saw in a Disney cartoon.

Never, thought Gary, *has his supercilious expression of superiority been more irritating.*

"Richards," Dearman began.

Now, suddenly, he was on a last name basis. Gary understood. More psychology. Gary was a battle-hardened bureaucratic infighter with many scalps on his totem pole.

"Yes, dear man." Gary insisted on the separation between the two syllables. The trick was to infuriate your adversary into making a mistake. Addressing Dearman by his last name with no Doctor, Mister, or Professor prefix was the equivalent of daring him to a duel. It succeeded in infuriating him. But he ignored the challenge. Avoided the mistake.

"Your report is exceedingly interesting and well written." Gary nodded, and Dearman continued. "You are to be congratulated on your detailed detective work on Miss Samson III. The eyewitness report from the Edith woman is the icing on the cake. All of us here have to admit that Miss Samson III had us fooled. She was destined for big things. You can imagine our disappointment and stupefaction when we learned that she was in cahoots with the traitor and those attempting to protect him."

Gary recognized the spin. "That's not exactly what the report says."

Dearman waved him off. "We are professionals. We know how to read between the lines, Gary." Back to first names. Reeling him in. Inviting him back onto the team. "But we did find some major problems and inconsistencies. I think you should have a chance to edit these out before I formally file the report."

Gary didn't react. He waited. His eyes were dark shadows under the ceiling light that accentuated the sharp angles of his cheeks and chin.

"All this speculation about Senator Brown and these foreign bank accounts should probably be eliminated."

Now it was Gary's move. He leaned back and pretended to think it over. Clasped his hands. Declared. "It's not speculation. It is fact. I have the certified account information. Moreover, the entire argument of the report is that the murder of Papachristou and the actions of Madison Samson III, Ranger Wilde, and the American gang were to protect Senator Brown, the mole."

Alvin Dearman shifted uncomfortably in his seat. Shook his head dismissively. "Senator Brown is out of our league. He is untouchable. The accounts are there, but there is no link to them and the money paid for the leaked intelligence. We have no doubt that he would never betray his country. He is one of our country's fiercest patriots and one of the Company's greatest defenders. We have to settle for what we can prove. The traitor and Madison Samson III conspired to betray our beloved country for money. Madison Samson III then used her position in Paris to cover her tracks. End of story. Let's leave it at that."

As skilled as he was, Gary was no match for Dearman's position and power. He decided to give it one last try. "There are so many holes in that story it makes a Swiss cheese look like a gold bar."

That was when Dearman gave himself away. "Only you and I know about the holes. We can tell the story any way we want."

Up to then, Dearman had been using "we" when discussing the Company's point of view, as if it had gone before a committee and been discussed. Gary understood that only Dearman had seen the report. He also understood that Dearman has made his decision. The decision was final, and there was no court of appeal. It was over.

"Gary, get that report back to me before the end of next week. I'll need it for the committee meeting."

*   *   *

PARIS

Brad was disgusted. Chuck was angry. Gary was resigned. His trip to Washington was a dead end. "The game's over, guys. There's nowhere else to go."

Chuck was staring at the floor. "Everything Dearman said is false. We do have proof of a direct link between the spy money and Brown's accounts."

"There is no direct link," Gary said. "We only know that some of the spy money went into an account that also paid out to Brown and his family. The Junior account could have other perfectly legal inflows. Without the full information set on the Junior account, it smells bad, but there is no proof that payouts to Brown and family are related to any illegal activity. If the Company wanted to pursue this line of inquiry, it could do so legally. But it doesn't. Director Dearman made that very clear."

"Well, how about the accused traitor? We know he received the documents from Papachristou, who got them from Mario Irigoyen."

Gary shook his head and scarfed up another coffee-soaked sugar cube. "Sorry, Chuck. We know that but have no proof. Irigoyen never came through on his promise to deliver the proof he has."

Brad tossed his package of Gitanes onto the table. "We've got nowhere to go. The buck stops at Dearman's desk. He's protecting his reputation and anybody else involved in the spy scheme. How would it look if word got out that Senator Brown had been involved for years in a scheme to sell top secret intelligence right under the CIA's nose? The alternative case is open and shut, and protects them all—except the accused traitor and Madison. The accused traitor and his accomplice, Madison, conspired to sell the intelligence. Any witnesses to the contrary were eliminated. Eyewitnesses, including Edith and Brad, saw Madison as an active participant in several of these murders."

"Unfortunately, guys, that's the way bureaucracies work. They protect their own. In this case, they had to sacrifice the 'traitor' and Madison to save themselves. Now, we can all go home and relax."

"Not really." Brad's voice was soft as he sipped his coffee. "We know from Irigoyen that the mole, Brown, has made a deal with Rega, the man who replaced Irigoyen as the power broker in the Argentine government, to continue with business as usual. The worst news is that Chuck and I are in the crosshairs of some very unsavory characters—Ranger Wilde and the Argentine Anticommunist Association. They're not gonna stop coming after us just because Alvin Dearman says the game is over."

The room went silent while they let that sink in. Gary broke the silence. "You're right, Brad, and there's not much I can do to help."

Chapter 40

The French had killed four members of the AAA and rounded up ten others in the vicinity of the quarry. Their investigation revealed that there were three or four other members unaccounted for. Gary confirmed that there was no one corresponding to the description of the two gangbangers who'd tortured Brad, the two who called themselves Cangrejo and Chispa—Crab and Sparky.

Brad figured that even if they were on the loose, they were on the run, more worried about avoiding the French dragnet than getting revenge. Ranger was another worry. Gary confirmed that he was in London courting investors. For the moment, then, it looked like the danger level was under control. Still had to be careful.

Brad hadn't accessed his apartment since he'd moved in with Samantha. She had been over several times to check things out and reported that the various traps she had placed at the door and around the apartment remained undisturbed. He donned his grungy student disguise and entered his building from the back through the university parking lot and over the wall. He took the stairway to the second floor. The small piece of cardboard was undisturbed, barely visible in the doorjamb an inch off the floor. Reassured, he slipped inside and waited at the entrance, searching the darkness and listening.

Rather than turn on the lights and run the risk of alerting anyone who might be on the lookout, he let his eyes adjust and used a pin light on his keychain to check out his surroundings. He started with the bedroom, then the kitchen and the sitting room. Everything seemed to be in place. He opened the bathroom door. The light flashed on. Momentarily blinded, he jumped back and rolled to the left. Crashed into the table. Grabbed it and threw it in the path of the oncoming shadow.

"Brad James. It's you. Didn't recognize you dressed like a bum."

Bathed in the light from the bathroom, Brad perceived the outline of a female form brandishing a weapon of some kind. The female form wasn't familiar, but the voice reminded him of something or someone. "It's me, Madison Samson III. From the Company."

Brad's heart was pounding like a piledriver. His eyes were adjusting, but he didn't see Madison Samson III. He saw a busty, blonde sex bomb with a voice like Madison Samson III. Words were unnecessary. His expression said it all.

"Relax, Brad. it's really me. We have to talk. I'll explain everything."

*   *   *

When Brad got to the part where the bathroom light flashed on, Chuck was roaring with laughter. "Oh, man, I wish I could have seen that."

Brad chuckled and nodded appreciatively. "I almost had a heart attack. Jeezus F. Christ. What a homecoming!"

"How'd she get past all the traps?"

"She's a security expert, man. She teaches that stuff. Anyway, she has metamorphosized." Chuck blanked out. Brad explained. "In other words, she changed. From a plain-Jane overachieving bureaucratic wannabe, she is now a busty, blonde sex bomb. She even moves different."

"Yeah, well, how does she talk?"

"She talks like a busty, blonde sex bomb who has been used and abused. Here's what she told me. The field agent working for her, who is accused of being the traitor, brought her a huge file of classified documents claiming they came from Georges Papachristou. These documents were a treasure trove of national intelligence that included transcripts from cabinet meetings, diplomatic exchanges, military plans, names and pictures of agents and informants, secret operations, strategies, plans, budgets. She brought the file directly to Alvin Dearman, her mentor, and her boss."

Brad stopped to let his words sink in. Made a big show of rubbing out his cigarette in the ashtray. Sat back and continued.

"Here is where it gets interesting. Dearman took a cursory look through the hundreds of pages of information and agreed they had a big security problem. He told her the Papachristou story was a fake. Said that Papachristou worked directly for him and had not reported any documents or security breach. He told Madison he would check this out and get back to her. Meanwhile, the big-haired blonde threw Papachristou off the balcony of the Argentine embassy reception center. When Dearman got back to Madison, he concluded that her agent was the traitor attempting to cover his tracks by bringing in the docs. He had Papachristou murdered by his accomplices to keep him quiet. Dearman made her change her report. Then he sent her to Paris to investigate the Papachristou death. Told her to work with Ranger and his group to find out what they were up to. When she reported they were killing people, Dearman told her to get as much evidence as she could against them."

Chuck was shaking his head. "Let me guess. When the accused traitor's claim of innocence became credible and the American gangbangers got blown out of the water, Dearman abandoned her. Denied he told her to change the report and collaborate with the gangbangers. Then he claimed her activity with the gangbangers was because she was in cahoots with the 'traitor' and was eliminating witnesses."

"You got it. She wants revenge. But she's on the run, which explains her new look. She hinted that Dearman would rather have her killed than going through the Company's bureaucratic procedures. Seems she has some kind of leverage on him. In any case, she is officially 'on leave' and not suspended. For her, this is confirmation he has put out a contract on her."

"Can she help us?"

"Doesn't look like it. She's a fugitive running for her life. Outside of the secret leverage she has on Dearman, she's pretty limited in what she can do. She has a lot of gossip on him. That's about it. Says he's a closet sado-pedophile and that she can prove it." When Chuck didn't react, Brad added, "That means he gets off on torturing little kids. Everybody whispers about it, but no one dares make an accusation. The few who tried had their lives ruined along with the lives of their children he abused."

There was a long silence before Chuck asked the obvious question. "Do you think we can trust her?"

"Don't know. We'll see. For the moment, it looks like Ranger and Brown are gonna get away scot-free with murder and treason.

We'll be sitting ducks. Our last chance at Ranger will be at Samantha's conference next week."

Chapter 41

Gary flipped off the TV. Ever since Dearman's report confirming the guilt of the "traitor," that insufferable windbag, Senator Jake Brown, was on every channel crowing about the treason he unearthed and his unwavering patriotism.

It annoyed Gary, but that wasn't what had him worried. Dearman's report included specific references to traitorous activities in Paris undertaken with the express purpose of undermining the investigation and protecting the "traitor."

That was what had him worried. Because when he'd come into the embassy that morning, there had been an urgent request for him to contact Langley. This he did, and he was confronted with an order to report on the activities of assets James and Hall over the last month.

Dearman was spinning the information on the offshore accounts uncovered by Brad and Chuck as a treasonous attempt to subvert the investigation.

There was no way Gary could deny their role in uncovering the accounts. He had headlined it in his report to Dearman.

So the big bureaucracy was going to grind up and destroy the two persons who had dared to defy City Hall.

*   *   *

"You are officially under investigation for treasonous activities. You are going to be interviewed and probably sent back to the States." Gary was really down. His shoulders were slumping. His eyes were bloodshot. His mouth was taut.

Brad was in battle mode. His adrenaline was pumping and his mind was whirling a mile a minute. Anger was not an option. That would come later. For the moment, he had to block this perfidious accusation and prepare his counterattack.

"Here's the way it's gonna work, Gary. If anyone wants to see either of us in person, they will communicate their request in writing. If we decide to accept, we will give them a time and a place." He turned to Chuck. "How does that sound?"

"I like it," Chuck said.

Gary's body language was screaming "No, no, no!" His words were more diplomatic. "Not sure that's gonna fly. Dearman is managing this personally. He is the second most powerful person in the CIA."

"We're in France, Gary. It was less than ten years ago that the French kicked the U.S. and NATO out of the country. I'm not sure how much clout Dearman has over here. One thing is for sure. He has less clout here than he does in the U.S. In the U.S.—and that includes the embassy—we are dead meat. Meanwhile, we'll get some legal representation to see what our rights are."

Gary almost spilled his coffee. "Don't do that. This is top secret."

Bingo. Brad had the information he needed. Dearman wanted

to avoid publicity. That would be Brad's ace in the hole. In fact, it wasn't even an ace, but it was the only card he had.

*   *   *

Brad and Chuck sat there looking at each other. Chuck broke the silence. "We're in the shit up to our cheekbones. The bad guys are going free. Ranger and the AAA are out to kill us. The CIA is accusing us of treason, and if we don't go along, they might just try to kill us, as well."

"We've got one last hope. Ranger's coming to Paris next week for the conference. We know where he'll be staying. We can take him down. That'll make one less gangbanger to worry about. Maybe we can make him talk. Get some leads on where to go next."

The door opened. Samantha had arrived. She wasn't smiling. "Hi, Chuck." She just stood there. Brad could see she was upset. She looked at them and shook her head in disgust. "All that work. All that effort. For nothing."

"What happened?"

"Ranger called. He canceled. He's not coming to the conference."

Now they had nowhere to go. They were going to have to end their crusade and worry about themselves.

Samantha said she would have to leave Paris but would continue to pursue Ranger and Jake Brown, probably from the UK and the U.S.

Brad and Chuck said they would continue to play defense against Ranger and the AAA while they tried to clear their names with the CIA.

They were pessimistic. They couldn't safely leave France and the potential political protection it offered. But if they stayed in France and tried to continue with business as usual, they would be in constant danger from Ranger and the AAA—maybe even the CIA.

Chapter 42

After a sleepless night of tossing, turning, and uninterrupted concentration, Brad came up with two potential leads that had not yet been fully investigated and might pan out. They were long shots, at best. Following them up involved leaving the relative political security of France and traveling to the UK.

He informed Chuck and Samantha that he would be absent for a few days and to lay low until he returned. The motorcycle to the coast and hovercraft to the UK would be the means of transport least likely to attract attention. He planned to stay no more than twenty-four hours. If his name was on any kind of a watch list, he would be in and out before anyone could react.

Except for getting used to driving on the wrong side of the road, the trip to London was uneventful. He scored a room at his favorite hotel in Hampstead. From the red telephone booth across from the metro, he inserted his coins and dialed the number. It answered on the third ring. The same voice and the same accent as in Paris. *"Sì."*

"Hello. I'd like to speak to Madame Papachristou."

"She's not available. Who is calling?"

"Do you remember the caller who said, 'There is a team of Americans preparing to attack you in a few minutes. Prepare yourself.'?"

Long silence. "Yes."

"That's who's calling."

Long silence. Whispering. A woman's voice. "This is Greta Papachristou."

"Good afternoon, Mrs. Papachristou. This is Brad James. We met in Paris. I would like to speak to you in person."

"It would be a pleasure."

Forty-five minutes later, Brad was ringing the doorbell of a six-story stone building overlooking Regent's Park. The door opened onto an antechamber with a massive steel door and a battery of cameras mounted around the perimeter. From the loudspeaker: "State your business."

"Brad James to see Greta Papachristou. She's expecting me."

The massive steel door swung slowly open without a sound. Brad stepped inside and was met by Head Honcho. The handshake was firm. The greeting was warm. *"Bienvenido, caballero* (Welcome, sir). *"*

They took the elevator to the third floor, where they exited into the most magnificent sitting room Brad had ever seen. In the middle of this marvelous room glittering with Claude Dalle crystals, Laurento Leathers, and impressionist originals, sat Greta Papachristou. She rose and took Brad's hand into both of hers. "Thank you so much for coming."

The meeting was short and successful—beyond Brad's wildest dreams. When Brad outlined the situation, Greta Papachristou understood immediately. She seemed almost relieved to deliver the documents Brad described. Then her expression changed. She wrinkled her forehead and reached into a brown envelope. "These photos might interest you as well."

She spread a packet of black-and-white photos on the crystal cocktail table. Brad picked them up one by one. He read the text. He studied them carefully. This wasn't a simple game changer. It was a whole new ballgame on a new field with different rules and different teams. There was a hint of triumph glowing in her eyes as she gathered the photos into the envelope and handed them to Brad.

He left the meeting with a treasure trove of documents that would prove the "traitor's" innocence and directly link Senator James "Jake" Brown to supplying the top secret intelligence and receiving payment for it. Far beyond that, she gave him information that, if corroborated, would shake the CIA to the very roots of its foundations.

Unsettled by the new revelation and deep in thought, he didn't notice the three men who followed him into the underground.

*   *   *

Back in his hotel, Brad secured the documents in the waterproof panel of his rucksack and made the snap decision to go straight back to Paris. There was no time to lose. He changed into his leathers and grabbed his rucksack and helmet. The room was prepaid. He went directly to the elevator to the underground parking lot.

The lights in the parking lot switched on automatically when the elevator doors opened. As he was about to exit, some scuffling sounds over by his bike warned him. He stepped back into the elevator and pressed *ground floor.* At the ground floor, he slipped out of the elevator, entered the stairway to the underground parking, and waited in the shadows behind the wall.

Two sets of footsteps clomping up the stairs confirmed that his intuition had served him well. He let the first gangbanger fly past him, push open the door, and rush into the lobby. The second gangbanger wasn't so lucky. His face caught the full force of Brad's helmet on the end of a home-run swing. He flipped backwards down the stairs to the tune of some disgusting cracking and crunching before he came to a stop on the landing.

Realizing his mistake, the first gangbanger came rushing back into the stairway and suffered the fate of his inanimate partner. He ran into the full force of Brad's helmet on the end of his second home-run swing. The dude did not go down immediately. Just stood there immobile, out on his feet. An axe chop with the helmet to the top of his head brought him to his knees. He fell forward onto the stairs.

Brad threw him down to the landing on top of his partner, donned his helmet, and shot down to the parking lot. He stepped into the light for a split second, then did a forward roll to the nearest car. He waited and listened. No movement. No sound. Pretty sure he was alone, he crept toward his bike. The sound of the elevator told him that he would soon have company. He jumped on the bike, cranked it, and careened up the exit ramp.

Out on the highway, Brad was trying to make sense of what had just gone down. He figured that Ranger had the Papachristou house under surveillance and picked him up when he went over there. They'd followed him on the underground to his hotel. He cursed himself for letting his guard down. Once they knew his address, a small tip at the reception desk would have been enough to get his room number and license plate information.

Then it hit him. If there were two guys watching his motorcycle, there must have been others keeping an eye on the hotel entrance.

That was who was in the elevator when he got away. Maybe…

He checked his rearview just in time. A big Bentley was bearing down on him. He couldn't outrun it, and traffic was thin. He took the first off-ramp, ran a red light, and cut down a side street.

The Bentley was right behind. Another couple of side streets took him to a dead end and the entrance to a park, too small for a car. He cut in and drove a hundred yards up the hill. A car door slammed. The car sped off.

He turned off his headlight. He figured that he had a guy on foot behind him and that the car had gone to block him at the other end of the park. Right again! The Bentley was waiting when he got to the other exit.

To the right was a sign for Saint Mary's Church Cemetery at the entrance to a well-worn footpath. He cut in. Drove to the back and laid his bike down behind a tombstone. Tall trees with drooping branches swaying in the breeze cast menacing shadows roaming around the graves. Gave him some cover as he sneaked back to the entrance. He waited. A car door slammed. It was the Bentley. Now there were two of them out and on the prowl.

He fingered his Beretta. If he had to shoot, the sound would wake up the whole neighborhood and attract a lot of unhelpful attention. Best to avoid it if possible, but if the gangbangers had firearms, he would have no choice. Firearms in the UK were even more of a no-no than firearms in France.

He did have a choice. The first gangbanger creeping up the footpath was holding a knife. Brad pocketed his Beretta and grabbed his helmet. Went on the attack.

The gangbanger was fast. He dodged and slashed. Drew blood on Brad's shoulder. Brad parried the next thrust with his helmet and followed with a front kick to the knee. Only partially successful. The gangbanger cursed and struck again.

Brad brought his helmet down on the knife hand, slipped to the right, and drove his elbow into the gangbanger's cheek. Swung back to the left with his helmet and caught the gangbanger on the back of the head. The gangbanger dropped the knife. Fell to his knees. Brad scooped up the knife and drove it into the gangbanger's neck.

Gangbanger number two was charging. Brad rolled to his right. Came up on his feet. Number two charged again. Slashed. Got some ribs, but Brad's roundhouse was already launched.

The dude never saw it coming. Caught him on the temple. Staggered him long enough for Brad to throw a side kick to the knee. Number two screamed. Grabbed his leg and perished as Brad drove the knife into his throat.

The show was over. Time to exit, stage left. Brad went for his bike. A flashing blue light on the street told him the cops had arrived.

Chapter 43

LATE MAY 1975, ISLAND OF JERSEY

It seemed like a blast from the past. There on the modest fishing boat stood the huge mountain of a bearded man still garbed in what was once a beautifully embroidered blue gentleman's jacket. His voice was still deep and gruff. "Brad James and his woman! It's a sight for sore eyes." His manner was friendly, and the light Irish lilt lent the touch of sincerity Brad had been hoping for.

"Indeed it is, Blackie."

The giant beamed when Samantha said hello. He jumped onto the dock and tenderly took her small hand into his gnarled paw. "Lord be praised for the pleasures he provides. Your presence is a godsend, lovely lady." A short bow. "At your service."

Samantha loved it. This confirmed it for her. Blackie was a human charm machine.

"Have you traveled to Jersey lately?" asked Brad.

"Can't say that I have, and can't say that I've missed it, either."

Brad lifted his rucksack. "There are ten thousand reasons in this bag to make you miss it."

Blackie broke into a beaming smile and a big belly laugh. "I'm already startin' to wax nostalgic, lad. When do we go?"

"As soon as can get your shrimper seaworthy."

"This is a sea ship worthy of whales, and it's always ready to ride the waves. Are we talkin' the same place as before?"

"Any chance of you getting us in closer to town?"

"We're not leavin' it to chance, lad. It's the good Lord that'll guide us." Blackie ushered them onto the boat, gave the signal to his matelots, and they weighed anchor.

Brad was a landlubber, but the sea held no fears for him. Samantha, on the other hand, had proven herself susceptible to seasickness. This time, she'd had the foresight to bring some pills with her. The sea was calm, the stars were bright, and the moon was on the rise. Brad put his arm around her waist. She leaned into him. They didn't need to speak. They just enjoyed.

When the lights of Saint Helier appeared, Blackie came on deck. "We'll be landin' soon. You'll be goin' ashore in a spot popular with young lovers." A theatrical wave of his hand. "I'll be bettin' you'll know how to play it." He checked his watch. "I'll be back for you at midnight. If you're not there, a few thousand more reasons could convince me to come back two hours later."

"It's a deal." Brad feared he might need that option.

A rowboat took them the last four hundred yards to lovers' lane. Brad had the good sense to take off his shoes and roll up his pants before exiting the boat. Samantha took off her sneakers. She was dressed in her Smith alter ego black sports outfit and could neither take off her leotards nor roll them up. They would just have to get wet.

They crossed the beach and climbed to a grassy knoll surrounded by tall trees. Samantha whispered, "We can wait here until the sun comes up. St. Helier is just a hop, skip, and jump down the road."

A cranky voice broke the silence. "Who goes there?"

They had decided that Samantha would do all the talking since her English accent would attract less attention. "Who's asking?"

"Conrad, the gatekeeper. All is well?"

"All is well."

"Cheers."

"Cheers."

*   *   *

Crowcroft's office was a three-story house near the town hall. They decided that Samantha would be the one to pitch him. She was unknown and unlikely to draw attention. The meeting was set for 10:00 a.m.

Brad waited at the rendezvous point by the beach. When Samantha didn't show up by midday, he began to worry. When one o'clock rolled around and she was still not there, he was anticipating a catastrophe. He moved to where he could observe the rendezvous point as well as the approach to the rendezvous point and waited. At 2:00 p.m., she was still not there. It was time to go into action.

He carefully checked out his surroundings for the nth time. There was absolutely nothing suspicious or out of the ordinary. No overzealous street cleaners or repairmen. Nobody loitering around. No vans or cars with tinted windows.

He was headed back to the town hall when a familiar image way down the street caught his eye. Samantha.

He went back and waited in the cover of his vantage point. Samantha reached the rendezvous point. Stopped. Signaled with folded hands that she wanted Brad to check she was not being followed.

After thirty minutes of her strolling around Saint Helier and him trying fruitlessly to spot some surveillance, he called off the exercise and approached her. "What's going on?"

She took his hand and continued her promenade. "Crowcroft convinced me that I should go to lunch with him. He said his activities were under intense surveillance by any number of clients, competitors, governments, and tax authorities and my appearance would have them all scrambling around trying to figure out what I was up to. Unless…"

"Unless what?"

"Unless they thought I was his new paramour. He said he had a 'well-deserved reputation as a ladies' man.' A cozy head-to-head lunch would label me as just another conquest. Made sense, so I went to lunch with him."

Brad took a deep drag off his Gitane and congratulated her with the admonition, "Don't improvise like that too often. My heart can't take it. I was sure something had happened to you. How did everything turn out?"

"Fine. He can get the proof of beneficial ownership, and the price is right." But Brad sensed her heart was not in it. "We have a meeting tonight at 10:00 down at the marina to make the exchange."

Brad agreed that 10:00 was just perfect—gave them enough time to get to the scheduled meeting with Blackie's boat but not have to wait around too long.

"Do you trust him?"

"He's a lawyer, Brad." She shook her head in disgust. "Of course I don't trust him."

They went to reconnoiter the designated meeting point. It was at the very end of the marina bordered by water on three sides. There was only one way in or out. Definitely not a place you want to be with a hundred thousand dollars in a rucksack and all kids of spy creatures creeping around.

*   *   *

At 8:30, Brad settled into his vantage point atop the tree-covered ruins of a medieval townhouse. From here, he could see the entire marina and the surrounding walkways and roads. At 10:00 sharp, Crowcroft arrived with his bodyguard and went straight to the meeting point at the end of the marina. At five after ten, Samantha arrived. She stopped at the entrance and signaled the two men to come forward. They declined and signaled her to come to the meeting point.

After several rounds of this signal sparring, Crowcroft and his bodyguard relented and came forward. They met Samantha and set off away from the marina toward the nook, where the money would be stashed. The discussion was animated. Probably because Samantha did not have the money with her and was making them take a long walk to retrieve it.

Brad had it and would place it in the site he and Samantha had chosen to protect them in case of a double-cross.

From his observation post, Brad saw two men in dark suits exit a car parked on the street running by the marina. They picked up the group of Samantha, Crowcroft, and the bodyguard and followed a safe distance behind.

Brad was thanking his lucky stars they had been prudent and taken precautions. He slipped out of his observation post and slid down the embankment, where he placed the rucksack behind the wall of the ruins he had been using as an observation post. He walked a block down the street and took up a position with line-of-sight to the wall.

Samantha and Crowcroft went behind the wall while the bodyguard stood guard outside. Crowcroft counted the money. Samantha verified the documents and secured them in the waterproof compartment of her rucksack.

Less than five minutes later, Crowcroft came out with the rucksack and disappeared with his bodyguard. The two dark suits took their cue and moved in on Samantha behind the wall. She had seen them coming.

Swinging from a crossbeam, Samantha's feet came down hard on the first dark suit coming around the corner. He stumbled and attempted a counterattack. She rotated back, changed her grip, and flew forward feetfirst into his unprotected face. He went down, and she landed on top of him with her knee in his gut. He was out for the count.

Brad was on the second dark suit before he had time to react. A long front kick to the back brought him to his knees. A side kick to the neck laid him out. Brad was afraid he had broken his neck. Fear confirmed. No pulse and no breath. The verdict was in. He was dead.

The first dark suit was coming to his senses just as Brad finished tying up his hands. "Not too tight, I hope."

"Fuck you."

The guy was American. There wasn't much time for discussion. Brad was going to have to improvise. The sidewalks were empty, but Samantha was keeping watch just in case.

Dark Suit tried to get to his feet. Brad slapped him down. "I want some answers."

"Fuck you."

Brad turned to the body of the second dark suit, grabbed the guy's neck, and with a theatrical flourish snapped it again. Of course, the dude was already dead, but the first dark suit didn't know that. And now he wanted to talk. "I've got answers, man. What do you want to know?"

Brad found out they were Ranger's men. There were more of them in town, in Paris and in London. They all had his picture. They all had the order to bring Brad James to Ranger Wilde. There was a big bounty on his head.

Brad shifted his attention to Samantha and Crowcroft's information. In that split second of inattention, Dark Suit jumped to his feet in an acrobatic exploit that surprised even Samantha. He executed an impressive backflip, his right foot catching Brad's chin on the way up.

Brad was stunned. Dark Suit went for Samantha. She slid underneath his spinning roundhouse kick. Came up behind him with a pointed rock that she buried deep into his brain.

Car doors slamming and voices on the street announced the arrival of more gangbangers. Brad pointed to the embankment leading to his lookout post. Samantha scrambled up the slope like a frisky mountain goat. Brad was close behind.

The gangbangers were having a problem figuring out what had happened. Brad and Samantha took advantage to get far enough away to feel safe. They had more than an hour to get to their rendezvous with Blackie's boat.

They went first to the tree-covered knoll from where they could scope out the beach scene. Nothing to report. The beach was deserted and the rowboat and matelot were there waiting. They broke cover and ran for the boat. They jumped into the boat just as lights from the highway behind the beach announced the arrival of some traffic.

The matelot grabbed the oars and began to row. Slamming doors and flashing lights coming from the highway shattered the silence. Brad turned to see six men racing down the dunes toward the beach. He heard the shots, but the gangbangers were too far away to cause any damage. That wouldn't last for long. They could run faster than the sailor could row. He pushed Samantha down, then crouched down himself.

The shots were getting closer. Brad saw the sailor slump down over the oars. He had taken a bullet to the shoulder. The waves were driving the rowboat toward the beach, and Blackie's fishing boat was three hundred yards out to sea.

There was no choice. Brad took Samantha's hand. "Swim for it."

Samantha slipped over the side and set out for the fishing boat on a strong, steady crawl. Brad threw the sailor over the side and jumped in behind. He cupped his right hand under the sailor's chin and started side-stroking it for the fishing boat. It was going to be a long swim. He was also hoping that the gangbangers had not brought their swimsuits. He started to worry when he made out the buzzing of an approaching motorboat.

Chapter 44

LATE MAY 1975, PARIS

Gary wanted all the details. Brad explained that once they had abandoned the rowboat and started to swim for it, they were all but invisible from the beach. The gangbangers continued shooting indiscriminately in the direction of the drifting rowboat, but the shots were nowhere near endangering them. Brad told him he thought they were goners when he saw the motorboat bearing down on them, splashing around in the water. His relief was boundless when he recognized Blackie at the helm.

Back on the fishing boat, Blackie gave Brad a powerful pat on the back. He had saved his sailor. "Yer earnin' yer place in paradise, laddie," he declared. "I'll be puttin' my thumb on the scale when the good Lord is weighin' yer good deeds."

There was no doubt in Brad's mind that Crowcroft had betrayed them. It wasn't really a double-cross. Crowcroft had honored his end of the deal and delivered the information Brad had requested and paid for. All Crowcroft did was make a side deal with the gangbangers about the time and place of the meeting.

Brad hadn't explicitly ruled out a traitorous side deal in their negotiations. In fact, it had never even occurred to him. He naively figured it was a given. Crowcroft was a lawyer and a businessman. He did deals. As a businessman, he had a reputation for scrupulously respecting the terms of every deal. As a lawyer, he had a reputation for concealing ambushes in the fine print. The fine print in Brad's deal had not ruled out sharing the rendezvous point with the gangbangers. That was how Brad tried to rationalize the fact that Crowcroft had tried to screw him twice. The third time, Brad would do the screwing.

Brad concluded it was blind bad luck the gangbangers had surprised them on the beach. They were probably just driving up and down the coast looking for something suspicious. They hit pay dirt when they saw the rowboat heading for Blackie's fishing boat.

Brad had studiously omitted mentioning Samantha's role in the adventure. Samantha wanted to remain out of the picture, and Brad saw no compelling reason to paint her in. He almost screwed up and spilled the beans several times, but Gary was too engrossed in the information Brad had delivered to notice.

At first, Gary refused to believe it. How could Alvin P. Dearman, the long-serving deputy director of the CIA, be a traitorous spy? The ramifications were limitless. The potential consequences devastating—for Gary, for Brad, for the CIA, for the country.

Brad argued the evidence he had obtained from Crowcroft was undeniable. The El Gordo account had one source of income— documented payments from the agent of a foreign government, Mario Irigoyen, in exchange for classified top secret information on the U.S. government. It had one beneficial recipient: Alvin P. Dearman.

Combined with other evidence, such as Dearman's surprising decision that the agent who initially discovered the security breach was actually the traitor, his refusal to consider the proof that Senator Jake Brown was selling classified information to the same foreign agent paying into his El Gordo account, his support for the assassination squad, his rush to discredit Brad and Chuck, the agents who had unearthed the proof against Brown, all this contributed to one obvious conclusion. Alvin P. Dearman was the traitor.

Brad also argued that meticulous reinvestigation of other past security glitches would surely point more fingers at Alvin P. Dearman. Gary had no choice but to accept the obvious. The looming dilemma for Gary was what to do about it.

Gary massaged his eyes and reached for a sugar cube. He dipped and ate. Shook his head and wrang his hands. His eyes were bloodshot. His shoulders slumped. "I just cannot get my head around this. It's overwhelming. Who would believe it?"

Brad said, "I believe it. And I'm hard to convince. We have to decide on how to proceed."

"That's just it, Brad. What are the choices? We could go through regular channels. Of course, that's a nonstarter. Dearman would kill the story along with us. We could go public, but that would make us look like disgruntled troublemakers and probably end up as a he-said-she-said stalemate and an end to our careers, if not our lives."

"Isn't there an oversight committee or something like that?"

"Yeah, we could try that with the politicians in Congress, maybe. We'd still be whistleblowers, and the politicians are even less reliable than the journalists. It's a symbiotic relationship. One hand washes the other. We have to think about whether we want to risk our necks."

Brad had already made up his mind on that. His reputation and future were on the line. The problem was to find a solution that did not conflict directly with the Company and all the players and institutions that depended on it for their well-being. He finally had to accept that fighting City Hall was a losing strategy. They had to find a way to work *with* City Hall.

Brad said, "We can go over Dearman's head. William Colby is the director of the CIA. He's Dearman's boss."

"Colby would never agree to that." Gary was unambiguous.

"I don't mean like a direct appeal to Colby against Dearman. Look, Colby's under pressure from Congress and the media to adopt a more open policy about U.S. intelligence activities. There's the Senate Church Committee and the House Pike Committee. We can use those investigations to justify a presentation to Colby."

"Be more specific."

Brad's brain was rocking along at full speed. His eyes were shining, and he was grinning the grin. "Something along these lines. One of our team has been contacted by a committee about testifying. When Colby says this is Dearman's remit and asks why we're coming to him and not going directly to Dearman, we say the testimony is about Dearman."

Gary shook his head. "Not gonna fly. No credibility. Who would be a plausible person the committee would contact? Surely not me. I have absolutely no official knowledge about the Papachristou affair. Remember, I was removed from the investigation. Surely neither you nor Chuck. You also were officially removed from the investigation."

"How about Madison?"

"She's been fingered as a traitor and suspended."

"No, she hasn't. She's officially on vacation. Says she has proof that Dearman forced her to change her original report to accuse her subordinate of the treason and then forced her to participate in Ranger's cover-up activities."

The astonishment brought Gary back to life. "What are you talking about?"

"Telling it like it is. I talked to her. Dearman set her up. She's in town, and she's burning with anger—to put it mildly."

"Has a committee contacted her?"

Brad raised his eyebrows, and gave Gary the exasperated how-can-you-be-so-naïve look. "Of course not. But Colby doesn't have to know that. And Madison will go along if anyone asks. Like I said, she's one wrathful woman, burning with anger and hungry for revenge."

Gary relaxed. He looked pleased. His voice was strong. "I think you've got something there. Leave it to me. I'll have to work on my presentation and decide on the best way to approach Colby. CIA Directors are busy people. Since the committees are taking up most of his time, the best way is probably to just say I have information on the committee's activity. I'll have to talk to Madison."

"That might be easier said than done. She's in disguise and on the run. She says she's too much of a threat for Dearman to let her live. Came to Paris because she knows the terrain and because she thinks anyone Dearman has hired to take her out will be easier to recognize in Paris than his home terrain in the U.S. I personally think she's here because this is the only place she has any support."

Chapter 45

Gary's simple query to Colby's office about information on contacts with the congressional committees generated an immediate invitation to a meeting. That in itself was an optimistic eye-opener. Colby was scheduled to be in Paris the next day for an informal meeting with his French vis-à-vis and offered to stop by Gary's office afterward. Gary was surprised Colby had agreed so readily.

The meeting went like a charm. Gary had prepared his presentation carefully. It was complete and succinct. Colby spent a long time examining the documentary evidence. His questions were incisive and precise. He was a big-league pro and didn't give anything away, but Gary had the strong impression Colby was shaken.

Gary worried a little that he could somehow discover the truth about the committee's supposed contact with Madison, but it was just the bait to get Colby to bite. Once Colby saw the extent of the evidence on Dearman, whether or not he was tricked into learning about it would be a minor concern. Gary was pleased with how the meeting had gone down. A strong professional current had passed between the two men.

As he was leaving with copies of the evidence, Colby told Gary, "You know how sensitive this is. Keep it under your hat until I get back to you."

Gary took that to mean that Colby was going to give this dossier top priority. He shivered when he thought of the profound consequences Colby's handling of the matter would have, not only for the personal circumstances of all the individuals involved, but for the security of the United States and the world.

*   *   *

VIRGINIA, USA

Dearman got wind of Colby's meeting with Gary before Colby had even left Gary's office. It set his alarms flashing. Then Colby made an amateur's mistake. He asked Dearman's office for the file on Madison Samson III.

The conclusions Dearman drew were obvious to him. First of all, he was under suspicion. Secondly, Madison Samson III was a key element in the investigation that would follow. Third, Madison Samson III must have somehow escaped to Paris.

He had to find her and eliminate her. Her recordings of their meetings were loaded guns aimed directly at his heart. It was the only remaining major threat. He had closed out his Jersey accounts and moved the funds to another tax haven. If push came to shove, he could question the authenticity of the transactions as well as his knowledge of them. But there was nothing he could do to blunt an attack by Madison backed up by the recordings. He would be grass, and she would be the lawnmower.

There was also that pervert, Ranger. He worked for Jake as well as him, and he knew that Dearman was in cahoots with Jake.

Ranger, however, was like the abominable snowman—often discussed, rarely seen, never captured. He signed for nothing. He had no foreign income or accounts. Both he and Jake paid him into his unique U.S. account. All his other income from his investment consulting was paid into this account. Nothing there. His role as leader of the gangbangers could be a problem, but it could easily be dismissed as misconceived hearsay. He did not live with the gangbangers. He did not ride with the gangbangers. He was careful to never be present at any of their illegal operations. And, perhaps most importantly, most of his gang was in a foreign jail or dead and buried. Only Madison Samson III could link Ranger to the gangbangers.

The pressing problem, then, was to find and eliminate little Miss Madison Samson III. All this time, he had been searching in the wrong place. She was in Paris. With her out of the way and the traitor in the Soviet embassy, his story of their conspiracy would be bulletproof.

There were some minor loose ends that might need attention, depending on how things panned out. Greta Papachristou was one of them. There had been some activity at her residence in London. He was not sure what it was, but the interloper got away from Ranger's men. Security would have to be tightened up to keep that from happening again. Otherwise, there was no way to get to her without missiles, tanks, and a small army. Dearman would have a word with her father. He was one of Dearman's most reliable sources of information.

The two pesky part-timers in Paris could also be a problem. The treason charges against them wouldn't be enough to get them out of the way or keep them quiet, especially if they were allowed to testify. They were popping up all over the place, and they claimed to have eyewitnesses to some of Ranger's assassinations.

Dearman decided to contact Ranger Wilde and instruct him to use his network to find Madison Samson III and make her and her tapes disappear along with James and Hall, the two troublesome part-timers.

That left the encounter Ranger's men had in Jersey with the beautiful dark-haired woman with an English accent who met with Crowcroft, asked questions about Jake Brown, and killed two of Ranger's best men. He had run checks in France, the UK, and the U.S. She was not on the radar.

Crowcroft had been extremely clear. Dearman's name had not been mentioned. The query was about that windbag Brown. If that was the extent of the contact—and there was no evidence to the contrary—Dearman had nothing to fear. Crowcroft had guaranteed that the information he had provided was worthless. As a master manipulator, Dearman knew that a high price for worthless information would bring the buyer back for a refund and revenge.

He recognized Crowcroft as a pure profit-inspired businessman and did not trust him. He would have his men keep a close eye on Crowcroft to see if the buyer did come back. If she didn't, he would know that Crowcroft had lied.

The information wasn't worthless. The question, then, would be whether or not Dearman's financial interests had been compromised. Highly unlikely. Close to impossible, even. Better to be certain. He considered having Crowcroft interrogated but dismissed the idea as counterproductive for the moment. This was not the right time to draw attention to the offshore financial center of Jersey.

His next step was to start some rumors. Sow seeds of doubt.

Chapter 46

"I laid the case out," Gary said. "Dearman used his privileged position to gather marketable intelligence. He passed it onto Senator Jake Brown. Jake Brown used his close relationship with Perón to sell the information. Jake Brown's intermediary was Ranger Wilde. Perón's intermediary was Mario Irigoyen. Wilde and Irigoyen would have regular rendezvous where Wilde would deliver the information and Irigoyen would deliver two cashier's checks for the agreed amount. Wilde would deliver the checks to Georges Papachristou. Perón then sold the information on to his cronies in other countries. Papachristou deposited the checks in the Junior and El Gordo accounts. From the information we have, it looks like the split was 70/30. Seventy percent of the amount was the check deposited into El Gordo, Dearman's account, and thirty percent was the check deposited into Junior, Jake Brown's account. Mittel managed these accounts."

"Simple, economical, and secure," Brad said. "What was Colby's reaction?" That was what interested him.

"He asked a lot of questions and wanted to see proof. He was concerned, but noncommittal. It did surprise me how much he knew about the Papachristou murder and the events in Paris. He took notes when I gave him my analysis."

Chuck chimed in, "What was your analysis?"

"I told him that the foolproof system they had in place blew up when Perón died and his intermediary, Irigoyen, got overthrown. They feared that Irigoyen would use his knowledge of the scam as a bargaining chip to save his life. Unfortunately for them, he got away before they could eliminate him, and he managed to communicate evidence of the espionage to Papachristou. Papachristou was next guy up the chain who also had evidence of the security breach. So they took him out and made it look like suicide, even though he was a high-ranking agent."

"Do you think he was in on the deal?"

Gary sighed and shook his head. "I doubt it. Papachristou probably did not know the source of the money he was depositing into the Junior and El Gordo accounts. When he found out, he passed evidence of the espionage up the line to the agent who was accused as the traitor. He wouldn't have done that and would still be alive if he were in on it. Anyway, the chain was broken by Papachristou's death. Madison was sent to Paris with orders to make sure that the chain was completely broken. The pictures appeared and the rest is history."

"Yeah, that's when Madison went from an innocent investigator into an active participant in the cover-up."

Gary turned to Chuck. "It's interesting you'd say that. Colby said the same thing. He said that either she did that to cover her own tracks, or she was under orders and unwittingly compromised herself to cover up for the real culprit."

"You told him that she was on the run from the real culprit, Dearman?"

"I did, and he said, 'That remains to be seen.'"

"What about us?" Brad asked. He and Chuck were unmentioned so far in the analysis.

Gary was ready for this question and brightened up as he answered. "I managed to keep you out of it as much as possible. No offense intended, but you guys would be considered low-value losses. Put into context, that means that if you can be blamed for anything, you will be blamed. Just like in the army, the buck stops with the lowest rank. The less said about you, the better. Colby is a CIA man. He's also a politician and a prominent member of the establishment. When he makes his decisions, his very last priority will be theoretical justice. He will worry about the effect on the CIA as an institution and what is best for the country. Establishment men often confuse 'best for country' with 'best for themselves' and/or 'best for the establishment.' In mathematical terms, this means that he will maximize the welfare of the CIA, the establishment, and himself with a weak constraint of theoretical justice. In laymen's terms, it means that he will find every reason he can imagine to limit the punishment of these two worthless traitors to a secret slap on the wrist."

Chuck was starting to get worked up. He was clenching his fists and squinting at Gary. "This is a big load of contented cow manure."

Brad cut him off. "No, Gary's right. In Colby's scheme of things, we're nothing more than background noise. This is bad. We can't be perceived as enemies of the establishment. At the moment, we're accused of being traitors because we dug up the info on the offshore accounts. As Gary never ceases to say, 'You can't fight City Hall.' Let's try and make ourselves disappear as background noise. We can spin the story about how the offshore accounts were discovered. We can say Madison ordered it. They'll believe it. She's already a suspect. Squelch the treason accusation. Get ourselves back onto the establishment train. Then we can see what Colby does. Whatever it is, both Dearman and Brown will be in weaker positions than they are now."

Chuck was reluctant, but he agreed. With a caveat. "We can't wait too long. It'll be too late once the game's over and the fat lady sings."

Gary interrupted. "There is something more pressing. I have to warn you. Somehow, Dearman found out that Madison is in Paris. He has sent one of his top black-op teams to track her down. Most pressing and more worrying, the black-op team has two other unnamed targets."

That was a mind-blowing conversation stopper. Brad and Chuck exchanged glances. Brad made it public. "So you're saying Chuck and I—the valueless, low-on-the-totem-pole, background-noise boys—are the 'unnamed' targets of the CIA's top assassination team?"

Gary hung his head like a whipped dog. "Yeah. Can't explain it."

"Any idea of who these guys are? Description? Anything?"

"Just hearsay. The leader is charming, handsome, a great athlete, elegant, epicurean, speaks five languages fluently, has pulled off some impossible exploits. In short, he's a legend. Nothing on the others."

"Stop there, Gary," Chuck said with a sneer. "It'll be easier if I go out and buy Ian Fleming's books." Chuck had gone head-to-head with all the North Vietnamese "legends." He knew that the reality rarely matched the myth.

Brad was more pragmatic. "Where did this info come from?"

"Some of the guys back at Langley. It's just a rumor. Don't know where it started. Might have no truth to it."

Brad fired up a Gitane and started blowing smoke rings. Finished off his coffee. Looked at Gary. "Whether it's true or not, we have to take the rumor seriously. Make it difficult for these guys to find us. Chuck and I are still in hideout mode. I'm on vacation from the Barbary for another two weeks, and Chuck has a secret apartment somewhere. I'm renting a room and rarely accessing my apartment. When I do, it's from a secret entrance. Madison is even more secure. She's holed up somewhere under an assumed name. The only starting point for the assassins is the embassy, and you're the only link to any of us. If this guy is half as good as his reputation, you and your big redhead will probably not be able to lose him. Can't take a chance. So all meetings are off. We communicate through drop-offs one through five. If we need more drop-offs, we start over again with the same one through five. Agreed?"

They all agreed, and Gary took off. When he left the building, a pair of soft dark eyes in a handsome face observed him from the café across the street.

Chapter 47

Brad and Chuck decided it would be wise to keep their meetings to a minimum and communicate by phone. Their phones were registered to other people and the risk was low.

Chuck was the first to leave. A pair of soft, dark eyes in a handsome face watched him from the café across the street. When Brad left the building, he set out toward the metro and saw a good-looking guy observing him from the terrace of the café. It was something in his eyes. Gave him the creeps.

He took the metro deep in thought. The black-ops team could be a big threat. It would have the advantage of knowing a lot about them. They knew nothing about the black-ops except legendary hearsay—most of which might have been invented on purpose to throw adversaries off the trail.

Brad left the metro at Havre-Caumartin and went into Au Printemps to get some socks and underpants. He also had to take a leak. As he was exiting the men's room, he caught a doe-eyed guy observing him from across the room. Gave him the creeps—for the second time in one day. That set his alarm off.

After making his purchases, he took the elevator to the top floor, exited, and took the stairway back down. He would surprise anybody running up the stairs after him. There was nothing. At the fourth floor, he took the elevator down to the metro level. Believing he was clean, he wanted to make sure and spent the best part of the next hour hopping from metro to bus to boutique to boutique.

Back at Samantha's, he called Chuck. "I think I might have seen one of the black ops. The only thing I can tell you is that he's creepy looking. Can't be sure, but I think he picked me up at the safe house. Must have followed Gary. Stay cool. I've got a plan."

*   *   *

LEVALLOIS-PERRET 92

For the third day, Edith was at the café by the safe house bright and early, ivory-handled walking stick by her side, Gitane between her lips, cup of espresso in her hand. Brad told her to be on the lookout for a doe-eyed dude who looked like a weirdo. Her job was to get a picture of him.

To this end, Brad had supplied her with a camera hidden in a decorated cardboard box. All she had to do was aim the box and push the button. Brad warned her emphatically, "Do *not* get greedy and try to follow him. He is a dangerous assassin."

Her answer was, "Goddamn weirdo assassins. Had 'em comin' outta my ears. Half the bosh Nazis were weirdo assassins. The other half were perverts."

Edith had hobbled around the area every day before going to the café. Nice area. Lots of young preppie families bustling around mixed with lots of oldies sitting in the park soaking up the sun. She fit right in.

Brad reasoned that the safe house was the only contact point available to the black-ops team. He was sure that the black ops would spend some time hanging around trying to get lucky and spot one of their targets accessing the safe house. Edith agreed that was plausible, and she would handle it.

She handled it. There were four guys. One of them was the weird-looking guy. Sometimes they came in alone, sometimes in pairs. There was at least one of them in the café from nine in the morning until four in the afternoon. Her strategy was to spend an hour in the café in the morning, leave and do some shopping that had her pass by the café several times, go to another café down the street from where she could observe the first café, go back to the first café, run some errands, go home.

After three days of this, she had pictures of the four men she'd fingered as surveillants and was about to call it a day. In walked the doe-eyed dude. Outside of his eyes, it wasn't his looks that were weird. It was the aura emanating from his persona.

These would be Edith's last set of pictures. She fumbled around for her camera box. Put it in place. Snapped four good shots and got up to leave. Doe-eyes was watching her intently. She felt the creepiness. Maybe he had noticed something. She would make him regret it if he bothered her.

Doe-eyes strode over to her table. That irritated her. She looked him in the eye. In perfect slightly accented French, he said, *"Vous partez, Madame* (Are you leaving, ma'am)?"

Edith felt his malevolence. Made her shiver just like the Nazis did. *"Oui, petit, je te laisse la place bien chaude* (Yeah, sonny, I kept the spot warm for you)."

Chapter 48

Senator James "Jake" Brown was featured on all the news programs: ABC, NBC, and CBS. There he stood, microphones in his face, flapping those gills like a winded trout.

"I knew all along that there was a problem in the CIA. First, they let a traitor get away with selling our most secret information. Then they tried to cover it up to protect those responsible. Now I am hearing there is witch hunt for a scapegoat at the highest level. I will not stand for this incompetence, subterfuge, and unconstitutional activity. I am calling for transparency and accountability and an immediate end to this criminal behavior."

His bald head was glistening with perspiration, and his shaggy eyebrows were wriggling around like hairy caterpillars with each word he spoke.

One journalist shouted, "Are you involved?"

It was out of the blue, and Jake was taken completely by surprise.

He took a three-count before blasting out a blistering, "No!" and ending the conference.

Dearman switched off the TV. It was obvious that Jake and the journalists had gotten wind of Colby's investigation. Jake knew he was on the firing line.

An in-depth investigation would inevitably lead to him and his offshore accounts. The journalist's question suggested that he was already a suspect. It looked like his strategy would be deny, discredit, and attack the investigation to nip it in the bud. Might get a sale. This strategy had served him well in the past.

Dearman would have to be more nuanced, but the more Jake babbled on, the better it was for him. More attention to Jake. Less attention to him.

He had some favors to call in and some strong arguments for special treatment. The deputy director of the CIA was privy to many secrets of the high and the mighty—that is, those who would be judging him. He would know how to use those secrets.

*   *   *

PARIS

Edith's pictures revealed what Brad and Chuck were up against. One guy was Cangrejo, another Sparky, the third the doe-eyed dude, and finally, an anonymous pistolero. Edith confirmed that the doe-eyed dude was just another pistolero. So the vaunted black-ops team was composed of nothing more than the remnants of Rega's AAA pistoleros, which meant that Ranger was somewhere in the mix.

Brad figured that Ranger was the legendary "charming, handsome, a great athlete, elegant, epicurean, multi-language-speaking" agent Gary had described. The four gangbangers Edith had photographed definitely were not.

The question now was how to use the information Edith had

brought them.

She told Brad that the doe-eyed dude smelled of evil just like the Nazis. She advised him to stay away from him. Chuck wanted to go on the attack. Brad did, as well, but could see too many reasons why that would be a losing proposition.

First, and most importantly, they were outnumbered and outgunned. Second, they no longer had the backing of the U.S. establishment. On the contrary! These guys had been sent *by* the establishment.

Brad thought it was better to lie low until Colby's investigation was completed.

Gary had already managed to put the accusation of treason against them on hold. He had appealed directly to Colby, and Colby had acquiesced immediately with no discussion—probably a good sign. If Colby's investigation led to strong reprisals against Dearman and Brown, the black-ops team would no longer have any backing. They might simply go away.

Of course, Brad recognized this as wishful thinking. Ranger— and Cangrejo, to a lesser extent—had personal scores to settle. Nevertheless, at the worst, they would be crippled by their loss of government support.

Brad had met with Madison earlier in the day to give her the pictures of the team sent to hunt her down. She agreed that Brad and Chuck should keep their heads down until the conclusion of the investigation.

She said that was exactly what she was going to do even though she was a material witness for the investigation and the conviction of Dearman and Brown. Coming out to testify would be the equivalent of a death sentence before she ever got to court.

She thanked Brad for the pics and said she was going offline and not to contact her unless it was a matter of life and death. Too dangerous. She would initiate any contact from here on out.

*   *   *

Mario Irigoyen was feeling pretty chipper. His security deal with Rega was holding firm. That was indispensable, but the main reason for his good humor was that Rega was losing his control over the country. Argentina was out of foreign currency, and it would be years before the agricultural sector could correct the situation by ramping up output and increasing exports, especially of beef, their major foreign currency earner.

The "beef cycle" was at the point where producers were holding back cattle from slaughter in order to increase herd size. Prices were sky-high, and output could still barely meet local demand, much less leave anything over to export. No Argentine politician, not even the great Juan Perón, had survived this kind of predicament. Mario figured his return to the Argentine political scene was imminent.

There would be a struggle with the generals, but Mario was counting on Isabela to put them in their place and open the door to him and the leftists. His dealings with Cangrejo had been increasingly cordial as Rega's position weakened. He congratulated himself on having been able to avoid angering the Americans and supplying evidence that would have contradicted their narrative about the "traitor."

He'd had to sacrifice Brad James on the altar of a goodwill gesture to prove his sincerity to Rega. But even that hadn't turned out too badly. James had managed to turn the tables on Cangrejo and sic the French on the AAA. He would have given anything to see that.

It was time to start his comeback. In his next meeting with

Cangrejo, he would begin negotiating the guidelines and outlining the things he and the AAA could accomplish together. He would also have to meet with Ranger Wilde.

*   *   *

Ranger Wilde was unhappy. He shouldn't have been. He was sitting in the catbird's seat, right where he always wanted to be. The deputy director of the CIA, Alvin P. Dearman, needed him to hunt down and eliminate the "loose ends" threatening Dearman's freedom.

United States Senator James "Jake" Brown needed him to liaise with Argentine strongman José Lopez Rega to protect his anonymity and maintain the lucrative information/access business with Rega. Rega needed him for that as well, but most of all, he needed Ranger to keep an eye on Mario Irigoyen, a threatening rival. Mario Irigoyen needed him to stay alive.

The source of Ranger Wilde's unhappiness was Brad James, the guy who'd killed his soulmate and lifelong lover. The guy who was responsible for tipping off the authorities about the Papachristou murder and the espionage arrangement deal with Perón. The guy who'd blasted his new gang, the AAA, to smithereens. Brad James was still alive when he should be dead. The showboating American was en route for a painful death.

Chapter 49

LATE MAY 1975, WASHINGTON, DC, USA

The sun was out. The birds were chirping. The bees were buzzing. Washington was in bloom, and Alvin P. Dearman was still calling the shots. He took a sip of his marguerita, leaned back in his dining chair on the garden terrace of his favorite restaurant, and smirked the satisfied smirk of a serial scammer celebrating the improbable success of his most daring hoax.

His sessions with William Colby, CIA director and his superior officer, had been uncomfortable and antagonistic. Dearman was fighting for his life. Colby was fighting for his career. Colby's evidence was incontrovertible proof that Dearman had been betraying his country for at least the last five years. It was all there in black and white. Yet Dearman had managed to turn the evidence to his advantage.

He began by reminding Colby that they were in the business of manipulation and deceit. He brought up memos and reports congratulating him on past devious plots to manipulate and deceive a long list of enemies as well as friends.

"Bill," Dearman said, "manipulation and deceit is my job. I've been doing it for over thirty years and I do it better than anyone else. What you have there is just another one of my most successful schemes."

William Colby knew bullshit when he smelled it, but he could see that Dearman was arguing from a position of principal. It was Washington's "panacea principal," the principal of plausible denial. There was no record of Dearman having initiated what he claimed was a disinformation scheme. In fact, just the opposite was true. Dearman had gone to great lengths to keep the scheme secret. Dearman claimed that the sensitivity of the scheme required total secrecy—plausible denial.

When Colby inquired about the proceeds from this super-secret, super-sensitive scheme, Dearman replied that it had gone into an account that he used to make secret payments to his super-secret agents—no proof of that, but plausible denial. When Colby pointed out that the agent who had been fingered as the traitor was actually completely innocent, Dearman replied that the agent had to be sacrificed for credibility—collateral damage for plausible denial.

This was how it went for the whole interview. There was an argument for plausible denial for almost every point Colby raised. For the minor points that had no element of plausible denial, such as fingering Brad, Chuck, and Madison as traitors, Dearman wrapped himself in the mantle of humility and admitted that his zeal had perhaps driven him to go overboard.

At the end of the interview, Dearman knew that he'd checkmated Colby. He also knew that testimony by Madison and the two part-time pests in Paris could undermine his defense based on Washinton's panacea principle of plausible denial. It only worked when everyone in the system would be better off by business as usual. If trying to maintain the false façade became too costly, such as credible evidence and witnesses to the contrary, those with the most to lose would abandon ship with the rest of the rats. Conclusion: Madison and the two Parisian pests had to go. He was confident that Ranger would see to that.

*   *   *

MCLEAN, VIRGINIA, USA

Senator James "Jake" Brown was comfortably ensconced in the padded leather armchair of his paneled drawing room. His shoes were off and there was a tumbler filled to the brim with Southern Comfort on the end table beside him. There, on the wide-screen TV, he saw himself featured on CBS news. A gaggle of journalists were thrusting microphones in his face. Pious as the pope, his bushy brows were caterpilling around as he sanctimoniously sermonized on the state of the nation.

"We are at the crossroads of our democracy. There are enemies all around us. There are traitors in our midst. We are allowing our enemies and these traitors to corrupt our institutions and run rampant over our beloved country. We have a traitor in the Soviet embassy down the street. He should be jailed and put to death. Yet here he is in interviews on national news shows, footloose and fancy-free, claiming his innocence and accusing our loyal leaders and civil servants who sacrifice their lives to the service of their country, of corruption and betrayal. This is unacceptable. This cannot be allowed. I am unbending. My love for this country is too strong. I will not stop until this traitor and all his cohorts are brought to justice."

Jake was mildly pleased. He gave himself an eight out of ten. He could have focused his penetrating gaze more effectively, and his wording could have been improved, but all in all, he was still crushing it.

A small sip of Southern Comfort set him to analyzing his interview with William Colby. Colby had been named CIA director, whose mission was to adopt a more open policy about U.S. intelligence activities through collaboration with the Senate Church Committee and the House Pike Committee. He was in one of those rock-and-a-hard-place, devil-and-the-deep-blue-sea positions. His mission was to take action against the very agency he was heading. He would be reporting to politicians who were posturing for transparency but were terrified that transparency would produce too much truth and poison their under-the-table double-dealings. None of them would take kindly to Colby doing his job as described. Jake was one of these.

What did Colby have on him? He had some bank records showing that Jake had some shady offshore income. Washington had been rife with rumors like this about him ever since he was first elected and took his first kickback. At the time, he was new to the game and made some rookie mistakes. That asshole FBI special agent, Sam Smith, spotted them and almost ruined it for him. Jake's sons had handled that one, and this episode taught him how to deal with criminal accusations. You deny. You kill your accuser. You stonewall on providing evidence. You attack the system and you paint yourself the victim. If you scream loud enough and long enough, your adversaries eventually tire of the conflict and slowly drift away, leaving you free to proclaim victory and the moral high ground. It was a recipe that had never failed.

This time would be no different. He was one of the most powerful members of the Senate. No one would want to cross him. He denied everything Colby presented to him. He demanded a list of witnesses and accusers. Denied. But he knew they included Perón's intermediary and some anonymous elements of the CIA.

He already knew, however, that his main target was Irigoyen, and he had already made the deal to have him eliminated. Ranger would identify and eliminate the remaining anonymous elements from the CIA.

*　　　　　*　　　　　*

PARIS

Mario was starting to relax, but he couldn't stop thinking about trains and light at the end of the tunnel. No need to get out ahead of himself. Time was on his side. His meeting with Cangrejo, the boss of Rega's AAA in Europe, had gone well and he was looking forward to many more. Ideology was not a problem. Cangrejo and his men were mercenaries. The main issue for them was money, and Mario had plenty of that from his days as chief financial officer for Perón. They smelled the end of Rega and were looking for new masters.

Mario had hesitated before revealing his hideout. He had weighed the pros and the cons. The pros won. Inviting Cangrejo into his hideout was a win-win situation. It was a strong signal of trust, and even if Cangrejo turned out to be untrustworthy, the hideout was impenetrable for all practical purposes. It would also please Rega to see Mario working with Cangrejo as evidence that their deal would be successful. The one-hundred-million-dollar Bellweather SA bank account was a powerful guarantee, especially insofar as Rega knew he would be needing that money in the near future. Finally, Mario is reassured by the knowledge that Rega does not do "personal."

Mario leaned back in his armchair in the corner of the sitting room of his studio apartment hideout on the protected fourth level of the underground parking lot. He was anxious to get outside for some fresh air. It is so quiet down here. Quieter than usual. His bodyguards were probably too tired to move. It has been a long day.

The cat he kept around to catch the occasional wayward rat was nowhere to be seen. Probably off on a hunt. Mario lit up a Cuban Cohiba and slugged back a shot of Chivas Regal. The solitude was relaxing. It was interrupted by a light tapping sound: tap-tap de tap-tap, tap-tap. In Mexico, it meant *"Chinga tu madre, cabrón* (Screw your mother, asshole)."* In Argentina, it meant the same thing.

Not funny. He left the apartment and went into the empty garage. Checked out the first aisle. The tapping picked up the pace and got louder. He looked down aisle 1. Empty. The sound was coming from the next aisle. It was louder. Faster.

Aisle 2 was empty. Tap-tap de tap-tap, tap-tap.

Mario shivered. Called out. *"Hé, cabrones. Donde estan* (Hey, assholes, where are you)?"

Waited, listened. Silence. Only the tapping, going faster and faster. He was perspiring now. And he was worried.

"Donde estan?"

No answer, and now he was really worried. The tapping was just around the corner. It stopped. He waited. A dark figure emerged from the shadows. Took form. Two innocent brown eyes, square jaw, smiling lips. A walking nightmare reeking malevolence and perversion.

Mario had nowhere to hide. Flight was his only chance. He dashed back to his studio. Doe-eyes followed, slowly tap-tap-tapping along. Inside the studio, Mario hit a button that activated the metal store that served as a door. It closed before Doe-eyes could jam it.

Doe-eyes began to pry it open with a tire iron. Mario rushed to the back corner of the studio. He flipped a switch, and a small trapdoor in the ceiling opened. He climbed onto the dressing table, used the coat peg in the wall as a step, and crawled through the trapdoor onto the third level of the underground parking lot. He managed to slam the trapdoor shut before Doe-eyes could break through the studio's metal store.

This level of the garage hosted only vehicles owned by Mario and his men. The emergency car was parked right where it should have been. The keys were on the back tire, right where they should have been. The only things missing were the guards. A closer look shows they were not missing. They were dead, stuffed in a corner. That explained how Doe-eyes had accessed his super-secure bunker.

Mario was on his own. There was a .38 under the driver's seat. He took it out, checked it. Stuck it in his belt. Cranked up the car. Drove up the exit ramp. In the rearview, he saw Doe-eyes running up from level four. Too little. Too late. Mario was out of there, on his way to another safe house.

He drove carefully. No reason to attract attention. He had heard of this doe-eyed dude. He was Rega's legendary right-hand ops man. That the dude was obviously out to kill him changed the whole basis of his analysis. He had assumed that Rega did not do personal. That is now obviously false. He had assumed that Rega's greed would keep him alive. That also was false. This new paradigm completely scrambled Mario's carefully laid plans. It also magnified his exposure because the Americans had hooked back up with Rega's men. That meant that now he had no plan, and the *gringos* after him.

Chapter 50

*J*AMES *'JAKE' BROWN THROWS HIS HAT IN THE RING.*

The headline in the *Herald Tribune* was a screamer. Brad grabbed the last copy. This, he had to read.

He paid for the paper and took a table on the terrace of la Rotonde. A thumbs-up to Jean-Pierre, the waiter, signaled he'd have his usual, a *grand café crème et deux croissants-beurre* (a big white coffee and two butter croissants).

Three bites into his first croissant and two paragraphs into the article, Brad was in stitches. Jake Brown was going to run for president. You couldn't make it up. It was hilarious—until you thought about it. Then it was terrifying. The guy was as crooked as a corkscrew. The whole country would be for sale.

Brad checked his watch. It was 11:00 a.m., about time for French philosopher Jean-Paul Sartre to go into the Dôme tobacco shop cross the street for his daily dose of nicotine. For some reason, the strange-looking man intrigued him. Brad had run into him once, literally, at the tobacco shop. He looked like a rabbit and had the breath of a bear.

Brad was watching closely as Sartre slipped into the shop, but a fleeting glimpse of the doe-eyed dude entering the Café du Dôme next door drew his attention and made him smile. They were watching Montparnasse as well as the safe house in Levallois. This was good news. His plan of drawing out the opposition was working.

Time to hustle out of there before they organized and came after him. His motorcycle was parked in front of the Barbary. When the light on Raspail turned green, he finished off his coffee and moved out.

Doe-eyes was moving as well but had to wait for the light to change in order to cross Montparnasse. Brad made it to his bike on Jules Chaplain before Doe-eyes got across Montparnasse. By the time Doe-eyes got across Raspail, Brad was long gone.

He was running late for the meeting. Gary and Chuck were waiting for him at a table in the back of the café. Chuck was radiating indignation. His mouth was set. He was scowling and mumbling under his breath. Gary was wearing his apologetic look and scarfing up sugar cubes he dipped in his coffee—a definite giveaway he was nervous. Brad ordered a *demi* at the bar and went over to the table.

Chuck was chomping at the bit. "Can you believe those rat-assed turncoats are getting a free pass and a promotion?"

Brad turned to Gary. "What?"

Gary held up his hands. "It's not that simple. Let me explain."

The explanation did nothing to alleviate the bad taste in everybody's mouth.

"It has been decided at the highest level," Gary continued, "that prosecuting Dearman and Brown would do the United States more harm than good. Dearman and Brown vowed to fight the charges. They are longtime high-ranking public servants. They have plausible arguments. They have supporters. It would be a political fiasco. Our country's international reputation would be damaged beyond repair. As would the reputation of the CIA and its ability to protect America from its foreign enemies."

"Correction," suggested Brad. "Our country's politicians' and bureaucrats' reputations would be damaged beyond repair."

"Yeah, that too. Dearman has agreed to resign at the end of the year, but Brown is elected. He is unapologetic, and he is untouchable unless he's publicly accused. He has been appointed to head the Congressional Committee on National Security."

"How about Dearman?"

The words lodged in Gary's throat. "He has been named as presidential advisor on national security."

Chuck was fuming. Brad looked down and shook his head. It couldn't get any more ridiculous. The fox was guarding the henhouse. Getting mad was a waste of energy—energy he would save and use to get even. "So they're going to walk and get promoted."

Gary tried a little spin. "It's not all bad. We know who they are. We'll keep an eye on them. Identify their contacts. Feed them false information."

"You know that's not going to happen, Gary. Brown has already reactivated the arrangement he had with Perón. He can do some real damage if he's head of the Congressional Committee on National Security."

"I'll have to look into that."

"Look into this, as well." Brad flipped the *Herald Tribune* with the headline on Brown's presidential candidacy.

Gary just said, "Yeah, I know," and shook his head.

Chuck wanted to know what would happen to the agent holed up in the Soviet embassy.

Gary looked down and hunched his shoulders. He was embarrassed. "Nothing. He's collateral damage. The whole story blows up if we exonerate him."

Chuck was about to explode when Brad popped the sixty-four-thousand-dollar question. "What about us?"

There was a long count of many Mississippis while Gary squirmed around and wrang his hands before answering. "Colby agreed to exonerate you and Chuck and Madison, but Dearman would not agree to let it go. The consensus agreement was you are still officially guilty of treasonous acts, but you have also been officially pardoned. That status shelters you from any legal jeopardy, but it also eliminates your eligibility to get back on the payroll. You have been officially terminated as of yesterday."

Both Brad and Chuck came out of their chairs. Gary held up his hands. "Hold it. Hold it, guys. The game's not over. I've got your back. I'm fighting for you."

Brad lowered his chin and gazed up at Gary through raised eyebrows in the classic Gallic are-you-shitting-me expression. "The toothpaste's out of the tube on that one, Gary. You know it as well as I do. City Hall is circling the wagons. My main concern is somewhere else right now, though. You do know there's a team of Argentine-American gangbangers in Paris whose explicit mission is to kill us, Madison included? We have to get rid of these guys. Now we have no support, no resources, nothing at all to help us fight them off. Any ideas? Or are we going to be 'collateral damage'?"

Chuck jumped in. "We've gotta get all the information we collected into the public domain. Once it's out there, the government will have to prosecute Dearman and Brown."

Gary cleared his throat. "That's something else I have to make you understand. That information, and all information pertaining to the Papachristou affair, has been classified top secret. If you provide it to anyone, you'll be prosecuted under the Espionage Act."

Dumbfounded, Brad and Chuck looked at each other. There was nowhere else to go. They were on their own. The meeting was over. Gary got up and slinked off.

Chuck was in a rage. They had just been screwed over—royally. He wanted to go kill and destroy. So did Brad. But they needed a plan, a plan that would preserve their personal safety and restore their tarnished reputations.

Brad had one. It was daring and risky and would require the help of Madison and Samantha. He was afraid they might refuse.

*   *   *

The meeting to discuss Brad's plan had taken longer than expected to organize. Madison could only be contacted between 10:00 and 10:15 a.m. at a number that rang at a telephone cabin somewhere in Paris. Otherwise, she was incommunicado.

She refused to meet at any safe house run by the Company. "They're not safe for me. They will be checking every hideout you have—even the ones you don't have."

They settled on café number one from a list of five she had given him when they ran into each other at his apartment the other night. It was a back room in a café on a side street not far from the Moulin Rouge. She was really playing it safe. Her obsession with security drove home the danger they were in. Madison knew the workings of the CIA inner sanctum and the creatures that inhabited it.

Samantha showed up in her Smith alter ego getup. It was rocky going between the two women at the beginning. In fact, Madison almost walked out when Samantha showed up. That would have blown up the whole deal.

There was some sparring and some sparks, but at the end of the day, they cooled off and began to bond.

Brad breathed a heavy sigh of relief when he saw the two women were bonding and starting to get along like old bosom buddies, even though it was the first time they had met. The whole operation hinged on them working as a team. Brad and Chuck had been a team for many years.

It took two hours and some heated discussion, but they had a plan everyone could buy into. Samantha and Madison would go to the U.S. for Dearman and Brown. Brad and Chuck would handle Ranger and his gang of American and Argentinian mercenaries.

The time frame for Samantha and Madison was six days—three days to reconnoiter and set up their operation, and three days to execute. Knowing that international calls were scrupulously monitored, they developed a simple code to remain anonymous when they communicated with each other. Samantha generously volunteered to finance the U.S. operation.

Madison decided to fly to Montreal, rent a car, and drive to their rendezvous point in Virginia. She said her new identity was "airtight" but would be even tighter with the relaxed border controls between Canada and the U.S.

Samantha decided to fly directly to New York, where she had access to a car through her foundation.

Chapter 51

LATE MAY 1975, MCLEAN, VIRGINIA, USA

McLean is a beautiful residential community in Fairfax County, Virginia. Its proximity to Washington, D.C., the Pentagon, and the Central Intelligence Agency makes it a magnet for wealthy residents such as diplomats, members of Congress, and high-ranking government officials. They lived on quiet lanes in luxury homes nestled in woodlands dotted with schools, swimming pools, and tennis courts. Senator James "Jake" Brown lived at the end of the quietest lane, in the most luxurious house, surrounded by the thickest woods.

Madison knew McLean well. She used to live there for many years. She knew that any kind of sustained surveillance was out of the question. She and Samantha had each taken a room in a nice motel just off Interstate 66 near Centreville. It was far enough away from her old stomping grounds that she was unlikely to run into anyone she knew. Her busty blonde disguise was great, but it was not perfect. Better to be safe than sorry.

Samantha also knew McLean quite well. She had lived there as a little girl before her family was slaughtered and had been back many times since. Brad had agreed not to inform Madison of the reason for her war against Jake Brown. So Madison didn't know how familiar Samantha was with McLean. Samantha decided to leave it like that and let Madison take the lead for the moment. Her time would come.

When they met downstairs, Madison suggested they step outside. "Any hotel within a hundred-mile radius of the CIA could be bugged. We even have to be careful in restaurants. I also parked the car I rented in Canada in a public garage and rented a car with Virginia plates. Foreign plates attract attention. We'll use it around McLean. I know I sound paranoid, but trust me, I know what I'm talking about."

"No problem. How do you want to proceed?"

Madison produced a map of McLean. She pointed to the woods around Jake's house. Samantha knew the area well. "These woods are riddled with walking trails. We can park the car at the shopping center right here." She pointed to the spot on the map. "It's about a mile walk through the woods to Jake's house. We can get in close. Check out the security, sight lines, neighbors, dogs, things like that. We won't be able to pass by more than twice. Neighbors are sensitive to unknown people and suspicious activity."

Samantha could only agree.

*   *   *

The reconnaissance walk was uneventful. The woods were magical with evening coming down. Birds were singing their last notes, and the night creatures were announcing they were on the move. It was the perfume of the sylvan aroma that summoned the nostalgia and memories of times past—for both women. By the time they arrived at Brown's house, they were both in the moment.

The nearest neighbor on either side was at least twenty-five yards away, obscured by trees and foliage. There were no dogs visible or audible.

Brown was alone, puttering around in the kitchen. On the second pass by, Madison pointed to the greenhouse where Brown did his gardening. They were ready.

Samantha was headed for the house when she heard the sound of a car approaching. She stepped back into the shadows and saw a police car driving slowly down the lane with a spotlight, searching right and left. It was too late to retreat, so she dived down and lay flat on the ground. She felt the spotlight bathing her body in its yellow rays. The car stopped.

*   *   *

Samantha hugged the ground. The cop exited the car. Turned off the spotlight and peered into the darkness. He took a few steps on the sidewalk toward her.

She was ready to blow the whole operation and make a run for it. He stopped, leaned against a tree, and extracted a pack of cigarettes from his shirt pocket. He lit up and gazed up into the sky. Samantha exhaled a soft sigh of relief. He hadn't spotted her.

She figured this dead-end lane was the end of his round and he was taking a break before he got started on his next one. She was right. He finished his cigarette, rubbed it out on the tree trunk, got back into his car, and drove slowly off, still rotating the spotlight from right to left.

Samantha walked up the path onto the porch and rang the bell. Madison reckoned the only sure way into the house without triggering an alarm was through the front door. They timed their intervention so that it was early enough in the evening that a neighborly visit would not be suspicious.

She saw the curtains move. Heard footsteps. The door opened a crack, with Brown peering around the edge. He was wary, but Samanatha was unthreatening and alluring.

"Excuse me, Mister Brown, my dad sent me to give you this. They delivered it to us by mistake." She held out an envelope addressed to Brown that Madison had prepared back at the motel, canceled stamp and all.

Brown shook his head and opened the screen door. Samantha seized the opportunity and gave Brown a violent shove. Taken by surprise, he fell back into the house. Samantha rushed in after him and stunned him with a kick to his ribs.

Madison, who had been hiding by the side of the porch, followed Samantha. She took advantage of Brown's momentary weakness to plunge a syringe full of anesthesia into his neck. He grabbed the syringe, tried to rush forward, stumbled, stopped, struggled to speak, waved his arms, and sank slowly to the floor.

Madison rushed to the alarm panel and made sure all the cameras were off. She recognized the system and was relieved because there was no recording device. She went to the window and studied the area while Samantha went through all the rooms in the house to make sure they were alone.

A sophisticated lock on the cellar door prevented her from going down. Because their plan called for nothing in the house to be disturbed, she couldn't break it. Madison tapped some keys on the alarm control panel, and the cellar came up on the screen. There was nobody in there, but it was full of documents.

Since Brown was known for going incommunicado on the weekend, they counted on having the whole weekend before them. In other words, it probably wouldn't surprise anyone if he didn't answer the door or his phone. Just to make sure, they turned out all the main lights.

They bound Brown's hands and feet, dragged him into the kitchen, and stuffed him in the corner where he was not visible from the outside. The anesthesia Madison had administered would last at least two hours.

They went into the greenhouse and got a lucky break. The flowerbeds were made of plastic and measured six feet long, four feet wide, and four feet deep. They were fitted into slots on a network of rails so they could be moved around easily.

The ingenuity of the system impressed Madison. It would make their job mush easier. At the back of the greenhouse, there was a compost pit of rich soil about six feet deep, eight feet long, and four feet wide. It was only half full, but it took them better than twenty minutes to transfer eighteen inches of soil from the compost pit into an empty flowerbed.

Back in the kitchen, they wrapped Brown tightly from head to toe in the plastic sheets they extracted from their backpacks. They cut a small hole at the mouth so he could breathe and dragged him to the greenhouse, where they lowered him face up.

Madison had fashioned a rubber breathing tube with a plastic mouthpiece, which she fixed into place through the hole in the plastic. They used the soil from the flowerbed to bury him, making sure the nozzle of the rubber tube remained free. Twenty minutes later, Senator James "Jake" Brown was buried under eighteen inches of rich topsoil. His only link to the outside world was the nozzle of a barely visible rubber breathing tube.

They waited. It didn't take long. The top layer of soil trembled slightly. Jake was awake, discovering the constraints of his newfound reality. Another short wait, and then it came. The nozzle moaned out the echo of an eerie wail that died in short sobs of desperation. There was a second one. A third. A fourth. Each one weaker than the last. Then, nothing.

They fist-pumped each other and topped up the pit with a few more inches of topsoil from the other flowerbeds. The game was on. Madison returned to the house to manage the alarm in case of a problem. Samantha stayed in the greenhouse to keep an eye on her host. They had twelve hours to wait.

Chapter 52

LATE MAY 1975, MCLEAN, VIRGINIA, USA

Saturday is a busy day in McLean, Virginia—shopping, yard tending, children shuttling, and anything else that couldn't be done during the work week. The neighbors were out and about, and Madison and Samantha would have to be very careful as they moved between the main house and the greenhouse.

It was 9:00 a.m. Madison went to the front window and checked for prying eyes. It was all clear at the front. At the back door, she checked again for prying eyes or any potentially compromising presence. All clear. She slipped out and joined Samantha in the greenhouse for the resurrection.

It took only five minutes to clear the soil covering Senator Brown's head. There was movement. They peeled back the layers of plastic. His eyes were wild. He was trying to scream with a voice that had worn itself out thousands of hopeless screams ago. A severe warning was, nevertheless, in order.

"One sound out of you and I'll put you back in the ground."

Samantha's impassive delivery was convincing. Senator James Brown ceased his silent screams, but his eyes were still wild and he was still hyperventilating.

Samantha continued. "I am going to take you out of your grave. But before I do, I want you to know that failure to comply with my orders will trigger your return to the grave. Only this time, there will be no breathing tube. There will be no discussion. There will be no second chance. Do you understand the rules?"

Brown's voice was a hoarse whisper. "Yes. Who are you?"

"You might remember the Smith family, the one your sons massacred. I have been sent by them to seek justice."

It took a few seconds. Brown was still hysterical from his prolonged stay in the grave. This new info made him tremble even more uncontrollably. He started to sob. "No, please, no. I'm sorry. It was a mistake."

Samantha nodded. "You are right. It was a mistake. It was a big mistake."

It took another ten minutes to extricate Brown from the pit and another five to strip off the plastic wrapping. Outside of having soiled his pants, he didn't look much worse for the wear. Madison had brought paper, pen, and a writing pad from Brown's office. She placed them in front of Brown and untied his hands.

Samantha said, "In your best handwriting, I want you to write exactly what I dictate. Understand?"

He was hunched over, and his bushy eyebrows were wriggling around. "Yes, yes."

Samantha began to read. The sharp ring of the doorbell interrupted the dictation. Samantha and Madison exchanged worried looks. Brown's eyes glowed with hope.

Madison put a knife to Brown's throat. "One sound. One damn sound and I slit your throat from ear to ear."

Brown nodded, and his eyes went dead. Samantha sneaked a look through the window. It was a handsome woman with a square jaw dressed in a pantsuit.

"I know you're in there, Senator. Please answer. This is important." She knocked a few more times. "Okay, I'm coming in."

Madison kept the knife on Brown's throat. Samantha positioned herself to take down the intruder. She heard the woman fumbling in her bag. Then, "Shit, I left the keys in the office." The woman turned and headed back to her car.

Madison and Samantha relaxed. "Who was that?"

"My office manager. We had a meeting scheduled for this morning."

Madison nodded to Samantha. "She says she's coming back. We'll have to hurry." Samantha turned to Brown. "Start writing." She began to dictate:

I am Senator James Brown. This is my confession. Fifteen years ago, FBI agent Sam Smith discovered I was taking kickbacks from foreign governments. To keep him from denouncing me, I sent my two legitimate sons, along with my illegitimate son, Ranger Wilde, to murder him and his family. I then used my influence as a United States senator to illegally have them acquitted. Since then, I have continued to sell classified information to foreign powers. Most recently, Alvin P. Dearman, deputy director of the CIA, and I entered into an agreement whereby he would supply me with highly classified information I would sell onto Juan Perón, the president of Argentina. The proceeds from the sale of this information were split between Deputy Director Dearman and myself—seventy percent for Dearman, thirty percent for me—and deposited in offshore accounts on the island of Jersey. I swear on the Holy Bible that all this is true, and I pray that Almighty God will forgive me.

"Now date it and sign it." Samantha compared the dated and signed document with other documents Brown had written. The writing was the same. She pushed another sheet of paper in front of him. "Copy it and sign again."

Brown's trembling hands made it slow going. When he finished,

Madison bound his hands.

Madison took Samantha aside and whispered in her ear. Samantha shook her head and smiled. "Senator Brown, I understand you have a videocassette recorder in your office. Let's take a look at it."

Madison untied Brown's feet, then ran interference to make sure the coast was clear. Samantha followed with Senator Brown in tow. Brown seemed to relax a little in the confines of his office. Madison examined the videocassette recorder and asked Brown, "What do you use this for?"

"Private interviews and campaign messages, things like that." His voice was making a comeback.

"Where do you sit?"

Brown pointed with his bound hands. "Right here."

"Sit."

"Why?"

Samantha whipped around and stared at him. He sat down. She handed him the document he had just written. "Start reading when I give you the signal."

Brown started to protest. "This machine costs a fortune. You don't know how to operate it."

"Silence, Senator." Samantha shot a quizzical look at Madison.

Madison nodded her head. "Don't worry. I've used this type of machine many times."

Samantha gave the signal, and Brown began to read. When he finished, Madison extracted the cassette and inserted another. She pointed to Brown and said, "Read."

Samantha was curious but said nothing. Madison repeated the operation but left this last cassette in the machine. Samantha understood. Whoever found Brown would also find the recording, as well as a signed written copy of the text. Samantha and Madison would take away with them an original signed copy, as well as two recordings of his confession.

Madison stood in front of the sobbing senator. She held a small yellowish pill between her thumb and forefinger. "Given your experience with foreign intelligence, you have probably seen one of these before. It's a cyanide pill. It's almost entirely painless, for all practical purposes, and you are dead within seconds. My colleague argued against giving you a choice. My arguments prevailed."

She held out the pill. Brown extended his bound hands and grasped it.

"We are giving you a choice. You can bite into the pill and swallow. Or you can go back to your tomb in the greenhouse as before, with one difference. This time, there will be no breathing tube. You have sixty seconds to decide. If you cannot make up your mind, my colleague will decide for you. She favors the tomb."

Brown's eyes glazed over. Samantha felt his faltering hope evaporate as the reels of his life flashed through his mind. She checked her watch.

"Sixty seconds. Stop. Too late, Senator Brown." Then, to Madison: "Let's take him back to the greenhouse."

That was the signal. Brown screamed, crammed the pill into his mouth, and bit down. Samantha had exaggerated when she said he would be dead in seconds. It took a couple of painful minutes, and it showed in the expression on his face.

They made sure he was dead, then set about cleaning up any evidence of their presence. They wiped down all the surfaces they might have touched and stashed their tools, plastic wrapping, masking tape, the envelope they used to gain entry to the house, cassette recordings, and signed confession in their backpacks. In the greenhouse, they returned the compost pit and flowerbeds to their original appearance.

Samantha went from the greenhouse back into the woods, where she waited for Madison. Madison went back into the house and turned on the alarm.

The sound of a closing car door froze her in place. She peeked through the front window. The square-jawed woman in a pantsuit was back, and she had a key.

Madison hurried down the hallway to the back door. The doorbell rang. The key turned in the lock. A pause. "Alvin! My God! What has happened?"

Madison slipped outside and hightailed it into the woods, where Samantha was waiting. "Run for it. We have a problem."

Chapter 53

LATE MAY 1975, THE BLUE RIDGE MOUNTAINS OF VIRGINIA, USA

Alvin P. Dearman loved his little lake house nestled deep in the heart of the Blue Ridge Mountains. It was his secret hideaway. Ownership, insurance, utilities, everything was in the name of his company on the island of Jersey. There was no way he could be traced. Strict privacy was exactly what he needed until things calmed down. The lucrative side game he had been running with the foreign spies was over, but who cared? He had more money than he could spend in a hundred lifetimes. All of the proof linking him to treason had been buried in classified files that would never be opened and could never even be discussed. He would be retiring on a full pension at the end of the year, complete with public service awards and professional accolades. He was really looking forward to his position as presidential advisor on national security.

Everything was coming up roses. The only cloud was that jackass, Jake Brown, who hadn't been able to keep his mouth shut and wanted to continue dealing secrets to the enemy. He had even wanted to run for president. His suicide was suspicious, but timely.

His antics no longer posed a threat. Jake Brown was somebody else's problem now.

Alvin had two weeks of total freedom to look forward to. Everyone had been notified he would be incommunicado for the next fifteen days. The fridge was stocked, the television was hooked up, and the boat was prepared. Fishing, gardening, and reading would be his only occupations.

*   *   *

Madison had a hunch. It was a long shot, but she had to give it a try. She might never get another chance. The little lake where she was headed in the Blue Ridge Mountains of Virginia provided perfect cover for someone wanting to hide out or "get away from it all." It was so secluded that even the inhabitants needed a map to find their way around. Actually, that was because it was secluded and because the inhabitants only lived there for a couple of weeks or months in the summer, not really enough time to get acquainted with the complex terrain. If they knew each other at all, everything was on a first-name basis. It was the closest thing to "incognito" she had ever seen.

She remembered a request from Alvin P. Dearman that came across her desk to sign off on a security system for a safe house on a secluded lake in a secluded part of the Blue Ridge Mountains. The request itself was routine procedure for high-security safe houses, but it attracted her attention because of its location and because the company that owned the house was registered on the Isle of Jersey.

She had been curious enough to take a weekend to drive out and inspect it herself. Everything checked out, and she thought no more about it—until now. It would be perfect cover for secret meetings…or for someone who wanted to go off the radar.

After taking care of Jake Brown, Alvin Dearman was next on her list. And she was running out of time. He was a phantom. She used all her contacts and came up empty-handed. He was away for fifteen days, and no one knew where or how to get in touch. The secluded safe house was a long shot. She was pressing her luck by hanging around in the U.S., but she had to give it one last try before leaving the States for good. This was it. The drive was scenic and restful. The rest was more than welcome after all the shenanigans in McLean with Jake Brown.

The thought of it gave her goosebumps. It had been a close call. She had been able to exit Brown's home before the square-jawed woman in the pantsuit found her. Once inside, the woman immediately smelled a rat and emergency-called the police.

Madison and Samantha barely had time to access their car before the sirens began wailing. Roadblocks were going up as they drove out of McLean. A search of their car would have revealed Jake Brown's impossible-to-explain videos and written confession. They'd escaped by the skin of their teeth.

She nearly missed the turnoff to the lake. The sign was old and rotten with rust. The road little more than a twisting, badly paved byway. Side roads were unpaved and marked with wooden arrows. About two miles in, the road forked right and left. She remembered the general store with a gas pump was a mile down to the left. The house of interest was to the right a half mile down.

She turned around and doubled back. Took the first side road to the left. A hundred yards down, there was a trail cutting into the woods. She backed in far enough to be invisible from the main road and parked the car facing out behind a thick barrier of underbrush.

This would serve as her base. It was unlikely anyone would take this trail so late in the day. Even if they did, it was already dark enough that the car hidden by the underbrush would be invisible to the naked eye.

She swept away the traces of the car tracks and covered the license plates with a set of fakes. A change into her all-black nightwear, and it was time to go.

Sunset on the lake was always beautiful. This evening, it was exquisite. Fiery red with highlights of purple, pink, and blue. Just bright enough to facilitate her excursion through the woods to Dearman's house. It took more than thirty minutes for her to get into a position where she could observe it.

There was Dearman on the porch, laid back in a recliner and sipping some kind of cocktail. A thick steak was sizzling on the charcoal grill. Looked like he was savoring the moment.

When she was certain he was alone, she broke her cover and stepped onto the porch. Dearman wrenched himself out of the chair, eyes wide, shoulders hunched. "What are you doing here?"

"Hello, Alvin. What kind of a greeting is that? Aren't you happy to see me?"

"How did you find me here?"

"I remembered the security system I signed off on a few years back."

Dearman remembered running the place through the Company to make it look legit in case anyone started asking questions. In fact, it was legit, and he was the only one with access or even knowledge of its existence.

"What do you want?" He eyed the twelve-gauge stacked in the corner. Madison caught it.

Dearman hesitated, then went for the gun. His clumsy attempt succeeded only in overturning the grill. Steak face up on the floor, embers strewn all over the place, Madison on top of him, knife at his throat. She pushed him inside. Duct-taped him to a kitchen chair.

Her movements were slow and deliberate. Her jaw was set, and her eyes were focused. "I'm here to even the score, Alvin. You ruined my life. Manipulated me. I trusted you."

"You stupid female. I created you. Without me, you would still be in the typing pool. I'm giving you one last chance. You cut me loose and get out of here, and I will forget this incident. Otherwise, I will have the book thrown at you."

There was smoke coming from the porch. The wooden planks were on fire. Dearman swiveled to see the flames that were spreading to the curtains in the living room and crawling up the walls. "You have to hurry."

Knife in hand, Madison stepped forward to cut him loose. She hesitated. He was panicking. "Get me out of here. That's an order, you stupid slut."

The flames were roaring through the salon. The heat in the kitchen was becoming unbearable. Madison took a step back and observed the nasty little creature jiggling around in front of her.

"What are you waiting for, woman? Cut me loose!"

A flick of the knife severed the tape binding his hands. A second flick freed his torso. He sprang off the chair and head-butted her in the gut. Stunned by the violent reaction, she fell against the sink. The knife dropped from her hand. A kick to her ribs left her breathless and semiconscious.

"Burn in hell, bitch."

Dearman turned toward the back door. Too late. The ceiling collapsed and left Dearman's leg trapped by a burning beam. He was screaming for his life.

"Help me, Madison! Help me!"

It was too hot, too dangerous, too late. She threw open the

picture window. Turned back. "Goodbye, Alvin."

The flames were closing in. It was time for her to go. She left Dearman screaming for his life. By the time she got back to her car, the whole house was engulfed in flames. Smoke was billowing through the trees up to the sky. Dearman was silent. Mission accomplished. She pumped the gas. Turned the key. The motor was dead.

Chapter 54

Brad exited the metro at the Montparnasse station and walked down the boulevard toward Raspail. This was the third straight day he was coming into the Montparnasse area where he was certain the gangbangers were watching for him.

His movements were always the same. He crossed Montparnasse in front of the Café du Dôme and then crossed Raspail after looking into the Café de la Rotonde and greeting his waiter-friend, Jean-Pierre. From there he went straight to Wadja's, a restaurant bar on a small side street popular with the aspiring artists in the area. After a quick beer, he went from there straight to his apartment on rue d'Assas.

So far, there had been no sign of surveillance. Neither he nor Chuck nor Edith nor Doris had noticed anything out of the ordinary. The lack of success made Chuck want to ditch the current plan of drawing the gangbangers out into the open. His plan was to be more proactive along the lines of the search-and-destroy tactics they had employed up to now. Brad disagreed. He argued it would be extremely difficult to locate the gangbangers in the first place, and in the second place, if they did locate them, they would expose themselves to the French, who were also actively seeking the gangbangers after the shootout at the quarry. Chuck was reluctant but had to agree.

Brad almost missed it. Edith was looking in the window with two fingers rubbing her chin and her thumb wagging left to right. That meant there were two gangbangers at each end of the street.

He finished his beer and went outside. Took his time lighting up his Gitane to get his bearings. The two gangbangers at the Montparnasse end were in plain sight, lounging against a car. There was nothing to see at the other end. The façade of the last building was being sandblasted and was covered in scaffolding and protective plastic sheets. It was a good place for an ambush. Chuck was supposed to be watching it.

Brad turned left toward the scaffolding. The soft footsteps of the gangbangers creeping up from the rear made him smile. Crunch time was here.

Two men stepped onto the street from under the scaffolding. Cangrejo and Sparky. Both were sporting blackjacks and long-bladed pampa knives.

Brad stopped. Before they could move, Chuck's silhouette swinging a baseball bat surged from the shadows of the scaffolding. The first swing crushed Cangrejo's right jaw and sent him reeling to the pavement. The second smashed Sparky's snout and dented his forehead. He dropped to his knees and flopped on his face.

Meanwhile, Brad faked left and turned to face the two men bearing down on him from behind. He used his nunchakus to parry the attack from the first gangbanger and dodge to the left.

The second gangbanger was the doe-eyed dude coming in from the right. Brad popped him three times with the nunchakus and followed through with a front kick that dropped him. A stomp to the neck took him out.

Chuck slipped past on the left. His third swing was another home run to the back of the first gangbanger's head. He wanted to go for a few more swings while the gangbangers were still not moving, but Brad waved him back. Stick to the plan.

Brad checked their pulses. Alive. He waved toward the Montparnasse end of the street, where Doris was waiting. She went to the Cosmos café on the corner and had the barman call in a street fight. Brad and Chuck slipped off into the night.

Doris and her four colleagues came down and surrounded the unconscious gangbangers until the cops arrived. They told the cops what they had seen. The four men had been fighting each other. There might have been someone else, but they weren't sure. The cops carted the unconscious gangbangers off to jail.

*   *   *

Edith was waiting for Brad and Chuck, house red in the left hand, Gitane sans filtre in the right. It was one of those dreary old-fashioned cafés that hadn't been renovated since before the war. The owners were an old couple in their eighties, too healthy to retire, too stubborn to change their ways, and too happy to reunite with their war buddy.

Edith was glowing. "Goddamn, son-of-a-bitch. Spotted those spic shits the minute they came out of the metro. Can smell 'em a mile away, just like the goddamn Krautheads. Did you get 'em?"

"Worked like a charm, except Chuck was a little slow on the draw. I almost got skewered by the doe-eyed dude."

Chuck laughed. "Just testin' your reflexes."

Brad snickered and continued. "Doris had the cops there in less than five minutes. The gangbangers were alive, but still not moving. The blows they took could have been fatal. Chuck was swinging for the fences. Anyway, the cops carted 'em off, and Doris and her girls made sure the cops knew these guys were Argentines. They're responsible for the deaths of several French cops they shot it out with over at the quarry. When they get out of the hospital, they're going to spend many unpleasant years in the French penal system. They're no longer a threat to us, same as if we killed 'em ourselves. Only we don't have to worry about the French investigating who killed them. We're in the clear all the way around."

Edith leaned into Brad and cupped her hand around the side of her mouth. "You ever need any reinforcements, Mollie and Jeannot are hot numbers." She nodded toward the proprietors. "Many a Bosch perished at their hands. Goddamn it, remember it well. Good old days!" She was in seventh heaven.

Chuck tapped Brad's arm. "We've still got places to go and things to do. Let's get movin'."

"Okay, let's go. Bye-bye, Edith, we'll see you soon." Out on the street, they were about to part ways when Brad stopped. "One last thing. I heard from Samantha. Mission accomplished."

Chuck's eyes lit up. "Mission accomplished. That means I can bring Betty back."

"I don't know about that. Brown's dead. They have damning evidence on Dearman and Ranger Wilde, but no way to make it public. Dearman's still protected, and Ranger's still on the loose. Might be better to hold off until we get more details."

Brad broke off and headed back to his apartment on the rue d'Assas. There were a few things he wanted to pick up before returning to Samantha's place. As long as she was in town, he wanted put off leaving her safe house as long as possible. His apartment was only a fifteen-minute walk, and he had a lot of things on his mind.

This experience with the CIA was bothering him. It had destroyed many of the naïve illusions still lingering around from the days of his youth. He was going to have to come to terms with them once this Papachristou affair was over and done with. His faith in the system and those who manage it had taken a big irreparable hit. His moral compass would have to be readjusted.

As a security precaution, he passed by his building twice before entering. He hadn't noticed anything suspicious, but he felt uneasy. As a further security precaution, instead of going straight to his apartment, he unlocked the door to the parking garage and took the stairs down to level one. His Indian Arrow was still undisturbed right where he had parked it. Nothing else attracted his attention. He scrounged around level 2 for few minutes, took the elevator to the top floor, and then the stairs back down to his apartment on the second floor. All clear. He was still uneasy.

At the door, he saw both of his traps had been breached. The sliver of cardboard was no longer in the doorjamb, and the thin film of wax over the keyhole was broken. There had been an intrusion.

He flattened against the wall and pushed the door open. All quiet and nothing moving. The scent of an expensive perfume told him at least one of the intruders was a woman. The scent was fresh. She was either still in there, or it hadn't been long since she'd left.

The silence exploded in a strident scream. "Don't come in, Brad! It's Ranger! He's got a gun!"

It was Samantha, the blonde version. He peeked around the corner. She was kneeling in the center of the main room, hands tied in front of her. Her clothes were ripped, there were scratches on her face, and her eye was swollen.

"Come in with your hands up. I only want you, James. I'll let her go. Otherwise, I'll kill you both. Her first. Then you."

"Don't do it, Brad. He's a psychopath. He'll kill us both. He wants revenge. You killed his boyfriend, Charles Lumbers, the transvestite pervert with the big blonde hair."

There was a pop. Samantha screamed. Fell forward, blood seeping from her shoulder, staining her dress. Ranger had a silencer on his gun.

"That's just an appetizer, James. I'll put the next one in her knee. Be a man. Come on in."

Surrender was not an option. Neither was waiting. Brad went in on a front roll. Heard a pop and felt the whoosh of the bullet. Samantha took advantage of Ranger's temporary distraction to jump up and kick the pistol from his grip. It dropped to the floor, and she fell on it.

Ranger didn't have time to get the gun from under her, so he kicked her in the head to keep her from using it on him and jumped out of the way.

Samantha was out cold. The evil dude in motorcycle leathers was dancing around and pumping his fists like Cassius Clay. Slicked-back hair, chiseled jawline, straight nose, hooded eyes, even features. Ranger Wilde, sneering in the flesh. There was no time to wonder how he had found Samantha or how long he had been waiting for Brad to return to his apartment.

Ranger was brandishing an oversized hunting knife and began circling to the left. Face to face, he was larger than he seemed sitting on a Harley chopper. He also moved like a big cat.

Brad popped the nunchakus out of his pouch. He twirled them around and cut Ranger off from Samantha by moving to the right. Ranger feinted to the left and struck to the right. He was fast. Brad stumbled as he dodged.

Ranger followed his strike with a front kick that landed on

Brad's hip. Brad retreated and counterattacked. His nunchaku caught Ranger on his free hand. Ranger replied with a slashing blow to Brad's breastbone.

Brad was bleeding. Ranger was on the move. Dancing around, ever more confident. Ever more careless. Brad slipped to the side and threw a low roundhouse to Ranger's groin. Swept upward with his nunchakus and popped Ranger on the chin.

Ranger was stunned. His knife hand was exposed. Brad swung downward and smashed his thumb. The knife dropped. Brad slipped inside. Drove the butt of his nunchak into Ranger's throat. Dug his thumb deep into Ranger's eye. Ranger staggered, grabbed his throat, and fell gagging to the ground. Brad kicked him in the head. Ranger was out, half blind and helpless.

Brad rushed to Samantha, where she lay unconscious by the terrace. He cradled her head in his hands. Caressed her cheek. "Samantha, can you hear me?" Her eyes cracked open. She struggled to speak.

The moon was still low and the shadows were long. Brad saw the shadow before he heard the footsteps. Ranger was rushing him.

Brad threw himself to the left. Ranger crashed into the terrace guardrail. He fought to regain his balance, wheezing through his wounded windpipe, blood oozing from his mangled eye. Brad drove a front kick to his groin, a roundhouse to his head, and a two-fisted uppercut to his jaw.

Ranger fell to his knees but refused to give up. He struggled to his feet and charged. Brad caught him under the armpits and leveraged his momentum to propel him over the guardrail. He nosedived to a hard landing on the concrete walkway two stories below.

Brad turned to Samantha. She was conscious and surprisingly alert. The bullet had gone through the meat in her shoulder and lodged in the wall. Minimal damage, and she was barely bleeding. Brad was more worried about the damage Ranger had done to her eye when he kicked her lights out. The socket might be fractured. It would take a specialist to fix the eye. A nurse could dress the bullet wound.

"We have to get you fixed up. Think you can walk?"

Samantha gave him a thumbs-up and a confident nod. "We have to clean this place up before we go."

She was back in the game. Brad was relieved. He gathered up Ranger's weapons. The hunting knife and the .38 with the silencer might come in handy. He'd keep them over at the safe house. He put the spent shells in his pocket and used a heavy dose of Mister Clean to wipe away the blood stains. The only lingering evidence of Ranger's visit were the two bullet holes in the wall. A small dose of plaster left over from the wall work in the bathroom covered those up—imperfectly, but good enough not to attract attention.

Brad's chest wound was superficial. Some rubbing alcohol and a couple of Band-Aids took care of it. He looked over the terrace to check on Ranger down below. Shock and awe! Ranger was gone. The guy was worse than a cockroach.

Brad rushed downstairs. Checked the walkway. No sign of Ranger. No blood. Nothing. Checked the sidewalk right and left. Nothing. There was no way Ranger could have escaped under his own power.

Some commotion a hundred yards down the street by the rue Vavin attracted his attention. He closed in on two couples standing around staring at Ranger's dead body. Ranger had somehow managed to crawl all that distance before he finally ran out of gas. Brad was satisfied there was no way Ranger's body could be linked to him or his building. He decided to let the good Samaritans take care of it.

Back at his apartment, Samantha had cleaned up and was ready to go. He wanted to know how Ranger linked him to Samantha. "Mario mentioned we knew each other. Ranger took it from there."

Brad exhaled and shook his head. "Mario is dangerous. Let me get you to a nurse friend of mine who can dress your shoulder. Then we'll get you to a doctor for your eye."

"Don't need a doctor for that." Her eye was looking better. "We'll see what the nurse says. Let's go."

Chapter 55

LATE MAY 1975, MCLEAN, PARIS

Gary made a succinct summary of whole Papachristou caper. Deputy CIA Director Alvin P. Dearman and U.S. Senator James "Jake" Brown had made a deal to betray their country and sell top secret information to Juan Perón, the president of Argentina. Ranger Wilde, Senator Brown's illegitimate son, was the intermediary for the Americans. Mario Irigoyen, Perón's power broker, was the intermediary for the Argentines. When Perón died, Irigoyen lost power to his rival, José Lopez Rega. Disgraced and on the run, the Americans feared he would disclose their treasonous conspiracy and decided to assassinate him. Irigoyen figured the motive to kill him would disappear if the treasonous conspiracy became known to others.

That was where the trouble started. Irigoyen passed evidence of the conspiracy onto Georges Papachristou, a close friend of Perón, who agreed to pass it on to the CIA. Unfortunately, both Irigoyen and Papachristou had only partial information. They did not know Dearman was involved as the major player. When Dearman saw the conspiracy had been outed, he used his position of authority to cover it up.

He had the information classified top secret and accused the agent who brought the information on the conspiracy of being the traitor and trying to cover his tracks. Then he had Brown assemble a gang to go after Irigoyen and Papachristou, the only two with firsthand knowledge of the conspiracy. The gang headed by Brown's illegitimate son got Papachristou as a fake suicide, but Irigoyen escaped and Papachristou's wife got proof her husband was murdered. Dearman sent his protégée, Madison, to collaborate with Brown's gang, supposedly to find out what was going on and solve the problem.

Brad and Chuck got sucked into the affair and dug up proof that both Dearman and Brown were involved. One thing led to another, with the result that the French ended up wiping out Ranger's gang. When Ranger went over to the Argentines, the French wiped them out as well. The last four in that gang were captured several nights ago, fighting with each other over by Montparnasse. Finally, Ranger, Brown's bagman and enforcer, was beaten to death the same night in the same area.

Gary eyed Brad. "Strangely enough, that is the same area where you work and live."

Brad faked a concerned expression. "Yeah, so what's the end to the story?"

Gary stared at Brad before continuing. "The big news is that Senator Brown took his life last weekend."

Brad and Chuck tried to look surprised. "What happened?"

"He took a cyanide pill. The kind we use in the Company."

"How about Dearman?"

Gary's smile was ambiguous. "Dearman burned to death last week in a fire at his summer home."

That surprised Chuck. "Do you think he was murdered?" A long silence. "By the Company?"

"I honestly don't know. Looks like the fire was an accident, but there is evidence of foul play. Everything is hush-hush."

"What about Madison and the falsely accused traitor in the Soviet embassy?"

Gary squeezed out a timid smile. "There's nothing we can do for the traitor. He made some strong, unfounded accusations against his country."

Chuck was visibly disgusted. "Everything he said was true."

"Yeah, I know, but a political decision has been made at the top of the pyramid. On the bright side, Madison has been completely rehabilitated, and so have you two guys. All suspicions and accusations have been completely expunged from your records. It's like they never happened. You are as pure as the driven snow. Nevertheless, Madison has decided to leave the Company. She's going to emigrate to the UK and start up a security agency. I suppose you guys are still with me, though."

Chuck answered for both of them. "We'll get back to you on that."

*   *   *

The *Herald Tribune* ran a front-page story on the suicide of Senator James "Jake" Brown. There was nothing about his espionage activities or his responsibility for the massacre of Samantha's family. The official storyline was that he was terminally ill and wanted to go out on his own terms. The president ordered flags to be flown at half-mast, and the Senate was planning a special ceremony in honor of his long, faithful dedication to the service to his country.

Samantha sneered when Brad read that to her. "He pleaded and sobbed and begged. He went out on my terms. And he definitely did not serve his country."

"What about the videocassette and the suicide note he left behind?"

Samantha made a thought-provoking reply. "As we suspected, City Hall must have covered that up. We've got original copies of both. Now we have to find a creative way to make them public without tipping off the Company that we're the culprits. I'm working on that."

It was one of those bittersweet situations. She had achieved her goal but was going to miss playing the game. She still hadn't fully embraced the fact that her crusade was over and she didn't have anything lined up for act two.

There's something about the end of an era. Brad didn't want this to end. Neither did Samantha. But the era was over. They walked along the river with the shadows gliding by. They breathed in the atmosphere but saw only each other, the shining water, and the sky.

Hand in hand, they experienced the quiet glory of the Cathedral Notre Dame and the splendor of the Tuileries. It was daybreak beneath the Eiffel Tower when they kissed their last goodbye.

Samantha jumped into the first taxi at the stand on her way to the airport. Brad jumped onto his bike parked by the metro. He was headed for a workout at the dojo and a recording session in the afternoon.

Epilogue

THREE MONTHS LATER

Rumors had begun to circulate after the local television station in Jefferson City, Missouri, broadcast a ninety-five second video of the deceased Senator James Brown confessing to murder and treason. The FBI immediately raided the station and confiscated the video.

Then the local newspaper in Evanston, Illinois, published a letter signed and dated by Senator Jake Brown confessing to the same crimes. The FBI raided the newspaper and confiscated the copy of the letter.

By this time, however, the cat was out of the bag. Other local TV stations and newspapers had received copies. They were broadcasting and publishing the information and scooping the national networks and big-city tabloids. NBC was the first national broadcaster to publish the video. *The New York Times* was the first major tabloid to publish the letter.

The *Herald Tribune* picked up the story and did an in-depth analysis. The government's reflex reaction was to deny the authenticity of the confessions and threaten the news agencies of spreading false information. That strategy came a cropper when the investigations of an army of researchers, lawyers, and journalists proved beyond the shadow of any reasonable doubt the confessions and the facts were authentic and true.

The politicians were the first to see the writing on the wall and began hemming and hawing and twisting themselves into pretzels attempting to distance themselves from anything to do with Senator James "Jake" Brown. The bureaucrats dived for cover and began purging their files. The name Brown began mysteriously disappearing from streets, roads, buildings, schools, and parks that had previously been proud to bear his name.

Mario Irigoyen, former Perón official and newly named professor at Columbia University, became an instant expert on the subject. He was difficult to avoid if you watched the news or the talk shows. As he had correctly foreseen, a devaluation of the Argentine peso chased José Lopez Rega from power. However, it was the military and not the leftists who took over. Mario was still out, but he was safe and had a comfy job.

The accused traitor was still being hounded by the bureaucrats, but he had filed a series of lawsuits that were shining unwanted light on the swamp and the creatures that haunted it. Dearman's estate was being challenged by a host of former CIA employees claiming they had suffered all kinds of financial, physical, and mental harm at Dearman's hands when they called attention to his professional and private misdeeds.

Brad and Chuck were going over every detail, congratulating themselves on how everything was working out. Betty came in with the coffee. "I saw Gary the other night at an embassy shindig. He says he misses you."

Brad looked at Chuck. They nodded. "Thanks, Betty."

She said, "Oh, by the way, Brad. This came in the office mail for you."

The handwriting was feminine. He pulled out a postcard featuring Marbella. There was no text. Just two drawings. The first was a target with an arrow in the bullseye. The second was a heart with an arrow through it.

It was signed: *See you soon.*

The following is an excerpt from *Cult Stalker* by Ephraim Clark, the first installment in the Brad James book series, also available from Glass Spider Publishing.

Prologue: The Prophecy

There were four of them—four handmaidens. They were solemn and silent, their movements slow and deliberate, gestures befitting the sacred ceremony. They bathed her and washed her hair. Special attention was paid to her hands and feet. The Prophet was particularly attentive to hands and feet. Her hands and feet were cleansed, massaged, and anointed with the holy oil. Each nail was painted pearl-white. Her thick, auburn hair was brushed carefully to the side and placed delicately to tumble over her right shoulder. There would be no makeup. There would be no clothes. There would be no sandals or shoes. She would offer herself exposed, defenseless, and pure.

Through the bars in her cell, she could see the red ball of the sun setting on the sea. It drenched the beach in a fiery mist that sparkled in the sand. She loved this sight, her faithful evening companion ever since she was chosen for the Prophecy's highest honor. Tonight, she would receive that honor. It was a lifetime honor with a lifetime commitment. Tonight, she would be consecrated into the Prophet's personal harem. She hunched her shoulders and shivered at the thought.

The harem was the Prophecy's inner sanctum. It was located in a separate compound surrounded by a brick wall twelve feet high topped by concertina wire. Only the Prophet, the Prophecy's small circle of high priests, and their accomplices were allowed inside. Only the Prophet, the Prophecy's small circle of high priests, and their accomplices were allowed to exit. Once inside, the harem's honored members would dedicate their bodies, their souls, and their lives to God and the Prophet.

Her body was prepared. It was time to prepare her soul. She was ready for her communion. She knelt before her prayer post and folded her hands. The handmaidens chanted soft litanies to the Prophet and His Majesty. The Prophecy's Priest of Priests approached. In his hand was the sacred white pill that would transport her for the next twenty-four hours to a parallel reality, a reality of vivid colors and soothing sounds, a world of mystery and revelation. When she emerged, she would be a new person in a new life in selfless service to God and the Prophet.

She closed her eyes and opened her lips to receive the "Holy Communion." The Priest of Priests placed the lozenge on the extended tongue, raised his arms toward the heavens, and whispered, "Go to God." She bowed her head, buried her face in her hands. With the subtlest movements of tongue and teeth, she surreptitiously expelled the lozenge into her hands folded over her face.

This was the crucial moment when all could be lost. Discovery meant death—slow death, agonizing death, death meant to torture, death meant to punish, death meant to deter any and all who would defy the Prophet and his holy cult, the Prophecy. She placed her folded hands under her chin and rose solemnly to her feet. Head bowed, she turned and shuffled to the single bed in the corner of her cell. She lay down on her back with her arms at her sides, the

lozenge held by the thumb in the palm of her hand. The eyes of
the Priest of Priests followed her every move. She closed her eyes
and pretended to embark on the voyage fueled by the explosive
drug in the sacred white pill.

They left her alone and locked the door behind them. The
countdown had begun. She had only a few precious minutes before
they would return. Her heart was pounding. Her limbs were paralyzed, and she was choking with terror. She struggled to control
the panic coursing through her trembling body and exploding in
her brain. Her life depended on it. Heretics were executed in a sa-
distic month-long ritual of mutilation and torture. The slightest
sound would bring her minders back to investigate.

She shifted her weight and arched her back in a contortion she
hoped would resemble a drug-fueled reaction—if anyone was
watching. She reached under the thin mattress of her bed and recovered the syringe and hypodermic needle she'd managed to con-
ceal. She had been hiding it over the two weeks of her "purification" period in the cell. It was filled with the drug administered for
purification or as a punishment for misbehavior. The drug was
powerful. A single drop caused intense pain and a paralyzing death-
like experience. A full dose was enough to kill a medium-sized
man. She had decided after her first injection that she would never
again misbehave.

She attached one end of a short string to a hair clip and the
other end to the syringe on the hypodermic needle. She then used
the clip to fasten the apparatus on the underside of the thick lock
of hair flowing down her right shoulder. It would be invisible—at
least she fervently hoped it would. She prayed it would.

They came for her and led her through the throng of chanting
worshippers to the magnificent altar in the Prophecy's cathedral.
Menacing shadows swayed over the flames of the ceremonial

candles lining the walls. The air, heavy with incense and anticipation, electrified the atmosphere. Excited the congregation. Intensified the trance. Step by step to the cadence of a hundred chanting souls she shuffled toward her destiny. She showed no emotion. She offered no resistance. She forced herself into a beatific state of submission. One false step—one slight hesitation, one off-key glance—and it would be the beginning of the hell that would end her life.

The ceremony was solemn and elaborate. The Prophet looked on as the Priest of Priests anointed her naked body, exposed, defenseless, and pure. The Prophet suddenly rose from his throne. Caught off guard by the unexpected move, she blinked. The Priest of Priests stiffened and stared. He had felt it. Did he see it? He was a man of exceptional intuition. She didn't move. She couldn't move. She was paralyzed by fear. The Priest of Priests moved closer, but he wasn't sure. He raised his hand.

The Prophet's impatience saved her. He stepped forward and took her hand. The chanting ceased. The Priest of Priests stepped back. The Prophet blessed his subjects, turned, and led the newly anointed addition to his harem into his private chamber.

There would be five days of celebration. The Prophet would be the first. She would pass each successive day with a different high priest. The order was designated by their rank. At the end of the fifth day, she would be consigned to the harem.

She could not wait five days. She could not wait one day. She had to act now.

The doors closed onto the Prophet's private chamber. It was spacious and opulent. There was a canopied bed in the middle of the room. Crystal bed tables on ornate bronze stands bracketed the bed. The ceiling was mirrored. At the foot of the bed, four steps led to a round, sunken bath the size of a small swimming pool. A large bathroom of pearl-white marble opened up behind the bed. The only other furniture stood in the far corner. It was comprised of a glass table on crossed glass legs adorned with two ebony black chairs.

On first inspection, she didn't see any entrance or exit other than the one leading to the altar. This was bad news because there was always someone watching the altar. She was confident, however, that there had to be another exit. Someone as crafty as the Prophet would never allow himself to be cornered in this room like a stupid rat.

The Prophet led her gently to the bed and had her lie down. He circled the bed and admired his prey. The hands, the breasts, the waist, the pubis. Everything was perfect. He stopped at the feet and stared. She counted ten Mississippis. Something was amiss. The Prophet's legendary sixth sense. Was he suspicious? She willed back the urge to sneak a quick peek. Discovery meant detention and a long, slow death.

The Prophet studied the perfect body. He took the right foot in his hand and began to examine it. He ran his forefinger around the elegant outline. Replaced it gently on the bed. He took up the left foot and examined it. His fingers caressed the suntanned toes and perfectly manicured, pearl-white toenails. He closed his eyes and let his tunic fall to the floor.

The first thing she noticed was his scrawny legs. They didn't go with the rest of his body. His torso was wide-shouldered with muscular pecs and abs. His beard was thick, black, and well-trimmed. His hair was long and thick and wavy. When he smiled through his sensuous lips, his white teeth sparkled in the overhead light and his eyes gleamed green. It was the eyes that had first attracted her. She thought they were inspiring. Now the only thing they inspired was fear and hate.

He was excited. She knew from the first time she met him he was interested. She was flattered. That was her first mistake. Her second mistake was to cultivate that interest. Her third mistake was when she eavesdropped on an explosive conversation between the Prophet and a mysterious, peculiar-looking middle-aged female FBI agent. She couldn't believe it! They were discussing how much money they were making from prostitution, drug dealing, and human trafficking. How their political cover was in jeopardy. Which clients they would have to sacrifice. And who would be the "fall guy" to justify the protection they were getting from the FBI. In fact, overhearing the conversation wasn't really a mistake. It was bad luck—bad luck she heard the conversation, and bad luck the conversation was so explosive. The mistake was that she let herself get caught.

The Prophet pulled her to her knees, then lay down beside her and had her straddle him. "Now you will ride the beast."

She started to ride. What he called "the beast" was surprisingly tame at first. She knew that a tame beast was not what she needed. She needed to drive the beast wild, and she was ready to use everything in her playbook to make sure this happened.

The beast began to respond. He came to life and started to react. The Prophet closed his eyes. She reached into her hair and pulled out the syringe.

He opened his eyes when she began her thrust. He was too slow. She hit the plunger when the needle hit his neck. He thrust forward and tried to scream. She covered his mouth. The drug washed through his body, which was paralyzed by intense pain, as he passed through the portal of his experience with death.

Strangely enough, the wild beast lived on, which caused her some difficulty when she tried to dismount. This worried her a little, but she didn't have time to dwell on it. She had to find the secret exit, if there was one, and put as much distance between herself and the Prophecy as she could.

She grabbed the Prophet's tunic and stepped into it. Too big. She hiked it up and tied it at the waist, giving her legs the freedom of movement she would need when she started to run. His sandals were a better fit. A quick reconnoiter of the room told her the secret exit must be in the back where the bathroom was located. She heard voices and movement coming from the cathedral. She froze. The voices drifted away. False alarm.

She raced to the bathroom. There was nothing, just the toilet and a ceiling-to-floor medicine closet. Panic was pounding. She was hyperventilating. She had to stay cool. She had to think.

A shadow fell across the door. Startled, she whipped around. There in the doorway stood the Prophet, buck naked with his arms outstretched, his eyes riveted on her sandaled feet. He reached for her. She dodged. He clutched her shoulder. She twisted free and seized the metal hand mirror from the washbasin. He lurched forward on unsteady legs. She pivoted right and took a full swing back to the left. The metal mirror crashed against the side of his head. He stumbled. She swung back to the right and caught the back of his head. He crumbled face-first onto the marble floor. A thin line of bright-red blood oozed through his hair and trickled down his neck.

Too noisy. Someone outside the room was calling to the Prophet. There was no time left. She returned to the medicine closet. Fumbled around. Found a hand grip. Pushed. Nothing happened. Pulled. Nothing. Jerked to the right. There was a click. Pulled. Felt something give way. Pulled again, harder. The bottom half of the medicine closet wall swung open. She fell to her knees and there, through the small doorway, she saw the highway that ran behind the compound.

She slipped outside, closed the door carefully behind her, and dashed for the highway. The compound was a long way from nowhere, and escape routes were few. The most obvious to her were also obvious to her pursuers. Remaining on the road was not an option. She ran for the mountains and started to climb.